Bella's Birthday Unicorn

Don't miss any of Bella
and Glimmer's adventures!

Unicorn Magic

BOOK 2: Where's Glimmer?

Unicorn Magic

- BOOK 1 -

Bella's Birthday Unicorn

BY JESSICA BURKHART

Illustrated by Victoria Ying

Aladdin

NEW YORK LONDON TORONTO SYDNEY NEW DELHI

ALADDIN
An imprint of Simon & Schuster Children's Publishing Division
1230 Avenue of the Americas, New York, NY 10020
This Aladdin paperback edition August 2014
Text copyright © 2014 by Jessica Burkhart
Cover illustrations copyright © 2014 by Victoria Ying
Interior illustrations by Victoria Ying
All rights reserved, including the right of reproduction in whole or in part in any form.
ALADDIN is a trademark of Simon & Schuster, Inc., and related logo
is a registered trademark of Simon & Schuster, Inc.
Also available in an Aladdin hardcover edition.
For information about special discounts for bulk purchases, please contact
Simon & Schuster Special Sales at 1-866-506-1949
or business@simonandschuster.com.
The Simon & Schuster Speakers Bureau can bring authors to your live event.
For more information or to book an event contact the
Simon & Schuster Speakers Bureau at 1-866-248-3049 or
visit our website at www.simonspeakers.com.
Cover designed by Jessica Handelman
Interior designed by Mike Rosamilia
The text of this book was set in Arno Pro.
Manufactured in the United States of America 1117 OFF
6 8 10 9 7 5
Library of Congress Control Number 2014936193
ISBN 978-1-4814-1105-9 (hc)
ISBN 978-1-4424-9822-8 (pbk)
ISBN 978-1-4424-9823-5 (eBook)

To Aly Heller,
for making magic with this series!

Acknowledgments

Thank you to everyone at Simon & Schuster for your enthusiasm over Unicorn Magic. Special thanks to Fiona Simpson, Bethany Buck, and Valerie Shea, and everyone on the sales team.

Victoria Ying, your illustrations couldn't be more perfect!

Also, thank you to Rubin Pfeffer and all my friends for your support.

Big shout-out to Team Canterwood! I hope you or a younger sibling enjoys this story.

Contents

1

Sleep? No Way!

"Bella! Time to get up for school!" Queen Katherine's voice came through the intercom system on Bella's wall.

From the window seat in her room, Princess Bella giggled at her mom's request. Little did Queen Katherine know that Bella had been up since the sun rose over the tall castle gates. In Bella's opinion, she had the best view of the castle grounds from her room in the North Tower. Early mornings were Bella's favorite time of day. She loved looking beyond the gates and over the Crystal Kingdom.

Bella got up, trotted to the intercom, and said, "Be down in a minute!"

She went back to her window seat, unable to tear herself away just yet. She looked at the lush green lawn and watched as the red roses, yellow daffodils, and purple lilies pushed up through the ground and opened into beautiful blooming flowers. Every night the flowers tucked themselves into their flower beds and slept under the giant moon. If Bella woke early enough, she could watch the flowers awaken, seemingly yawning and stretching as they reached for the sun.

A giant silver fish leaped out of the moat that surrounded the castle. The fish's fins glittered like a rainbow as it snapped at a dragonfly zooming over the water. The Protection Fish kept any unwanted intruders out of the water and helped the castle's royal guards. The fish were spelled to appear as menacing sharks to anyone who was not supposed to be on castle grounds.

The guards watched over the majestic grounds with fierce wolves. The wolves—almost twice the size of common gray wolves—had incredible senses. If a fierce wolf sensed danger, it would make eye contact with its prey. One gaze from a fierce wolf could hold an intruder in place. This gave a guard time to capture the paralyzed target.

In the center of the cobblestone driveway, the fountain flowed with clear water over the family crest sculpture. Thanks to a special shimmering spell, the water glistened as if it was filled with diamonds.

Toward the stables, the pastures were full of regal unicorns frolicking in the warm spring sun. Bella could watch the gorgeous creatures all day! She spotted two unicorns grazing together—one with its white coat, mane, and tail shaded green and the other tinted yellow. Kiwi and Scorpio. Her parents' unicorns. They stood out among the sea of white animals—only royal unicorns changed colors. The rest remained a dazzling white.

Unicorns were precious to Crystal and its neighboring kingdoms such as Menon, which related to the moon, and Foris, a kingdom filled with forests. In Crystal and the other kingdoms, a princess's or prince's eighth birthday was the most important birthday of all. The special celebration was a birthright that separated a royal from the regular townspeople.

Royals were born with an *aura*. King Phillip, Bella's father, had explained that an aura was a hazy light that glowed around a royal's body. Auras only showed themselves during a royal's eighth birthday and when a royal was being crowned king or queen.

Auras came in every color of the rainbow. One color, however, was one that *no one* wanted. Red auras meant the royal was dangerous. Evil. Even worse, a royal with a red aura wouldn't get the one special thing available only on his or her eighth birthday—a unicorn. It was tradition that royals were gifted with unicorns. If a royal did not get one, it left them not only without a best friend but also without a lifelong guardian.

Both of Bella's parents had amazing unicorns. Kiwi had been by Queen Katherine's side ever since her eighth birthday. Photos of baby Bella on Kiwi's back rested on the fireplace mantel in the main sitting room. Kiwi's best unicorn friend was Scorpio, King Phillip's lemon-shaded unicorn.

Bella headed to her canopy bed and straightened the lavender sheets and fluffy comforter. Lavender was one of her favorite colors. Sky blue—like her nightgown and slippers—was another. The colors made Bella happy even when she was in a bad mood.

She fixed her pillows on her bed and stepped

back to admire her handiwork. Even though she was a princess, Queen Katherine and King Phillip insisted that Bella make her bed. She didn't mind. Her two best friends in the entire universe, Ivy and Clara, did chores too. Ivy and Clara weren't from royal families, and Bella wanted to be as normal as her friends.

Ivy's father was one of the groundskeepers at Crystal Castle. Bella had met Ivy one day in one of the gardens—Violette Garden—when they were both six. The two had become instant friends. Bella had asked Ivy to bring any of her friends over to the castle whenever she liked. Ivy brought Clara over to the castle days later, and the three girls were soon best friends.

"This is *it*," Princess Bella whispered aloud. "My last morning as a seven-year-old."

She hurried over to her floor-length mirror and grabbed a brush off her nightstand. She ran it through her light-brown hair, so long it was down to the middle of her back.

Before Queen Katherine could call her again, Bella trotted out of her bedroom and darted down a staircase and into one of the castle's many hallways. Her slippers were silent over the stone floors as she hurried toward the dining room. It was a family joke that Bella had gotten lost in the castle every day until she'd turned six. Forty-two rooms and a dozen hallways would confuse anyone!

Bella sniffed the air, catching scents of her favorite breakfast foods like eggs and waffles. That made her hurry even faster! She got to the dining room, and Queen Katherine and King Phillip were already seated at the head of the table.

"Good morning, Bella!" King Phillip said. Bella's dad greeted her with a smile. "How did my favorite girl sleep?"

Bella slid into a velvet-cushioned high-backed

chair at the giant mahogany table. "Daaad!" she said. "Did *you* sleep at all when you were *this close* to your eighth birthday?"

Bella's father chuckled.

"So, I'm guessing you've been thinking a little about tomorrow?" King Phillip asked. He shared Bella's green eyes and brown hair. They both had pale skin. Bella had her mother's petite build. This morning, Queen Katherine's long, dark blond hair was in a loose braid down her back.

"A *little*? Um, only if 'a little' means every second of the day for, like, a week!" Bella answered. She felt like jumping out of her seat. "Turning eight is the most important day in my entire life! I can't wait!"

"Oh, Bells," her mom said. "It's a day that your father and I have been looking forward to celebrating with you since you were a baby."

"Tell me everything about Crystal's history," Bella said. "I want to hear it again."

"But we only just told you the very same thing *yesterday* morning!" Bella's father laughed.

"And the morning before that," her mother said.

The king, queen, and princess sat back as Thomas, one of the kitchen staff, pushed open the double doors from the kitchen and placed a plate in front of each of them.

"Thank you, Thomas," Bella said. "This looks delicious."

"You're welcome, Princess Bella," Thomas said, bowing his head.

Bella dug her fork into the scrambled eggs and eyed her waffle covered in strawberries and blueberries. With a mouthful of eggs, she stared at King Phillip with puppy eyes. "Pleeease," she said. "I promise, Dad—just one more time!"

Her dad put down his fork, smiling. "All right, Bella. I'll tell you the story one more time."

Bella clapped. "Yay!"

"A *very* long time ago, your great-great-great-great-grandfather King Scott, on your mother's side of the family, discovered a tiny piece of land," the king began. "To get there, he had crossed river rapids, survived dark forests, and scaled tall mountains. Finally he found himself standing amid a deserted space—a perfect spot right in the middle of a bunch of clouds! Now, King Scott had never stood among the clouds before. In fact, no one had! He was surprised to find the land was lush and plentiful. The grass there was the greenest he'd ever seen, the towering trees the tallest, and the fresh river that surrounded the land was the cleanest—it sparkled like a thousand diamonds in the moonlight."

"What about the sun?" Bella interrupted.

Her father winked. "The sun was perhaps the most important of all. The legend goes that the warmth of the sun, on the warmest and most beautiful morning where King Scott stood that following day, is what made unicorns from all the sky islands come to Crystal."

Bella could practically feel the sun's warmth on her cheeks when she closed her eyes and pictured the map of the four sky islands that hung in her classroom. They were giant pieces of land that floated high in the clouds and were only reachable from other islands when either a rainbow or moonbow spell was cast. Then the person who cast the spell could walk on the rainbow or moonbow to the other island.

Bella had traveled by rainbow once before. Never by moonbow. Walking on a rainbow felt a lot like walking up and then down escalator stairs.

Bella pictured the moonbows in her head. She had seen photos of them in her textbooks. Moonbows were just like rainbows except they flowed out of the moon and lit up the night sky with color.

"The beauty and magic of the sky," King Phillip

continued, "is why King Scott named our kingdom Crystal."

"You know the story by heart from here, Bells," King Phillip said. "King Scott encouraged his friends and their families to move to Crystal. They built houses, began families, and soon it was time to crown a king. Everyone in the kingdom wanted your great-great-great-great grandfather Scott to reign over all the people, since he'd discovered the kingdom."

"Then he was crowned king and our castle was built," Bella said. She put a forkful of tasty eggs into her mouth.

"Right," King Phillip said. "Your grandparents grew up here, and so did your mom. I lived in River Falls—a kingdom bordering Crystal."

Bella knew River Falls was on the same sky island as Crystal. There were so many kingdoms on each island that she couldn't name them all!

"Mom, you weren't much older than me when

12

Gram made *you* queen," Bella said. She took a bite of waffle.

Queen Katherine laughed. "I was *quite* a bit older than you. Your gram stepped down from the throne and passed her crown to me. That was around the time I met your dad."

Bella rolled her eyes as her parents made googly eyes at each other. *Ew!*

"What was it like when you were Paired to Kiwi and Scorpio?" Bella asked her parents.

A slight frown appeared, then was quickly covered by a smile on Queen Katherine's face. "Being Paired to Kiwi was one of the best moments in my life. When his aura turned green, I squealed so loud that I scared him!"

Bella giggled. "Dad?"

"I didn't squeal," King Phillip said. "But I was extremely excited to have a unicorn. Scorpio wouldn't let any of my friends ride him until I told him it was okay. He's still a very loyal uni-corn."

The large clock in the foyer chimed nine a.m.

"I think it's time for you to get ready for school," Queen Katherine said. "Ivy and Clara will be here soon. Ms. Barnes is already preparing your lessons in the schoolroom."

Ivy and Clara had been attending the local school, but when the king and queen had seen how much Bella loved being around the two girls, they had invited Ivy and Clara to attend school at the castle along with a few other kids Bella's age. Bella had been homeschooled by a tutor since kinder-garten, and now she couldn't imagine not having friends in her class.

Bella pushed back her chair and started toward her room. Footsteps quickly followed her.

"Good morning, Princess Bella."

"Hi, Lyssa," Bella said, stopping and smiling.

Lyssa was Bella's companion and handmaiden. She was a few years older than Bella—fourteen— and it was her job to help Bella get dressed and do homework, and make sure she had whatever else she needed. Lyssa had been by Bella's side for more than a year, and Bella loved her like an older sister.

"Let's get you dressed, shall we?" Lyssa asked. Together they walked to Bella's room.

"Something cheerful," Bella said. "You always know how to match the right clothes, Lyssa."

The blond girl smiled, tucking her long hair behind her ears. She wore a black skirt, ballet flats, and a collared light-pink shirt. Lyssa was one of the few employees at the castle who didn't have to wear a black uniform bearing Crystal's seal. Lyssa had told Bella that it was because Queen Katherine wanted Bella to forget that Lyssa was a member of the staff. Bella was glad, because the seal was *definitely* something that wasn't easy to ignore.

The Crystal seal was a giant diamond with two unicorns below. The rearing unicorns faced each other, and they stood on a scroll that read CRYSTAL KINGDOM.

Bella flipped on her closet lights and walked inside. The walls were bubblegum pink, with a coat of glitter paint that sparkled from the overhead chandelier and spotlights. Bella's clothes, on rotating racks, spun slowly so Bella and Lyssa could choose an outfit.

"Hmmm," Lyssa said, putting a finger to her lips. "How about . . ." She plucked a light-blue dress with white hearts from a rack and held it up for Bella's inspection.

"Yes, definitely!" Bella exclaimed. "And silver ballet flats? Would those match?"

Lyssa walked to the shoe racks, nodding. "Silver is perfect, Bella." Lyssa found the right shoes while Bella slipped out of her pj's and into the dress.

As she dressed, Bella couldn't stop thinking about what her father had said about his friends riding Scorpio. Bella wanted her unicorn to be loyal and love her, but she also wanted to give Ivy and Clara rides. Her nonroyal friends wouldn't get unicorns on their eighth birthdays. *I don't want them to think the unicorn is all mine and I'm never going to share,* Bella thought. That is, if she was actually Paired with a unicorn. The thought made her shudder. She'd never heard of a royal *not* getting a unicorn, but what if, for some crazy reason, she was the first?

"You're awfully quiet," Lyssa remarked. The older girl had pulled out a chair in front of Bella's mirror and held a hair brush.

Bella sat down, and Lyssa began brushing her hair.

"I'm just thinking about tomorrow," Bella said. "There's so much happening—the parade, the after-party, the Pairing Ceremony . . ."

"It's a lot," Lyssa said, nodding. "But remember that you've done big days like this your entire life. They've always been for your parents or grandparents, but tomorrow is *your* day. Celebrate—don't worry!"

Bella turned in her chair, reaching her arms up to hug Lyssa. "Thanks, Lys," she said. "You always make me feel better."

"What kind of help would I be if I didn't?" Lyssa asked with a grin.

"Bad help!" Bella teased back.

Lyssa put her hand over her heart. "That hurt, Bella," she said, pretending to be serious.

Bella, playing along, shrugged. "You always tell me to be honest. I mean, what if I didn't tell you that purple dress you had on last week was on backward?"

Lyssa's mouth dropped open. "Are you serious? Oh *no*! I can't believe it! I knew something was wrong—"

Bella turned around and grabbed Lyssa's hands. "Lys! I was kidding! I'm sorry! That dress was perfect *and* on the right way. I only brought it up because it was so cool that I wanted to borrow it one day."

Lyssa blew out a giant breath. "You scared me!" Laughing, she wrapped her arms around Bella. "Now I have to think about letting you wear it." She winked at Bella.

Lyssa left, headed for the classroom with Bella's schoolbooks. *I don't know how I'm going to concentrate on school today!* Bella thought.

When she heard the familiar chime of the doorbell, Bella realized that the answer to her question was easy! *And* standing right outside the front door to her castle.

Ivy and Clara, her two besties in the whole wide world, would be on Distraction Duty, starting now!

2

BFFs to the Rescue

"One day before you're older than Ivy and me!" Clara declared. She was the tallest of the three, and her long blond waves bounced as she hopped on tiptoes. Clara was the most outgoing and fearless of the group. In fact, Bella would never have even *met* Clara (even though Ivy had brought her to the castle) if Clara hadn't been brave enough to walk right up to Bella and say, "I know you! You're the princess! Is it fun being a princess?"

None of the other kids in Crystal had ever come up to Bella to talk to her the way Clara did. Bella admired how fearless Clara could be—she often wished she could feel even half as brave as her friend.

Now, all three girls walked down the castle hallway to the sunny room where their lessons were held every weekday. Six other kids of castle employees attended school in the royal classroom.

"You're so lucky," Ivy said. She tucked a lock of straight, chin-length blond hair behind her ear. "I can't wait to turn eight!" Ivy was the opposite of Clara—she was quieter and listened more. That meant Ivy always had the best gossip!

Bella nodded. "I wonder if I'll feel any different tomorrow."

"I bet you'll wake up at exactly midnight," Clara said. "Or maybe you won't be able to sleep at all! You're going to be Paired tomorrow!"

Paired.

The thought alone made Bella's stomach do backflips *and* rumble nervously at the same time.

"Do you think Troy will bring a toad to class again today?" Bella asked, quickly changing the subject.

Clara wrinkled her nose. "He better not, or I'll toss him in the moat!"

Laughing, Bella felt relieved. Her attempt to stop all Bella's Birthday Talk had worked.

Ivy rifled through the pages of her red notebook. "I wanted to show you guys a sketch that I made of the royal unicorns," she said. "But it's invisible now. Ms. Barnes must have activated the invisible ink spell until after our spelling quiz."

Ivy held up her notebook, its pages blank. Ms. Barnes often used invisible ink spells on test or quiz days so no one could cheat by looking at his or her notes. But she made sure that the spell only lasted until the exams were turned in. After, everyone's notes returned to normal.

"Definitely show it to us after," Bella said.

The school bell sounded from inside the classroom. Time to go!

The girls hurried inside the classroom and took their usual seats in the front row.

"Good morning, everyone," Ms. Barnes said. "As you may have noticed, all of your notebooks are blank and will be until we've finished our spelling quiz. I hope you studied last night."

A small groan came from the back of the room. Bella didn't have to turn around to know it was her friend Evan. He never studied and was always being asked to stay after class.

"Take out a fresh sheet of paper and a pencil," Ms. Barnes said from the front of the classroom. "We'll begin."

Ivy, Bella, and Clara didn't have a free second to talk the rest of the morning. Bella counted down the seconds until lunch period.

* * *

"Ah! I thought we would never get to talk ever again!" Clara said.

The three friends had grabbed their favorite table on one of the castle's back decks. A cheery orange umbrella stuck up from the middle of the table and shielded the girls from the sun.

Along with their turkey sandwiches and different side dishes, each girl had extra helpings of Crystal's famous "sunray pie." Bella didn't know exactly how the pie was made, but she did know that it contained sunray berries. Sunray berries grew on vines that stretched into the clouds and out of sight. The people of Crystal said the vines were connected to the sun.

When farmers picked the berries, they had to wear extra-dark sunglasses because the berries were so bright! They glowed sunny yellow, and inside the piecrust were circles shaped like the sun that made Bella feel happy the second she

25

took a bite. The pie tasted sweet—from the sun-ray berries—and refreshing, like lemonade, at the same time.

"I was trying not watch the clock, but I kept looking at it!" Ivy added.

Bella knew her friends wanted to talk about tomorrow—her birthday—but it was the last thing she wanted to bring up. This was the first time Bella noticed how very different *her* life was from her friends'.

Bella didn't feel lonely with kids her own age at the castle. But now she realized she would be on her own at her Pairing Ceremony—the biggest event in her life so far!

"Guess what? My dad said he's taking me to River Falls one day," Bella continued. She wasn't exactly lying to her friends—her dad had said that. But it was weeks ago, and she'd forgotten about it until now. "Dad wants to show me where he was born. I heard there are Fall Frogs that are as big as cats!"

"Whoa!" Ivy said. "That will be a fun trip! But I just learned about something way creepier than frogs. My sister's friend told us that these spiders called Anasi live deep the Crystal woods. They're prankster spiders—they appear to shift into whatever the person who's nearby is imagining."

"They can turn into *people*?" Bella asked, shuddering. "A spider-person! Ewww!"

Ivy and Clara made yeah-totally-gross faces too.

"But the spiders just create a vision—they don't really become something else," Ivy continued. "When the person gets close enough, the spider stops the trick and scares the person by showing itself as a spider."

"I can't think about creepy spiders anymore!" Bella said. Her skin felt crawly. "I'm so glad I've never seen one."

"I heard something too," Clara said. She clearly didn't want to be the only one who didn't have something to add about a new creature.

"One night I couldn't sleep, so I started to go downstairs for milk," Clara said. "My parents were talking and I stopped and listened."

"Eavesdropper!" Bella said, teasing.

"I couldn't help it!" Clara said. "It was too interesting. I heard my parents talking about an old lady who lives on the edge of town. She only comes out during big royal celebrations. They said she's so jealous that red smoke poofs around her. She travels with this band of, like, bad unicorns."

"Bad unicorns?" Ivy asked.

"Unicorns that probably bite your fingers off," Clara said.

With that, the girls all burst into giggles over their silly, scary stories of creatures and old ladies.

Lunch period was minutes from ending, and Bella sighed quietly with relief. She had managed to avoid talking about her birthday. She picked up her empty tray—even the tiniest crumb of sunray pie gone—and started to stand.

"Oh, Bells!" Ivy said. "What time should Clara and I come over tomorrow? I'm *so* excited!"

Bella stood slowly. "Six," she said, her tone a little uncertain.

Clara and Ivy nodded.

"Wow, your birthday starts early!" Clara said. "But I'll be up on time and at the castle by six a.m."

Oh no, Bella thought. Now she had to tell Ivy and Clara something awful.

"I actually meant six in the evening," Bella said. She paused, looking at her tray for a second. "I have the royal parade and press stuff to do before I get home for my party."

"Ha, ha," Ivy said, grinning. "You're joking,

Bella. What time do you *really* want us to come over?"

Bella wanted to cry. Sometimes being a princess was no fun at all!

"I'm so, so sorry," Bella said. "I've been *begging* my mom to make an exception this year so you can both be in the parade with me. But she won't budge. She keeps saying it's 'royal tradition' and we have to follow the rules."

Ivy and Clara sat unmoving. They both had huge frowns on their faces.

"That's such an old tradition!" Clara said. "We're your *best* friends! Your mom won't let us be in the parade at all?"

"We're not *royal*, Clara," Ivy snapped. "Don't forget that Bella is a princess. There are things that you and I—just regular people—can't do. I guess being with our best friend on her birthday is one of them."

Tears pricked Bella's eyes. The sunray pie swirled in her stomach.

"You guys have no idea how hard I've been fighting to change the rules," Bella pleaded with Ivy and Clara. "I agree—it's a silly tradition! I've been begging my mom every single day. I want you two there for every minute of my birthday. Especially this one."

Clara stood, not looking at Bella, and picked up her tray. "Don't waste your time, Princess. In fact, forget about coming to *my* eighth birthday party."

Ivy nodded, standing next to Clara. "Mine too. I don't want any royals at my party."

Ivy and Clara, trays in hand, hurried away from the table, leaving Bella in tears.

3

Princess Confessions

Later that afternoon, Bella flopped onto her stomach on her bed. She actually wished her teacher had assigned homework—she needed something, *anything*, to keep her mind from racing ahead to tomorrow. *And to stop me from thinking about how mad Ivy and Clara are at me,* Bella thought.

She changed into comfy after-school clothes— bright yellow leggings and a plain white T-shirt—then left her room to wander the castle's hallways. When Queen Katherine had taken the throne, she had completely redecorated. Bella's mom had told her daughter that she wanted the castle to feel "welcoming."

New rugs, all a warm, cherry-red color, covered much of the hallway floors. Beautiful wrought-iron candelabras lit by long ivory taper candles hung along the walls every few feet, illuminating the lovely artwork decorating the castle's royal walls. Even the dusty, old, heavy drapes that had hung over the large palace windows had been replaced by the queen with light, airy curtains.

Bella hurried up two flights of stairs to the main tower. She skidded to a stop in front of her parents' open bedroom door. Queen Katherine tilted her head toward the door where her daughter stood. She put the pile of mail in her hand down on her bedside table and smiled at her daughter. Queen Katherine waved Bella into the bedroom.

"I've never seen anyone move so slowly," her mom joked. Then she saw the look on Bella's face. "What's wrong, Bells?"

Bella crossed the room and sank into the cushy

white-and-blue comforter. It felt like she was sitting on pillows. She traced an index finger over one of the swirly designs.

She shrugged, not looking up. "Nothing. Okay, something. But it's silly."

"I love hearing about silly things," Queen Katherine replied. "Especially from you."

Bella looked up into her mom's hazel eyes and took a giant breath. "I'm scared about tomorrow," she began.

Queen Katherine put a hand on her daughter's knee but stayed silent.

"I'm nervous about the parade," Bella continued. "What if no one comes? I'll be *so* embarrassed—plus, it'll be upsetting to you and Daddy."

"Is that all?" the queen asked. "Are you sure there's nothing else bothering you?"

Bella frowned. Her mom knew her way too

well. *I won't get away with keeping anything from Mom,* she thought.

"I'm scared that I won't be Paired with a unicorn. What if one just doesn't exist for me?" Bella asked.

Queen Katherine tilted her head, smiling at Bella. "Sweetie, I have no doubt that a *very* special unicorn is waiting for you. He or she is probably in the royal stables right now, thinking, 'When am I going to meet Princess Bella?'"

Bella giggled. "You really think so?"

"I know so," Queen Katherine answered. "I want you to tell me these things, Bells. Whatever you're worried about—big or small—so that tomorrow will be as amazing for you as possible."

Bella chewed on the inside of her cheek. "There is one more thing. I feel bad having all of this attention on me, tomorrow, when Ivy and Clara will never have a birthday like mine," she said. "We got in a fight today because I had to tell them they couldn't be in the parade with me. What if they get so jealous that they decide to stop being my friends? There is so much about this birthday that they'll never have. I mean, getting a unicorn is such a *big* deal!"

Queen Katherine took her hand from Bella's knee and ran it over Bella's hair. The familiar gesture soothed Bella a little.

"Tomorrow is a huge day for you, Bells," Queen Katherine said. "But Ivy and Clara have never been jealous that you're a princess. They became your best friends knowing exactly who you are."

"I know, but they don't get to participate in anything tomorrow," Bella said. "They have to watch me in the parade, and they can't even come to the Pairing Ceremony because it's only for royals. They're *really* upset."

"They'll still be at your party after the parade," Bella's mom pointed out.

"But they're so mad," Bella said. "I don't even think they're coming to my party."

She buried her face into a pillow on her mom's bed. The queen wasn't going to budge, Clara and Ivy were going to stay mad at her, and tomorrow wasn't going to be half as special without her friends.

4

Happy Birthday!

Princess Bella was wide awake even before her rainbow-shaped alarm clock went off. Sometimes she liked to set her alarm instead of her mom waking her up.

Shortly after, there was a knock at her door, and Queen Katherine and King Phillip stepped inside Bella's bedroom.

"Happy birthday, Bella!" Queen Katherine, clad in a plush white robe, exclaimed. She hurried to Bella's bedside and kissed her forehead.

"Happy eighth birthday, sweetheart," said King Phillip. He ruffled Bella's hair after kissing her cheek.

"I can't believe it!" Bella said excitedly. "I'm *eight*! I thought I'd be up all night and counting down until midnight, but I fell asleep."

Her parents laughed.

"Throw on a robe and come to the breakfast table," Queen Katherine said. "Your favorite breakfast is ready."

Once her parents left Bella's room, she flopped back onto her pillow. *I'm eight! I'm eight!* she chanted over and over in her head. She had been dreaming about this day for as long as she could remember. It was time to get her birthday started! Then Bella remembered. Ivy and Clara. She had called them last night, but neither of her friends had answered.

You have to at least smile and pretend to be happy for Mom and Dad, Bella thought.

She put her feet into fuzzy pink slippers and pulled her terry-cloth robe over her matching shorts and T-shirt pj's. She dashed to the breakfast table. All of the castle staff—the chefs, gardener, stable workers, Lyssa, maids—had gathered around the table. They smiled and chanted, "Happy birthday, Princess Bella!"

Bella blushed as pink as her slippers. "Thank you," she said to everyone.

Color-changing streamers that twirled in the air hung from the ceiling and formed a canopy around the breakfast table. Glittery balloons flashed on and off as they floated from the floor to the ceiling and back down again.

Plates, ready to be filled, hovered at the start of a luxurious breakfast buffet. Fruit, waffles, eggs, bacon, and sausage filled silver trays. A glass filled itself with orange juice for Bella, and two mugs soon were brimming with coffee for her parents. Bella's plate, waiting in front of her, moved toward the buffet—ready to fill itself with whatever food Bella wanted.

"Ooh, this is so beautiful!" Bella said happily, clapping her hands. "Can we start eating now?"

Everyone laughed. King Phillip pulled out a chair for Bella and she took her seat, ready to dive into her birthday breakfast. Bella gulped her entire glass of juice first.

Lyssa poured Bella another glass of OJ, and the pitcher refilled itself. Bella glanced at the waffles and her plate wafted through the air, stopping in front of the waffles.

"Two, please," Bella said.

Two steaming waffles lifted from the silver tray and slid onto Bella's plate. Immediately, new waffles replaced the ones that had floated to her plate.

She grinned and looked at the fruit. Her plate was going to get a workout today!

After a delicious start to her birthday, Bella trotted up the stairs to her room with Lyssa.

"I can't believe I'm finally going to see my birthday dress!" Bella said.

Lyssa smiled. "You're going to love it!"

Bella eyed Lyssa. "I can't believe I haven't been able to convince you to tell me *anything* about it. Mom hasn't spilled one detail."

"Close your eyes," Lyssa said, taking Bella's hand.

She felt as though soda bubbles were bursting in her stomach.

She shut her eyes tight and let Lyssa lead the way to her dress.

"Okay! Open!" Lyssa squeezed Bella's hand.

Bella's mouth dropped open.

"Oh my gosh, Lyssa! It's gorgeous!" she squealed.

The blush-colored dress was satin, covered with a delicate layer of lace. Holding her breath, Bella slowly walked up to the dress and touched the cap sleeves. A satin sash cinched the dress's waist. Gray ballet flats covered in iridescent sequins were on the floor under the dress. A delicate silver chain with a letter *B* hung on the hanger.

Bella spun in a circle to look at Lyssa. "This was *so* worth keeping a secret! It's the best dress ever!"

Lyssa grinned. "Seems like you kind of like it."

"Only a little bit," Bella joked. "Will you help me get dressed?"

As Lyssa started to help Bella, the princess felt a pang of sadness. Normally, Bella would be snapping photos of her dress and sending them to Ivy and Clara. She couldn't even stand the thought that her two best friends might never see her dress.

Lyssa helped Bella change from her pajamas

into her dress. Bella slid her feet into the ballet slippers while Lyssa clasped the necklace around her neck.

Unable to wait another second, Bella turned toward her full-length mirror.

"It's the prettiest dress ever!" Bella sighed happily.

She twirled in front of the mirror, loving how the layers of her dress spun out in front of her. Her mom and the seamstress had captured everything Bella could want in a dress. The shade of pink was Bella's favorite, and the fabric swished around her knees. *I really feel like a princess today!* Bella thought.

"Bella?" Queen Katherine called, knocking on Bella's door.

"Mom, come in!" Bella faced the door, grinning. Lyssa stood back and clasped her hands.

"Oh, Bella!" Queen Katherine put a hand over

her mouth. The other hand held an old wooden box. It was a deep polished mahogany with gold corners and a gold lock. "You look *beautiful*."

Bella hurried over and wrapped her arms around her mom. "Thanks, Mom. I love my dress so much."

"It's perfect for your big day," Queen Katherine said.

Bella started to ask what was inside the box when her mom asked, "Would you like me to do your hair?"

"Yes, please!" Bella said, checking her ruffled hair—definitely not parade worthy—in the mirror.

She sat at the purple-velvet-cushioned chair with gold that twisted into vines to make the chair's arms and legs. Her mom put the box on Bella's bed.

"Lyssa," Queen Katherine said. "Feel free to leave and get yourself ready for the parade."

"Thank you, Queen Katherine," Lyssa said. She

bowed her head to the queen and winked at Bella as she left the room.

Queen Katherine took a large brush and ran it through Bella's hair, gently combing out the tangles. Bella watched in the mirror, hoping she'd be able to copy the look one day, but Queen Katherine was too fast. Within minutes, the queen had swept Bella's hair into an elegant half-updo.

"What do you think?" Bella's mom asked.

"I love it, Mom!" Bella said, looking at her hair in the mirror. "Thank you so much!"

Bella started to get up, but her mom placed a hand on her shoulder. "There's one more thing I need to do to finish your look," Queen Katherine said.

"Oh, okay." Bella settled back into the chair.

Queen Katherine appeared by Bella's side with the mystery box in hand.

"I think this will add a little sparkle," the queen said.

Bella turned in her chair, peeking into the box. Queen Katherine opened the lid and inside, resting on a blue pillow, was a glittering tiara. Not just *any* tiara either. Bella had a princess tiara that she wore during royal events and celebrations. *This* tiara was clearly made for Bella's birthday.

Bella's mouth fell open "Wow," she breathed. "I get to wear this tiara? Are you serious?" She clutched her chest and couldn't stop herself from bouncing on her toes.

Queen Katherine laughed. "Very serious. Your father and I went into the jewel vault this morning and retrieved it. This tiara was made the day you were born, and we've kept it under lock and key until your eighth birthday."

Bella stared at the diamonds, which shone and winked at her. The tiara had intricate swirls and curls that formed a heart at the center. A teardrop-shaped diamond dangled from the middle of the heart.

Queen Katherine took the tiara from its pillow and carefully lowered it onto her daughter's head. Bella couldn't stop staring at it—it was the prettiest thing she had ever seen.

"Now," Queen Katherine said, meeting Bella's gaze in the mirror, "you are ready for the parade."

Bella stared at herself in the mirror, trying to keep up her smile, but her chin wobbled.

"Oh, sweetie," her mom said. "What is wrong?"

"Today would be perfect if Clara and Ivy were able to celebrate with me. I'm happy, Mom, but I'm sad they're angry with me."

Queen Katherine leaned close to Bella's ear. "I wasn't going to say a word, but . . ."

When the queen finished whispering in Bella's ear, Bella let out a loud squeal.

"Mom!" she said. "This is the most magical day of my whole life."

"I'm happy to hear it," Queen Katherine said,

smiling. "You deserve one day to have whatever you wish."

Bella squealed again and hugged her mom tight. Her birthday was off to a perfect start!

5

Parade Princess

After one last check to make sure everything looked perfect, Princess Bella had dashed out of the castle and into a special carriage that took her to the start of her official birthday celebration.

Queen Katherine, King Phillip, and Bella had taken the royal carriage they used only for special occasions. It was powered by Crystal's pride and joy—the sun itself! The royal carriage needed only a royal driver to steer. The carriage glowed like a giant orb. Usually, Bella stared out the clear exterior with her nose pressed against the glass as they made their way down the winding roads from the castle to town. This time, she'd sat silent with her hands clasped in her lap. She was nervous *and* excited.

The royal carriage stopped at the beginning of the parade route. Tons of people were already lined up behind the shield spell on either side of the cobblestone road.

"Your mom and I will see you at the end of the parade, Bells," King Phillip said. "Have fun!" Her mom kissed Bella's cheek. "We're heading to our float just in front of yours."

Bella stepped out of the royal carriage, and flashbulbs popped. Her parents exited the opposite side with royal security. They wanted all of the attention to be on Bella on her special day.

Crystal's weather seemed to know it was Bella's birthday—sunlight beamed down, there wasn't a cloud in the sky, and the temperature was unseasonably warm.

Just like her mom had taught her, Bella stopped and turned to wave at the newspaper and TV crews. A dozen or so men and women had notebooks, giant cameras and recorders, and microphones. It was a little scary, but Bella remembered the security guards at her sides and the shield spell.

The location calmed Bella too. The royal carriage had stopped at the edge of town in a grassy field filled with daisies and clusters of wild tulips. Bella loved the pops of color. It looked like pieces of a rainbow had been sprinkled in the field! The parade floats had lined up, and Crystal's police patrolled the area with fierce wolves. None of the wolves had teeth bared, so no danger was near.

Now Bella could really see the sparkly line of the shield spell along the sides of the parade route. The spell glittered—a sign it had been cast by a royal—so none of the townspeople could break the barrier. Only a royal could disarm the spell.

"Princess Bella! A photo for the *Daily Crystal*?" a man with a camera asked Bella with a smile.

"Sure!" Bella said. The security guards moved off to the sides, and Bella smiled at the camera.

More flashbulbs popped as other reporters crowded in to catch a shot of Bella. She stood for a moment to let everyone get a photograph. Bella jutted out a hip, putting her hand on her side, and grinned.

"Thank you, Princess," the reporter from the *Daily Crystal* said.

Bella nodded. "Of course! I hope you got a good picture!" She may have spent her life growing up as a royal, but her parents had always been fiercely protective of her in the media. Until today, most of the media coverage centered on her parents.

The reporters laughed. "It's your birthday," a woman said, adjusting the lens on her camera.

"Pictures always come out good on someone's birthday."

Bella looked at everyone, taking it all in. The *Daily Crystal* was on the breakfast table every morning, and usually the only royals in the paper were her parents. Now it was Bella's turn.

"A quick question, Princess?" the *Daily Crystal* reporter asked. He let his camera hang around his neck and pulled out a small notepad. "My name is Dan, by the way."

"Sure," Bella said. "Pleased to meet you, Dan."

Inside, she smiled. Her parents would be so proud of her manners if they were here.

"First, I would like to wish you a happy eighth birthday," Dan said. "Second, I would like to know, what is your favorite part of this birthday?"

Other reporters scrambled to get out their gadgets to catch Bella's answer. Many of them pressed the bridge of their frameless glasses, and with the blink of a blue light, the glasses started recording wherever the reporter looked.

"My favorite part is having no school," Bella said. "So that I can spend the day with my best friends and family!"

Someone tapped Bella on the shoulder, and she turned around. Bella grinned when she saw who they were.

"You guys are here!" she said happily.

Ivy and Clara had been escorted to Bella. The girls all hugged as cameras clicked and flashes went off, but Bella ignored the lights.

"Your dress!" Clara said, her blue-green eyes wide.

"It's so pretty!" Ivy added.

"Thank you! You both look like princesses!" Bella told her friends.

She said a silent thank-you to Queen Katherine. Only the queen would be able to get beautiful dresses for Bella's best friends *and* make sure the girls could accompany Bella on her royal float.

"Can we talk to you for a minute?" Ivy asked.

"Please," Clara added. "We know you're busy, but we have to talk to you."

Bella nodded and took Ivy and Clara by their elbows and led them away from the crowd. She pulled them into a clear tent—it had been concocted with a sunshield spell. They could see out of the walls, but no one could see in. The sunshield spell gave the people a break from the sun if they entered.

Ivy and Clara hung their heads.

"Bella," Ivy said. "Clara and I are *so* sorry for what we said to you at lunch."

Clara nodded. "Ivy and I know that you're a princess and it would be silly of us to think you could change a tradition that has been in place for hundreds of years."

"But you *did*," Ivy said. "Your mom called our moms and told them how you wouldn't have a good birthday without your best friends."

Bella blinked fast, holding back tears. "I couldn't imagine spending today with you two mad at me *and* not in the parade or coming to my party tonight."

"Ivy and I were awful to you," Clara admitted. "But you and your mom not only got invites for us to be in the parade, but your mom also got us these amazing dresses."

"My mom did the whole thing," Bella said. "She told me at the last minute that you two were coming and asked if I wanted to help choose your dresses. At first, I thought she was kidding! You both were so mad at me that I didn't think you'd even want to come to the parade."

"We acted like spoiled brats," Ivy said. "We always wanted to be with you on your birthday."

She smiled. "Especially in dresses like these!"

"Ivy," Bella said, "I chose that emerald dress just for you because I know it's your favorite color."

Ivy's mouth opened and closed.

Bella turned to Clara. "I picked plum for you because it's your favorite fruit. I wanted to have a rose on the neckline because you love roses so much."

"I love my dress," Ivy said softly. "And I'm so sorry."

"Me too," Clara said.

"Though I wouldn't blame you if you didn't like *either* of us right now," Ivy interjected.

Bella half smiled and shook her head. "That's silly. Of course I still like you both. You're my best friends."

"We didn't act like it," Ivy said. "This is your day, Bella, and I'm so sorry I did something to make it less special."

"I'm sorry, Bella," Clara said. "Really sorry—I'm glad one of my best friends is a princess. I'm okay that I'm not one. But like the type of friend you are, you found a way to make Ivy and me feel like princesses too."

Bella's friends lowered their eyes and stared at the stones beneath their feet. Even though she was still a little hurt, Bella didn't want them fighting, and she certainly didn't want anything to be off with the three of them for the rest of her birthday.

"Hugs, already!" Bella said. She opened her arms.

Clara and Ivy looked up at Bella, their eyes wide. Squealing, they almost knocked her over with a giant bear hug. They pulled apart and smiled at each other.

"I need bestie power right now," Bella said. "All I can think about is the Unicorn Pairing Ceremony."

"You've got it," Clara said. "But are you sure

that you still want us to come over?" She fidgeted with the front of her dress.

"Yes, are you sure?" Ivy asked. "Clara and I talked about it on the ride over. You know that we are a million percent happy for you, right? We know we're not princesses, but we're not jealous of you, Bella. We would *never* be. You're our BFF, and we really want to come to the castle and party with you!"

Tears filled Bella's eyes. She didn't want her nose to turn red, like it always did when she cried, but she couldn't stop a tear from falling.

"Bella! Don't cry!" Clara said. "Is something else wrong?"

"Nothing—everything is so perfect," Bella said. "I knew you guys wouldn't be jealous, but a tiny part of me was scared that you would be. I don't want to lose you as my best friends just because of this silly princess thing."

"Never!" Ivy and Clara said at the same time.

All three girls laughed.

"You're stuck with us," Clara said.

"Forever," Ivy added.

Giggling, the three girls hugged again.

6

Smile and Wave!

Bella smiled as she walked toward her float. Security, almost enough for a royal wedding, walked beside her. The fight with her friends had been a nightmare. Now, everything could be about including Ivy and Clara.

Bella spotted her float before the guards could point it out. The second float in line shimmered and glowed with lavender and sky-blue lights and flowers. Light-blue fog settled above the float and sheer purple fog stretched around the bottom. Four tall posts, mimicking a canopy bed, had light-purple tulle draped from each of them and across the top of the float. At the front, lights in cursive script blinked HAPPY BIRTHDAY, PRINCESS!

An oversize throne in the middle of the float was just the right size to fit Bella, Ivy, and Clara. Bella knew from past parades that the floats were all preprogrammed to follow the parade route.

"Princess, please allow me to help you and your friends aboard," one of the guards said.

In no time Bella, Clara, and Ivy stood on the float. The girls grinned at each other. They had been instructed to keep a hand on the railing unless they were seated. Bella stood at the front of the float and Ivy and Clara were on opposite sides, practicing their parade waves. Bella had never seen bigger smiles on her friends' faces.

"It's time!" a man with a bullhorn called from atop a prancing unicorn. "People of Crystal, please join me in wishing Princess Bella a happy birthday! Let the parade begin!"

Queen Katherine and King Phillip's float lifted a few inches above the ground, hovering, and started forward. The king and queen stood at the front of their elegant red-and-gold float and began waving as soon as they reached the start of the crowd.

Here we go! Bella thought excitedly.

There was a crackle in the air and thousands of tiny lights—like fireflies—appeared at each corner of Bella's float. The lights whirled in circles and propelled the float forward. The cheers of the crowd grew louder and louder. Bella wondered if people in the next kingdom could hear the people chanting, "Happy birthday, Princess!" Nerves rumbled in Bella's stomach. *I can do this,* she told herself. *Just smile and wave! That's it!*

Ivy and Clara reached into the large buckets that hung beside them and grabbed handfuls of candy, including Sunstix—a stick of candy that

glowed in the dark and did the same to the person's tongue!

They tossed the treats into the crowd. Bella smiled as she watched little kids chase after the scattered candy. Watching them made her nerves evaporate. She dipped a hand into her own bucket and threw a bunch of sweets toward a group of young girls. The girls held a sign with glittery pink letters spelling WE ♥ PRINCESS BELLA! When they saw Bella had noticed the float, the girls released the sign, and the letters floated into the air before disappearing with a *poof* over the crowd and raining silver sparkles.

Behind the royal floats, royal soldiers led fierce wolves that performed tricks for the audience. All kinds of instruments floated down the parade route playing upbeat music. Bella couldn't see the performers, but she knew fire eaters, enchanted animals, and spell casters walked the route and entertained the crowd. Security guards walked beside the royal family. *This is a lot of security, even for a royal parade!* Bella thought. But the king and queen had always gone overboard on safety measures for Bella.

Bella's float wound along the parade route, and there wasn't one empty spot behind the shield spell. Princess Bella tossed as much candy as she could and waved and smiled for pictures. She looked behind her at Ivy and Clara. Both girls furiously tossed candy to keep up with the outstretched hands.

"This is so crazy!" Clara shouted to Bella.

"And ridiculously fun!" Ivy added.

"I'm so glad you're both here," Bella said.

"Happy birthday, Princess!" someone called from the crowd. A familiar voice.

She scanned the rows of people and saw Lyssa smiling and waving at her. Bella waved furiously at

Lyssa and almost hopped up and down at seeing her friend in the crowd.

She took a deep breath, wanting to remember the moment forever, and glanced up at the sky. And noticed something odd.

Bella blinked and shut her eyes, hoping when she opened them that what she had seen would be gone. But there it was—a giant, billowing plume of red smoke. The float turned a corner, and Bella realized where that smoke was coming from.

The Dark Forest.

7

Parade Panic

As soon as the crowd caught sight of the smoke, panic spread from person to person. People were pointing and shouting, Bella's celebration temporarily forgotten.

Any activity from the Dark Forest and the Blacklands was *not* good. Bella didn't know much about the Dark Forest or the Blacklands, but she did know one thing: *Never* go there. She had been taught since she could walk that the Blacklands and Dark Forest were dangerous and she was never to set foot on those grounds bordering Crystal. Bella had heard rumors about an evil queen ruling the lands, but her parents always said the same thing when she confronted them: "We'll tell you about it when you're older."

She really wanted to talk to her mom and dad, but they had their heads together on their float a few feet in front. The princess gripped the float's railing tightly, in shock that this was happening on her big day. Was that why there was extra security? Bella wondered.

"Your Majesty!"

"Is evil threatening Crystal? What shall we do?"

The townspeople shouted questions at the king and queen as they climbed down from their float.

"C'mon," Bella said. She grasped Ivy's and Clara's hands as a security guard helped them to the ground. "We have to find out what's going on."

The three girls hurried up to Bella's parents. "Mom?" Bella asked as she reached her mother's side. "What's going on?"

"Shhh, sweetie," Queen Katherine said. She placed a hand on her daughter's head. "Dad's going to address everyone. The smoke isn't anything to worry about."

"But—," Bella started, but she was interrupted by the crackle of a bullhorn.

Silently, Lyssa appeared at Bella's side. Since she worked at the castle, Lyssa was able to slip through the shield spell. Bella slipped her hand into the older girl's comforting grasp.

King Phillip, sword gleaming at his side, was atop the podium in the town's center.

"Kind people of Crystal," King Phillip said. Bella realized her dad was using his deep I'm-king-so-listen voice. She, Clara, and Ivy huddled together next to Queen Katherine.

"The smoke is merely a misguided birthday message to my daughter," King Phillip continued. "Neither you nor our fair kingdom is under attack.

As a precaution to ensure that everyone continues to enjoy this glorious day, extra guards will patrol Crystal's boundaries. Please go about your plans and do not let this act of childishness ruin the spirit of Princess Bella's birthday."

"Whew," Ivy said in a whisper. "Your dad doesn't seem worried, Bella."

"I was scared for a minute," Clara added.

"But who's sending the smoke signal?" Bella asked. "Why would it be a birthday message to me?"

She met her mother's eyes. Queen Katherine was worried. "I'm going to speak to your father," the queen said. "I'll be back in a moment."

Bella's mom was gone only moments, but it felt like hours before she returned.

"You two better say good-bye to your parents before you come to the castle for my party," Bella told her friends. She managed a smile despite her nerves.

Ivy and Clara nodded and started into the crowd. Since they were on the inside of the shield spell, they'd be able to cross over. Plus, it was time to drop the shield.

"Lyssa," Queen Katherine said as she arrived beside Bella, "please make sure the royal carriage is prepared for our ride home. Thank you."

"Yes, Your Majesty," Lyssa said, bowing her head. She squeezed Bella's hand before disappearing into the crowd.

"Mom?" Bella asked. "What's wrong? What was that?"

Queen Katherine lowered her hazel eyes to Bella. "It's nothing. Everything is okay."

"I can tell you're scared," Bella said, slipping her hand into her mom's. "Maybe we should cancel my party."

"Bella, listen to me," Queen Katherine said, leaning close to her daughter. "You mustn't worry.

Your father and I will protect you, the castle, and Crystal from anything bad. Today is your eighth birthday. Please let me do any worrying that needs to be done, and promise me you'll enjoy your party."

The queen squeezed Bella's hand. Bella watched the red smoke billow from the distance and couldn't help but cringe.

"Okay, Mom. I won't worry—promise."

Queen Katherine smiled and hugged Bella. "Good girl."

Bella hugged her mom and chewed the inside of her cheek, wondering if she could keep that promise.

8

What Red Smoke?

A couple of hours later, the weird red smoke was the *last* thing on Bella's mind. She was too full to think of anything but her stomach. Bella, Ivy, and Clara had feasted on delicious roast chicken, mac 'n' cheese, and all of Bella's favorite foods.

After dinner, the chefs brought out an eight-tiered cake—one layer for every year since Bella's birth. The gorgeous cake had been covered in light-purple buttercream frosting, and each layer was decorated with images of Bella's favorite things. Unicorns, flowers, and bumblebees floated in the air around the cake and looked real until you swiped a hand through them—and it became clear they were images projected in the air. Bella had almost stopped her dad from cutting the cake, because she loved looking at it so much!

After cake, the girls had watched a movie, but Bella hadn't been able to concentrate. She was too busy thinking about the waiting unicorns.

"I think it's time for presents!" Queen Katherine said.

"Yaaay!" Bella cheered. Now it was just Bella, her parents, and Ivy and Clara.

The first-floor living room overflowed with presents from Bella's family. The people of Crystal had come to the castle gates after the parade, leaving hundreds of flowers, small gifts, and cards for Bella. Bella had burst into giggles when one of the royal security guards had told her that someone had left a hen with a note explaining how fresh eggs would make Bella a healthy princess.

"This box is taller than me!" Bella exclaimed. She stood next to a box wrapped in dark-blue paper with glittery white stars. The bow on the box was the size of her head.

"That's from Grandma Margie," said Queen Katherine.

"Grandma M sends the best presents," Bella said. She smiled, thinking of her dad's mom. "I can't wait to open it."

Her eyes were trained on the presents that Clara and Ivy held. Her besties, still in their parade gowns, grinned.

"Can I open your presents first?" Bella asked her friends. Then she glanced at her mom. "In my room?"

Ivy and Clara looked to Queen Katherine for a yes or no.

"That's entirely up to Ivy and Clara," Queen Katherine said. "Perhaps they want to make you

wait, Bella, until the end of the evening." There
was a teasing tone in the queen's voice.

"Hmmm . . . maybe we should make you wait,"
Ivy said.

"Yeah, we could make you wait until you open all of your gifts," Clara said. "I'm sure you have *no* interest in opening our presents right now. . . ."

"Oh, *please*? You can't say no to the birthday girl," Bella said. "I'll be sad forever."

Queen Katherine, Ivy, and Clara laughed.

"Well, if you're going to be sad *forever,* then maybe we should let you open our gifts," Ivy said with a look at Clara.

Clara nodded. "If you'd only be sad for a day, okay, but not *forever!*"

"Yay! Let's go!" Bella cheered, dancing in the direction of her room. Ivy and Clara were right behind her.

The girls ran to Bella's room, kicked off their shoes, and hopped onto Bella's enormous bed.

"You can go first," Clara said to Ivy.

Smiling, Ivy handed a small box to Bella. It had

been wrapped with paper that kept changing from pink to purple, and there was a card attached to a curly purple bow.

Bella opened the card and read it aloud. "'Princess Bella, happy birthday! I'm so lucky to have you as my best friend! I hope this is the best day ever! Love, Ivy.'" Bella smiled at her friend. "Thank you so much. I'm lucky to have you!"

Bella ripped open the wrapping paper and found a silver photo frame dotted with colored gems. Inside was a photo of Ivy, Clara, and Bella with their arms slung across each other's shoulders as they grinned at the camera. The gems in the frame changed from red to blue to green in no particular order.

"Oh!" Bella said happily. "I love this picture! I remember when your mom took it, Ivy, when we had a sleepover at your house a few months ago. The frame is so perfect! Thank you!"

She hugged Ivy and got up to place the framed photo on her dresser.

"My turn!" Clara handed Bella a long, rectangular box. The white box was closed with a turquoise ribbon, and like Ivy's, there was a card taped to the top.

Bella took the pink envelope, opened the card covered with adorable unicorns, and smiled.

"'Hail Princess Bella! Don't get used to me calling you 'princess,' okay? Only on your BIRTHDAY! You're an amazing best friend, and I'm so happy this day is finally here! Xoxo, Clara.'"

"So you're really not going to call me 'princess' after this huge birthday?" Bella teased.

"No!" Ivy and Clara said at the same time. All of the girls burst into giggles.

Bella slid off the ribbon and lifted the box lid. She removed a sunshine-yellow cloth binder with a clear pocket in the front. She opened it and found pages of clear pockets, thick papers with color and different designs like swirls or rainbows, and some with words in glittery letters, like *SMILE!*, *BFFs*, and *SLEEPOVER*. The stickers flashed on and off so the words disappeared for a second before reappearing in a different color. The borders around the empty frames blinked and shone brightly.

"Oohhhhh! A friendship scrapbook!" Bella said. "This is perfect for all of us! We can fill the pages with pictures and pass it around."

Bella hugged Clara, who had a huge smile on her face. "I'm so happy you like it, Bells!" Clara said. "I thought it would be fun for us to keep memories in here."

Ivy climbed off the bed and searched through the CRYSTAL GIRL canvas bag that she carried everywhere. "Aha!" she said, holding up her camera.

"There's no better night to start filling the scrapbook! Say cheese!"

Bella and Clara said the magic word and grinned into the camera. Ivy left the camera floating in the air and scrambled to join them. The camera clicked and flashed.

"Print it!" Bella said.

Ivy plucked the camera out of the air and pressed a button. The photo appeared on Bella's bed.

Bella picked up the picture and slid it into the scrapbook. The photo, on repeat, captured the girls a few seconds before and after the photo was taken. Again Bella, Ivy, and Clara readied themselves for the camera, posed, and then giggled.

SLAM!

Though her mom was too far away for Bella to hear what she was saying, she heard Queen Katherine yelling downstairs. The voices of at least four or five royal security guards echoed up to Bella's room.

"What was that?" Clara and Ivy asked, looking scared.

"Stay here, okay? I'll be right back," Bella said nervously. She was off the bed and out the door before her friends could answer her. An uneasy feeling swirled in her stomach. Bella ran down a spiral staircase, through a long corridor, and skidded to a halt in the foyer.

"My Princess Bella, happy birthday, darling."

9

Queen of Mean

Bella stared at the strange woman who stood in the entrance to the castle. She had black hair cascading down her back, and the ends were bright red. Red lipstick stained the woman's mouth—one that smiled at Bella. But the smile wasn't real. Bella could see it in her eyes. They were black and without a trace of feeling.

At that moment Bella took in the guards surrounding the woman, swords drawn. In the middle of the circle, Queen Katherine stood next to her with a furious expression.

"Bella, go back upstairs," the queen said, her voice low.

The scary woman laughed. "Sister, you haven't changed at all in the years since we last gathered."

Sister?!

Bella took a closer look and realized that the strange woman looked exactly like her mom. Except a lot meaner. And with darker hair.

If this crazy woman was Queen Katherine's sister, that also meant she was Bella's . . . aunt?

Queen Katherine's head whipped away from Bella as she faced the woman.

"Speechless, Katherine? This whole"—the woman waved a pale hand at the guards—"mess could have been avoided had you sent me an invitation to Bella's eighth birthday. Silly of you and Phillip to think royal guards would keep me from my niece."

Bella's eyes widened when the woman said "niece."

"Did you see my birthday message to you, Bella?"

Bella frowned. *Birthday message?* "You?" she whispered. "You sent the red smoke?" She shook her head. "That would mean . . . you live in the Dark Forest."

The woman laughed. "More like I rule the Dark Forest, darling. I am Queen Fire, after all."

Queen Fire? Bella stared at her mom, but Queen Katherine's eyes were on her sister. Bella clenched her teeth. A cold feeling trickled down her back, and she wanted to scream at the guards to make Queen Fire leave. If this . . . relative . . . ruled the Dark Forest, she was dangerous. *Mom told me to go already,* Bella thought. *But I can't.* Her legs felt rooted to the ground.

"Darling girl, come give your aunt a hug,"

Queen Fire said, her black eyes trained on Bella. "I haven't had a glimpse of you since your birth."

"Mom?" Bella asked. "What is she talking about?"

Queen Fire's expression darkened. "You know nothing about me?"

Bella shook her head.

"We breathed not a word about you to Bella, Fawn," Queen Katherine said. "Bella didn't need to know of your existence."

Bella's mother turned to look at Bella. "Go upstairs now!" Queen Katherine's voice was sharp.

Bella hated to disobey her mother, but she wasn't going to leave her alone with guards and her apparently evil sister. *Dad, where are you?* Bella thought.

Queen Fire smiled and clasped her hands. "You were afraid, Katherine. Afraid that Bella might be like me. She certainly has my feisty spirit."

"I don't know you at all," Bella said, her heart pounding. "But if my parents kept you from me, they had a good reason. My mom doesn't want you here. And neither do I."

Queen Katherine shot Bella a look, but this time it was one of pride. Bella knew she would be grounded later for staying against her mother's wishes, but she wasn't going to let anyone upset her mom. Queen Katherine slipped away from her sister, through the circle of guards, and took Bella's side. Bella felt an instant rush of relief that her mom wasn't between the guards and Queen Fire.

Queen Fire took a step toward Bella, her long black dress skimming the floor. The royal guards jumped closer, their swords shining in the light as they pointed at the queen.

"You're young, my girl," Queen Fire said, almost in a trancelike tone. "Tell me you haven't worried about tonight."

Bella's mouth opened and closed. Suddenly she wished she'd listened to her mom and had left the room. Queen Fire was *right*—Bella had worried about the Pairing Ceremony, but why would Queen Fire expect her to have worried?

"I have my answer," Queen Fire said, a smile curling on her lips. "Bella, do you wish for something different from the life planned for you?"

"That's enough!" Queen Katherine exclaimed. "You will leave at once or—"

"Or what, Katherine?" Queen Fire asked.

"Or I will have you thrown into prison for trespassing!" King Phillip ran into the room, his sword at his side. His boots thundered on the marble floor. "Remove her immediately," he barked to the guards. "Make sure she never crosses the castle bridge again."

Bella swallowed. She'd never seen her dad so angry. The guards sprang into action, two of them taking Queen Fire by the upper arms.

"Fawn, if you *ever* set foot onto my property or speak to my wife or daughter, remember that you have been warned," King Phillip threatened.

The way Queen Fire looked at the royal family made Bella shiver.

"Don't worry about me, Phillip," Queen Fire said. "Your concern should be if and when Bella crosses the river and seeks *my* help."

"Out!" King Phillip bellowed.

"I'll see myself out," Queen Fire added. She opened her hands, palms to the sky, and the air crackled and a red cloud of smoke covered her. The guards coughed and scrambled in the smoke. But Queen Fire was gone.

"Bella." Queen Katherine placed a hand on her daughter's arm. "Are you all right?"

Bella took a few deep breaths before she looked up at her mom. "Yes. I'm sorry that I didn't go to my room. I know there were guards to protect you, but I don't trust her and—"

Queen Katherine knelt down in front of Bella. "I understand why you stayed. Thank you for wanting to protect me. I'm more concerned about you. I didn't want you to learn of Queen Fire this way."

"Is she really your sister?" Bella asked.

Queen Katherine nodded. "Bella, I'll answer all of your questions. I promise. But you have guests. Would you like to talk after Ivy and Clara have gone?"

Bella nodded, still shaking from the whole thing.

"Go upstairs and talk to Ivy and Clara," Queen Katherine said. She kissed Bella's cheek, and Bella hurried upstairs.

She reached her room and found her friends sitting wide-eyed on her bed.

"Everything is okay," Bella said immediately.

The three best friends hugged, then huddled together while Bella told them what had happened downstairs. When she reached the end of the story, Bella didn't even want to think of the words *Queen Fire* until she talked to her parents. It was too much, too fast.

10

Moonbow + Pairing Time = Good Luck?

The night air was warm, but Bella shivered. She sat on one of the stone benches outside between Queen Katherine and King Phillip. It was time to talk about Queen Fire before they made their way to the royal stables. Moments ago Bella had said good-bye to Ivy and Clara. Usually the girls would sleep over, but not tonight. Not with the Pairing Ceremony ahead. Both girls had hugged Bella tight and made her promise to call them first thing in the morning to give them all the details about her new unicorn. Thanks to Queen Fire's interruption, Bella hadn't had time to open her other gifts yet.

Bella looked up at the night sky. It twinkled with lights of thousands of stars. The moon, full and round, had given light to a rare moonbow. Usually moonbows were a symbol of good luck. Bella blinked up at the arch of colors that spread from the moon and lit up the sky. *I hope my aura is any of the moonbow colors except red,* she thought.

Her throat was tight. The visit from Queen Fire had rattled her, even though the rest of the evening had been perfect.

"I knew a bad queen lived in the Blacklands and ruled the Dark Forest, but I've never heard the name 'Queen Fire.' Until tonight," Bella began.

Suddenly the questions came to her mind rapid-fire.

"Mom, what happened to her? Why is she evil? Why didn't you and Dad tell me? Is she dangerous?" The questions tumbled out of Bella's mouth.

Queen Katherine took a deep breath. "Bella, this was not something your father and I intended to keep from you forever. We knew you would eventually learn about Queen Fire from a classmate or research. Your father and I always wanted the truth to come from us."

King Phillip nodded. "Queen Fire—Fawn—is your mother's fraternal twin sister. We do not speak of her because, yes, she is evil and she does have a grudge against our family."

"Why?" Bella asked.

"On our eighth birthday," Queen Katherine started, "Fawn and I were best friends. As close as sisters could be. We were both excited for our Pairing Ceremony that night, and I went first. My aura, as you know, turned green and I was gifted with Kiwi."

Pain flicked across the queen's face. "My sister's aura turned red. The first royal in history to have that color aura. It was something my parents had only read about in Crystal lore as a color of evil and darkness."

"Oh no," Bella whispered. "Did Queen Fire find a red unicorn that night?"

"No." Queen Katherine shook her head. "Red auras in unicorns do not naturally exist. My sister also became the first royal not to be Paired. She changed that day. The fun, caring sister I'd grown up with was gone. In her place was someone angry and jealous."

"I'm sorry, Mom," Bella said softly.

Queen Katherine lifted her head, looking out across the castle grounds at the fireflies that sparkled in the night. "At fourteen, my sister left the castle and never came back. I reached out to her, but she didn't want anything to do with me."

"Queen Fire," King Phillip said, squeezing the queen's hand, "began stealing royal unicorns—the special, highly trained ones that aren't Paired with a royal—and built a castle in the Dark Forest."

"What happens to the unicorns?" Bella asked.

"My sister's aura, which has now shifted to black, poisons the unicorns' minds," the queen explained. "They become angry, dangerous creatures. I think Fawn continues to steal unicorns because she never got one as a child."

Bella didn't know what to say. Red auras. Black auras. An evil queen who was her aunt.

Horror struck deep in Bella's stomach.

"Mom, Dad," she said. "What if . . . what if my aura is red?"

"No!" the king and queen immediately chorused.

"No, Bella," Queen Katherine repeated firmly. "That will not happen. My sister must have had something dark within her long before her Pairing Ceremony. You are my daughter—you are one of the most compassionate girls I've ever known, and I am sure you will not reveal a red aura."

King Phillip put a hand on Bella's knee. "Your mother is right. Fawn was a troubled girl who hid it very well from her sister and parents. You're nothing like that, Bella."

"My sister has nothing to lose, so she came here tonight to cause worry and doubt in your mind," Queen Katherine added. "Her own eighth birthday was so unhappy that she wants to make yours that way as well. Don't let her get to you."

Almost as if on cue, a unicorn whinnied from the stables.

Bella took a deep breath, nodding, and tried to believe her parents. She crossed all her fingers that a red aura wouldn't appear when she began the Pairing Ceremony. She didn't know what she would do if—

"Are you ready, sweetie?"

King Phillip's voice cut through Bella's thoughts. She hadn't even noticed that he and her mom had risen and were standing in front of her.

Bella nodded, slipping a sweaty hand into her dad's free cool hand. In the other, he carried a book—a very *old*-looking book.

The family approached the royal stables. It was one of Bella's favorite places on the castle grounds. Floodlights lit the stable yard and the stable entrance. The pastel-green paint on the stable's outside reminded of Bella of mint chocolate chip ice cream because of the black stable roof. All of the unicorns had been tucked away in their stalls for the night.

"Greetings, King Phillip, Queen Katherine," Frederick, the stable manager, said. "And happiest of birthdays to you, Princess Bella."

Bella's smile was wobbly. "Thank you," she said to the tall, brown-haired man.

"Follow me, please," Frederick said.

Frederick led Bella and her parents to a large arena inside the stable. The glass windows, usually where Bella loved to watch the unicorns' training, had been sprayed a frosty white. Bella couldn't see inside.

"The glass is frosted for your privacy during the ceremony," Frederick explained, as if he had read Bella's thoughts.

Frederick opened a door, bowing his head and waving for the royal family to enter ahead of him.

"You first, honey," King Phillip said. He released Bella's hand. Bella didn't realize how hard she'd been squeezing it!

She took a giant breath and walked across the dirt-covered floor. Ten gorgeous white unicorns stood in a line in front of her, each one held by a stable groom. The unicorns almost shimmered. Their manes and tails looked like silk and had a slight curl at the ends. A horn poked from under each unicorn's forelock—the mane across the unicorn's forehead. The horns weren't very long, since these were young unicorns. But each horn had a *very* pointed tip. A line etched into the horn swirled from the base to the top.

Frederick, Queen Katherine, and King Phillip formed a line next to Bella.

"Bella," Frederick said.

Bella tore her eyes away from the unicorns. "Yes?" she asked, looking past her mom.

"As the royal tradition goes, you are to start at the beginning of the unicorn line and make your way to the end. You will only need to pause for a second or two in front of each unicorn before the unicorn's aura color is revealed."

"My aura hasn't shown," Bella said, biting her bottom lip. "When will it?"

Frederick and Bella's parents smiled.

"Don't worry, Bella." King Phillip smiled. "Your aura will appear after I read a short passage from Crystal's *Royal Book*. Then you will approach the unicorns."

"Bella, please stand before your father and me," Queen Katherine said.

Bella clasped her hands together and tried to stop her knees from shaking. She moved in front of her parents, and Frederick stood off to the side.

King Phillip carefully opened the dark-brown book with the royal family crest on the front. He stopped on a page bordered in gold and looked up at Bella. Queen Katherine put an arm through one of King Phillip's arms and gave her daughter a reassuring smile. "You're ready," the queen mouthed.

My stomach doesn't feel ready! Bella thought. Her heart sounded like it was in her ears.

"Princess Isabella," King Phillip said formally.

He spoke with his this-is-very-important voice, like he had used during the parade.

"On April thirteenth," King Phillip continued, "this day in the Crystal Kingdom, you have reached the age of eight. With this birthday comes immense responsibility. You, as your royal ancestors before you, are about to participate in your Unicorn Pairing Ceremony."

Bella felt as though her dad was speaking another language for a moment. Or talking about someone else. *I can't believe this is my ceremony,* she thought.

"As the only princess of Crystal," King Phillip said, "you must acknowledge that you are in a place of great power and responsibility. Your kingdom looks up to you as its princess. If you feel that you are too young for anyone to look up to, this is untrue. Your actions will be watched with closer scrutiny by your kingdom. Your mother and I expect you to remember this and to be a kind, compassionate, relatable royal. Are you able to fulfill these duties, Princess Bella?"

"Yes, Father," Bella answered. It didn't seem like the time to say "Dad."

King Phillip smiled. "Wonderful. It is with great pleasure that your mother and I bestow upon you a chance to find a unicorn that matches your aura. This unicorn will serve not only as your unicorn to ride but as your lifelong protector. The unicorn Paired to you, Princess Bella, will be attuned to any danger around you and will fight to ensure your safety."

King Phillip closed the book and handed it to Frederick. He took Queen Katherine's hand.

"Princess Bella," Queen Katherine said, "please bow your head and repeat after me."

Bella dipped her head. *This is really happening!* she screamed to herself. She wanted to break into a dance from nerves and excitement.

"I, Princess Bella," Queen Katherine said.

"I, Princess Bella," Bella repeated.

"Ask my aura to reveal itself," the queen said.

Bella repeated the line.

"And wish it to glow while I seek my unicorn match," Queen Katherine said.

"And wish it to glow while I seek my unicorn match," Bella said.

"Aura, please present yourself now," Queen Katherine said.

Goose bumps covered Bella's arms.

"Aura, please present yourself now," Bella said.

"Raise your head, Princess Bella," instructed Queen Katherine.

Bella lifted her head. Only seconds had passed, but it felt like hours to her. Nothing appeared.

"Mom," Bella said, panic in her voice.

Before she could say another word, Bella felt a . . . *tingle* coursing through her body. She blinked fast as a light haze appeared before her. She looked down as the mist covered her hands, arms, and the rest of her body. She could feel it—her aura was about to appear!

The shimmery white soon tinted with the palest hint of lavender and kept getting darker and darker until it stopped at a royal purple.

"Ohhh!" Bella said, gasping. "It's not red!" She didn't know if she wanted to laugh or cry. She grinned instead.

"Bella! Darling, your aura is beautiful!" Queen Katherine said. Bella saw tears in her mother's eyes.

"Honey, that color is perfect for you," King Phillip agreed.

"It's so pretty!" Bella exclaimed, waving her hands in front of her and trying to touch the mist. But her fingers swiped right through the aura. "And it's one of my favorite colors!"

"Princess Bella," Frederick said. "Congratulations on your aura. It is time for you to meet the ten awaiting unicorns."

Frederick offered Bella his arm, and she took it. He led her to the beginning of the unicorn line. The king and queen tightly clasped their hands together at their sides.

Bella's pulse pounded in her ears. *Just because your aura isn't red doesn't mean any of the unicorns will match,* she reminded herself.

"Princess?" Frederick snapped Bella back to reality.

"Yes, I'm sorry," Bella said.

"Whenever you are ready, please begin the Pairing Ceremony," Frederick said.

Bella looked at the gorgeous unicorns. The creatures, like their grooms, stared straight ahead and didn't move. Not so much as a tail swished. Bella knew how much careful selection and training this group of unicorns had gone through to be here as potential candidates.

This was it.

Bella let go of Frederick's arm and took a few first shaky steps. She reached the first unicorn and stopped in front of it. She glanced into the unicorn's liquid brown eyes. *Are you my match?* Bella thought.

A soft pink haze spread quickly over the unicorn from head to tail. Disappointment gripped Bella's stomach. *It's only your first unicorn,* she told herself. *There are nine more.*

The groom holding the pink-aura unicorn led it away from the line and out of the arena.

Bella stepped in front of the second unicorn. Green.

The third unicorn turned purple before Bella even came to a full stop in front of it.

Nerves made Bella's stomach flip-flop. She

glanced at her parents. They both nodded, encouraging her with smiles.

Bella tried to smile back, but she was too nervous. *If I don't get a unicorn even though my aura isn't red, what will happen?* she thought. *There won't be another Pairing Ceremony.*

Bella lifted her head and smoothed her dress as she stepped to the fourth unicorn. The beautiful creature blinked as a yellow haze covered its body.

The fifth unicorn turned dark blue. Bella sniffed hard, determined not to cry. *But I'm halfway through,* she thought. She forced her feet forward to the sixth unicorn, almost not stopping. *I know there won't be a match,* Bella said to herself.

Her eyes were on the seventh unicorn when she heard gasps from her parents and Frederick.

Bella looked at the unicorn beside her. The

gorgeous animal's white body had covered itself in a white mist that was turning light purple. The purple deepened just like Bella's aura. Bella's heart seemed to stop—she waited for the aura to keep darkening, but nothing happened.

The aura began to float from the hindquarters forward. Bella's mouth was open as the aura floated over the unicorn's body and disappeared into the unicorn's horn. Before Bella could blink, the last bit of the haze vanished into the horn, and it twinkled with a violet light before turning back to white. Bella's aura evaporated along with the unicorn's. A purple tint remained in the unicorn's mane and tail.

"Oh!" Bella exclaimed. She threw her arms around the unicorn's neck. The unicorn's coat was soft, and it smelled like sweet hay. "You're my match!" Bella's eyes filled with tears, and she couldn't stop hugging her unicorn.

The groom holding the unicorn bowed his head. "Congratulations, Princess Bella. This guy is incredibly lucky to have you." He handed her a leather lead line—a tool for Bella to guide her unicorn. It was attached to a matching headpiece—a halter—that ran across the unicorn's muzzle and up behind his ears. The unicorn nuzzled Bella's neck. She giggled at the warm breath on her neck and the unicorn's tickly whiskers.

Her parents rushed over and threw their arms around Bella.

"Oh, sweetie!" Queen Katherine said. She hugged Bella extra hard. "What a perfect match!"

"You've got quite a unicorn here," King Phillip said. He reached out to the unicorn, who stuck her muzzle out for a rub.

A few happy tears slid down Bella's cheeks. "I was so scared! I didn't think any of them would match me!" The unicorn nudged Bella's arm and blinked at her with warm brown eyes. It was almost as if she was saying, *Don't cry.* "You're such a good girl," Bella said.

"You'll have to think of a name," said Queen Katherine.

"I've had eight years to think," Bella said. "I already know."

She looked at the unicorn before her—all *hers*—and grinned. "Her name is Glimmer," Bella said.

"Well, Glimmer," King Phillip said happily. "Welcome to our family!"

Bella threw her arms around Glimmer's neck, never wanting to let go.

HERE'S A SNEAK PEEK AT BELLA AND
GLIMMER'S NEXT ADVENTURE:
Where's Glimmer?

"Glimmer!" Princess Bella yelled before she burst
into giggles. The princess's unicorn picked up the
brush from Bella's hand and held it in her mouth.
The shimmery white unicorn shook her head,
sending her purple-tinted mane flying. It was like
she was teasing Bella. "Are you excited because
it's Saturday and I have all weekend to spend with
you?" Bella asked.

"She's sneaky," said Ben, a boy only a few years
older than Bella. Glimmer reached out her muzzle, offering Ben the brush. He took the brush, grinning. Ben had arrived a couple of days after Bella had

been Paired with Glimmer. He was the nephew of Frederick, the stable manager, and he had come from the neighboring kingdom of Foris as an apprentice of his uncle. It was up to him to teach Bella about unicorn care and riding. More important, he had been assigned to help Bella and Glimmer prepare for their upcoming Crystal Kingdom debut.

It was a beautiful, sunny day in Crystal Kingdom, the land ruled by Bella's parents, King Phillip and Queen Katherine. The air smelled like honeysuckle and roses. Ben had secured Glimmer to a post just outside the royal stables with a shimmering rainbow-colored rope that was also used to help lead her around. Bees and butterflies flitted through the air, looking like confetti. A few of the bees flashed neon yellow, almost like a flashlight being turned on and off. That meant the bees had sensed pollen in the air and were headed toward a sweet-smelling flower.

The butterflies in Crystal Kingdom were more beautiful than any others in the neighboring kingdoms. Crystal butterflies had wings lined with teensy sparkles that flashed and glittered like diamonds in the sunlight.

"Thank you for showing me how to keep Glimmer clean, Ben," Bella said, lifting her hand to shield her eyes from the sun. She eyed Glimmer—her very own unicorn—who had been a gift on her eighth birthday. A gift per royal tradition, of course. The unicorn's coat was super shiny, and her mane and tail were silky after Ben had helped Bella comb them.

"No problem, Princess Bella," Ben said.

"Ben, please," Bella said. "Just call me Bella."

"Okay, Prin—I mean, Bella." Ben smiled at her.

"Do you like taking care of the unicorns?" Bella asked Ben.

Most people did not have a unicorn. It was law in Crystal Kingdom and the surrounding kingdoms that the best unicorns were saved for the royal stables. Other unicorns ran free, and it was against the law for a commoner to capture one.

Ben laughed, looking at Bella. "I love it," he said. "Uncle Frederick has taught me so much already. I don't know much about the royal customs, but I do know about unicorns."

"Did you know someone royal in Foris?" Bella asked.

"My father worked in the royal stables at Foris Castle," Ben explained. "He had been training me so I could work in the stables someday too. But he broke his arm a few weeks ago working with a royal unicorn."

Bella's long brown hair swirled around her shoulders as she whipped her head around to look at Ben.

"Ouch! I'm so sorry! Is your dad going to be okay?" she asked.

Ben nodded. "He'll be back in the stables in a couple of months, but he didn't want me to lose any time. Uncle Frederick has been training and caring for unicorns even longer than my dad, so I'll be living with him until my apprenticeship is done."

Bella climbed the white fence and looked out over Crystal Castle's grounds. She loved watching unicorns frolicking in the lush pastures. But when Bella thought about the unicorns, it reminded her of her upcoming debut with Glimmer. It was going to be here so fast—this coming Wednesday morning! It was especially exciting because it was a holiday and there would be no school.

It was royal tradition that within the first month of a prince or princess being Paired with a unicorn, the pair presented themselves to the kingdom. Bella's parents had told her that the people of Crystal Kingdom were eager to see the princess and her unicorn.

Bella couldn't wait to introduce Glimmer to the townspeople!

Bella shifted her gaze back to Glimmer as Ben climbed the fence to sit next to her. She'd only been Paired with Glimmer a week ago, but she loved her unicorn more than anything in the entire Crystal Kingdom (well, except her parents!). Definitely more than all of the people in the other three sky islands. Bella had learned in geography class that sky islands were pieces of land that floated high in the clouds. The only way to reach another sky island was to cast a spell to create a rainbow or moonbeam to walk over as a bridge between two islands.

"I can't believe I got so lucky," Bella said. Glimmer pointed her cute ears in Bella's direction. "My eighth birthday was so scary!"

"How do eighth birthdays work for princes and princesses?" Ben asked.

"Well, every royal is born with an aura," Bella explained. "It's this kind of light that shows when a royal turns eight and when they are crowned king or queen. It can be any color of the rainbow." She paused, frowning. "Except for red."

"So red auras don't exist?" Ben asked.

"Actually, they *do*. But if someone's born with a red aura, it's a very, very bad sign. Have you heard of Queen Fire?"

Ben nodded quickly. "My uncle warned me about her. He told me never to enter the Dark Forest and explained that Queen Fire was, like, your family's enemy."

"Actually, Queen Fire," Bella said, taking a big gulp of air, "is my aunt. She is the first royal in history to be born with a red aura." She squeezed her eyes half-shut, peeking at Ben through her lashes. *I hope I didn't scare him by telling him a crazy evil queen is related to me,* Bella worried.

"Whoa," Ben said. "I didn't know Queen Fire was related to you. My uncle didn't tell me that part. That must have been scary for you when you waited for your aura to appear."

"It was!" Bella agreed. "My mom's is green and my dad's is yellow. Once I learned about my aunt, I got scared that my aura might be red."

Ben laughed, his brown eyes twinkling. "I haven't known you that long, but there's *no* way your aura ever could have been red."

"Thanks, Ben," Bella said. "Only my best friends, Clara and Ivy, know Queen Fire is related to me. I hope you don't want to stop teaching me now that you know."

Ben reached out a hand to stroke Glimmer's forehead. "No way. No evil queen relative is going to scare me off from helping you with Glimmer." He grinned, a mischievous glint in his eyes. "You've got a lot to learn, Princess."

Bella laughed. "Oh, really? Well, I'm glad you're sticking around then."

"Let's take Glimmer for a walk, and you can tell me more about being a royal," Ben said.

Bella nodded, and Ben untied Glimmer, handing the soft rope to Bella.

The three set off down a familiar path that wound through the castle grounds and circled one of the castle's many lakes.

"My aura appeared during the Pairing Ceremony on the night of my birthday," Bella explained.

"A Pairing Ceremony is where you're matched to your unicorn, right?" Ben asked as he walked beside Bella.

"Yes. I got this strange tingly feeling, and a purple fog surrounded me. It was my aura. Your uncle Frederick asked me to walk in front of unicorns that he had picked for me."

"He told me a little about that part," Ben said.

"Each royal unicorn glowed, showing its aura, and you had to keep going until you found one that matched you, right?"

"That's right," Bella said. She, Ben, and Glimmer continued walking through the cropped grass toward the lake. "I was getting so scared that none of the unicorns would turn purple. Then I stepped in front of Glimmer, and it was so magical. She changed from white to purple in seconds!"

"That is *so* cool! I can't wait until I'm old enough to help during a Pairing Ceremony." Ben got a faraway look in his eyes, as if he was picturing himself in Frederick's place.

"I felt this instant bond with Glimmer," Bella said. She reached up a hand and patted the unicorn's neck as they walked. "I'd been dreaming about my eighth birthday my entire life, and Glimmer has made me so happy."

Glimmer snorted and bobbed her head.

"I think she's happy too," Ben said.

Bella, Ben, and Glimmer reached the lake. A spell had been cast on the deep water so it was clear enough that the bottom of the lake was visible. Bella and Ben led Glimmer to the lake's edge and halted her. Glimmer watched Ben and Bella peer into the water, then turned her own gaze to the lake water.

"Ooh, look!" Bella said. "See those spiky blue fish?" A school of electric-blue fish covered in spikes swam near the water's edge.

"Yeah! Look over there," Ben said, pointing. "There's a huge dog fish at the bottom of the lake."

Bella's eyes followed Ben's finger. It took a moment before she spotted the dog fish. The white fish had dozens of black spots and barely moved as it crawled along the lake's bottom. It had floppy ears that covered its gills, and instead of a fish mouth it had a dog's snout. Dog fish were important to lake life—they ate all the dirty algae and helped keep the water clean. Dog fish reminded Bella of vacuum cleaners.

Glimmer pulled on the rainbow line, stretching her neck toward the lake. Ben nodded his okay, and Bella let Glimmer lower her head and take a few sips of water.

"Want to try taking Glimmer for a ride tomorrow?" Ben asked.

"Really? Do you think I'm ready?" Bella asked. She clasped her hands together and tried very hard not to jump up and down.

"Definitely!" Ben said. "I think you guys are ready."

"Yaaay!" Bella cheered. Glimmer lifted her head from the lake, and water dripped off her chin whiskers. Giggling, Bella hugged her neck. "Silly girl. We get to go riding tomorrow! Our very first ride together."

"My friends Clara and Ivy are coming over tomorrow," Bella said to Ben. "They'll be so excited to see me ride Glimmer for the first time."

The trio stayed by the lake for a few more moments before starting the walk back to the royal stables. For the rest of the day, all Bella could think about was riding. It felt like her birthday all over again!

Mermaid Tales

*Exciting under-the-sea adventures
with Shelly and her mermaid friends!*

Where's Glimmer?

Don't miss any of Bella
and Glimmer's adventures!

Unicorn Magic

BOOK 1: Bella's Birthday Unicorn

Coming soon

BOOK 3: Green with Envy

Unicorn Magic

- BOOK 2 -

Where's Glimmer?

BY JESSICA BURKHART

Illustrated by Victoria Ying

Aladdin

NEW YORK LONDON TORONTO SYDNEY NEW DELHI

This book is a work of fiction. Any references to historical events, real people,
or real places are used fictitiously. Other names, characters, places, and events
are products of the author's imagination, and any resemblance to actual
events or places or persons, living or dead, is entirely coincidental.

ALADDIN

An imprint of Simon & Schuster Children's Publishing Division
1230 Avenue of the Americas, New York, NY 10020
This Aladdin paperback edition August 2014
Text copyright © 2014 by Jessica Burkhart
Cover illustrations copyright © 2014 by Victoria Ying
Interior illustrations by Victoria Ying
All rights reserved, including the right of reproduction in whole or in part in any form.
ALADDIN is a trademark of Simon & Schuster, Inc., and related logo
is a registered trademark of Simon & Schuster, Inc.
Also available in an Aladdin hardcover edition.
For information about special discounts for bulk purchases, please contact
Simon & Schuster Special Sales at 1-866-506-1949
or business@simonandschuster.com.
The Simon & Schuster Speakers Bureau can bring authors to your live event.
For more information or to book an event contact the
Simon & Schuster Speakers Bureau at 1-866-248-3049 or
visit our website at www.simonspeakers.com.
Cover designed by Jessica Handelman
Interior designed by Mike Rosamilia
The text of this book was set in Arno Pro.
Manufactured in the United States of America 1117 OFF
6 8 10 9 7 5
Library of Congress Control Number 2014936192
ISBN 978-1-4814-1106-6 (hc)
ISBN 978-1-4424-9824-2 (pbk)
ISBN 978-1-4424-9825-9 (eBook)

BE YOURSELF.
IF YOU CAN'T BE YOURSELF,
BE A UNICORN.

Acknowledgments

So much gratitude to the amazing team at Simon & Schuster. First, I have to thank Alyson Heller, Editor of All Fantastical. Aly, you waved a magic wand over Unicorn Magic and also shared your wand with me. I wouldn't have written a fourth of the fabulous fantasy elements had it not been for you. You taught me a new way of writing, and I'm so grateful. Your aura is bright purple!

Thanks to Fiona Simpson, Bethany Buck, Mara Anastas, the sales reps, and everyone at Simon & Schuster who worked so hard on *Where's Glimmer?*

Special thanks to Rubin Pfeffer for handling everything businessy so I can write.

Victoria Ying, again you've created a dream cover!

Finally, thank *you* for reading all about Bella and Glimmer! I hope you like their latest adventure. ☺

Contents

Where's Glimmer?

1

Glimmer + Bella 4Ever

"Glimmer!" Princess Bella yelled before she burst into giggles. The princess's unicorn picked up the brush from Bella's hand and held it in her mouth. The shimmery white unicorn shook her head, sending her purple-tinted mane flying. It was like she was teasing Bella. "Are you excited because it's Saturday and I have all weekend to spend with you?" Bella asked.

"She's sneaky," said Ben, a boy only a few years older than Bella. Glimmer reached out her muzzle, offering Ben the brush. He took the brush, grinning. Ben had arrived a couple of days after Bella had

1

been Paired with Glimmer. He was the nephew of Frederick, the stable manager, and he had come from the neighboring kingdom of Foris as an apprentice of his uncle. It was up to him to teach Bella about unicorn care and riding. More important, he had been assigned to help Bella and Glimmer prepare for their upcoming Crystal Kingdom debut.

It was a beautiful, sunny day in Crystal Kingdom, the land ruled by Bella's parents, King Phillip and Queen Katherine. The air smelled like honeysuckle and roses. Ben had secured Glimmer to a post just outside the royal stables with a shimmering rainbow-colored rope that was also used to help lead her around. Bees and butterflies flitted through the air, looking like confetti. A few of the bees flashed neon yellow, almost like a flashlight being turned on and off. That meant the bees had sensed pollen in the air and were headed toward a sweet-smelling flower.

The butterflies in Crystal Kingdom were more beautiful than any others in the neighboring kingdoms. Crystal butterflies had wings lined with teensy sparkles that flashed and glittered like diamonds in the sunlight.

"Thank you for showing me how to keep Glimmer clean, Ben," Bella said, lifting her hand to shield her eyes from the sun. She eyed Glimmer—her very own unicorn—who had been a gift on her eighth birthday. A gift per royal tradition, of course. The unicorn's coat was super shiny, and her mane and tail were silky after Ben had helped Bella comb them.

"No problem, Princess Bella," Ben said.

"Ben, please," Bella said. "Just call me Bella."

"Okay, Prin—I mean, Bella." Ben smiled at her.

"Do you like taking care of the unicorns?" Bella asked Ben.

Most people did not have a unicorn. It was law

in Crystal Kingdom and the surrounding kingdoms that the best unicorns were saved for the royal stables. Other unicorns ran free, and it was against the law for a commoner to capture one.

Ben laughed, looking at Bella. "I love it," he said. "Uncle Frederick has taught me so much already. I don't know much about the royal customs, but I do know about unicorns."

"Did you know someone royal in Foris?" Bella asked.

"My father worked in the royal stables at Foris Castle," Ben explained. "He had been training me so I could work in the stables someday too. But he broke his arm a few weeks ago working with a royal unicorn."

Bella's long brown hair swirled around her shoulders as she whipped her head around to look at Ben.

"Ouch! I'm so sorry! Is your dad going to be okay?" she asked.

Ben nodded. "He'll be back in the stables in a couple of months, but he didn't want me to lose any time. Uncle Frederick has been training and caring for unicorns even longer than my dad, so I'll be living with him until my apprenticeship is done."

Bella climbed the white fence and looked out over Crystal Castle's grounds. She loved watching unicorns frolicking in the lush pastures. But when Bella thought about the unicorns, it reminded her of her upcoming debut with Glimmer. It was going to be here so fast—this coming Wednesday morning! It was especially exciting because it was a holiday and there would be no school.

It was royal tradition that within the first month of a prince or princess being Paired with a unicorn, the pair presented themselves to the kingdom. Bella's parents had told her that the people of Crystal Kingdom were eager to see the princess

5

and her unicorn. Bella couldn't wait to introduce Glimmer to the townspeople!

Bella shifted her gaze back to Glimmer as Ben climbed the fence to sit next to her. She'd only been Paired with Glimmer a week ago, but she loved her unicorn more than anything in the entire Crystal Kingdom (well, except her parents!). Definitely more than all of the people in the other three sky islands. Bella had learned in geography class that sky islands were pieces of land that floated high in the clouds. The only way to reach another sky island was to cast a spell to create a rainbow or moonbeam to walk over as a bridge between two islands.

"I can't believe I got so lucky," Bella said. Glimmer pointed her cute ears in Bella's direction. "My eighth birthday was so scary!"

"How do eighth birthdays work for princes and princesses?" Ben asked.

"Well, every royal is born with an aura," Bella explained. "It's this kind of light that shows when a royal turns eight and when they are crowned king or queen. It can be any color of the rainbow." She paused, frowning. "Except for red."

"So red auras don't exist?" Ben asked.

"Actually, they *do*. But if someone's born with a red aura, it's a very, very bad sign. Have you heard of Queen Fire?"

Ben nodded quickly. "My uncle warned me about her. He told me never to enter the Dark Forest and explained that Queen Fire was, like, your family's enemy."

"Actually, Queen Fire," Bella said, taking a big gulp of air, "is my aunt. She is the first royal in history to be born with a red aura." She squeezed her eyes half-shut, peeking at Ben through her lashes. *I hope I didn't scare him by telling him a crazy evil queen is related to me,* Bella worried.

7

"Whoa," Ben said. "I didn't know Queen Fire was related to you. My uncle didn't tell me that part. That must have been scary for you when you waited for your aura to appear."

"It was!" Bella agreed. "My mom's is green and my dad's is yellow. Once I learned about my aunt, I got scared that my aura might be red."

Ben laughed, his brown eyes twinkling. "I haven't known you that long, but there's *no* way your aura ever could have been red."

"Thanks, Ben," Bella said. "Only my best friends, Clara and Ivy, know Queen Fire is related to me. I hope you don't want to stop teaching me now that you know."

Ben reached out a hand to stroke Glimmer's forehead. "No way. No evil queen relative is going to scare me off from helping you with Glimmer." He grinned, a mischievous glint in his eyes. "You've got a lot to learn, Princess."

Bella laughed. "Oh, really? Well, I'm glad you're sticking around then."

"Let's take Glimmer for a walk, and you can tell me more about being a royal," Ben said.

Bella nodded, and Ben untied Glimmer, handing the soft rope to Bella.

The three set off down a familiar path that wound through the castle grounds and circled one of the castle's many lakes.

"My aura appeared during the Pairing Ceremony on the night of my birthday," Bella explained.

"A Pairing Ceremony is where you're matched to your unicorn, right?" Ben asked as he walked beside Bella.

"Yes. I got this strange tingly feeling, and a purple fog surrounded me. It was my aura. Your uncle Frederick asked me to walk in front of unicorns that he had picked for me."

"He told me a little about that part," Ben said.

"Each royal unicorn glowed, showing its aura, and you had to keep going until you found one that matched you, right?"

"That's right," Bella said. She, Ben, and Glimmer continued walking through the cropped grass toward the lake. "I was getting so scared that none of the unicorns would turn purple. Then I stepped in front of Glimmer, and it was so magical. She changed from white to purple in seconds!"

"That is *so* cool! I can't wait until I'm old enough to help during a Pairing Ceremony." Ben got a faraway look in his eyes, as if he was picturing himself in Frederick's place.

"I felt this instant bond with Glimmer," Bella said. She reached up a hand and patted the unicorn's neck as they walked. "I'd been dreaming about my eighth birthday my entire life, and Glimmer has made me so happy."

Glimmer snorted and bobbed her head.

"I think she's happy too," Ben said.

Bella, Ben, and Glimmer reached the lake. A spell had been cast on the deep water so it was clear enough that the bottom of the lake was visible. Bella and Ben led Glimmer to the lake's edge and halted her. Glimmer watched Ben and Bella peer into the water, then turned her own gaze to the lake water.

"Ooh, look!" Bella said. "See those spiky blue fish?" A school of electric-blue fish covered in spikes swam near the water's edge.

"Yeah! Look over there," Ben said, pointing. "There's a huge dog fish at the bottom of the lake."

Bella's eyes followed Ben's finger. It took a moment before she spotted the dog fish. The white fish had dozens of black spots and barely moved as it crawled along the lake's bottom. It had floppy ears that covered its gills, and instead of a fish mouth it had a dog's snout. Dog fish were important to lake life—they ate all the dirty algae and helped keep the water clean. Dog fish reminded Bella of vacuum cleaners.

Glimmer pulled on the rainbow line, stretching her neck toward the lake. Ben nodded his okay, and Bella let Glimmer lower her head and take a few sips of water.

"Want to try taking Glimmer for a ride tomorrow?" Ben asked.

"Really? Do you think I'm ready?" Bella asked. She clasped her hands together and tried very hard not to jump up and down.

"Definitely!" Ben said. "I think you guys are ready."

"Yaaay!" Bella cheered. Glimmer lifted her head from the lake, and water dripped off her chin whiskers. Giggling, Bella hugged her neck. "Silly girl. We get to go riding tomorrow! Our very first ride together."

"My friends Clara and Ivy are coming over tomorrow," Bella said to Ben. "They'll be so excited to see me ride Glimmer for the first time."

The trio stayed by the lake for a few more moments before starting the walk back to the royal stables. For the rest of the day, all Bella could think about was riding. It felt like her birthday all over again!

2

Better Than a Birthday

"Bella?" Bella's bedroom doorknob turned, and a girl with braided blond hair peeked inside. The girl smiled when she saw the princess. "Good morning."

Bella, sitting up in the middle of her already-made bed, grinned. "Lyssa! Oh, I thought you would never get here!"

The older girl looked at Bella's wall clock. The clock had a baseball-size pink crystal surrounded by twelve smaller crystals. Two light beams shot out from the center of the big crystal and formed clock hands.

"It's just after eight," Lyssa said, laughing. She

smoothed her gray skirt and teal blouse with pearl buttons. "I usually get here at this time."

Fourteen-year-old Lyssa had been Bella's hand-maiden for more than a year, but she was more like a big sister. It was Lyssa's job to help Bella dress, get to the castle's schoolroom on time, complete all her homework, and assist Bella in any other way she might need.

Bella hopped off her bed and threw her arms around the older girl. "I know, but today's *special*!"

"Really? Spill!" Lyssa said, hugging Bella back.

The princess let go of Lyssa and looked up at her. "Ben said . . . I get to *ride* Glimmer today!"

"Oh, wow! Bella, this is so exciting!" Lyssa took Bella's hand and squeezed it. "Now I know why you already made your bed."

Bella nodded. "I already washed my face, too. I was waiting for you to come and help me pick out riding clothes before breakfast. Would you?"

"Hmmm." Lyssa tapped her cheek. "I don't know. . . ."

Bella made puppy-dog eyes at Lyssa.

Lyssa laughed. "Okay. I mean, I *guess* I'll help you." She flipped up the nearby light switch and opened Bella's closet door.

Both girls entered the walk-in closet. The bright-pink walls with a glitter top coat always made Bella feel cheerful. Racks of shoes were lined up along the walls, and Bella's clothes spun on rotating display racks. A crystal chandelier hanging from the ceiling cast tiny rainbows on the walls.

"Here are your clothes for riding," Lyssa said. "You'll need a pair of riding pants."

"How about the black ones?" Bella asked.

Lyssa grabbed the pants and long socks, and the girls moved to the boots.

"I think these will be perfect," Lyssa said. She held up a black pair of tall boots.

"I love them," Bella said. "It was so cool of Mom and Dad to get me riding clothes when I got Glimmer. Otherwise, I'd have to ride in jeans and sneakers!"

"That wouldn't be too bad, would it?" Lyssa asked.

Bella slipped into the socks and pants. "I didn't think so, but Ben said I had to wear a shoe with a heel. And not a high heel. A boot heel. I'll have to ask him why today. He did say jeans were kind of tight and uncomfortable for riding."

Lyssa walked over to Bella's T-shirts, nodding. "That makes sense. What color shirt, Bells? This will be a day you'll remember forever! Fashion choices included."

"Ummm." Bella rolled her eyes to the ceiling. "Purple! I want to match our auras."

Lyssa handed Bella a purple tee with a glittery heart in the center and a jacket with pretty buttons.

She held it up with a flourish, and Bella grinned.

Soon Bella was all dressed. Lyssa brushed her hair into a low ponytail. "I think you're ready to ride!" Lyssa said. "Have *so* much fun, and tell me every single detail when you're done. Promise?"

"Pinkie promise," Bella said. She locked pinkie fingers with Lyssa.

After checking to make sure everything was in place, Bella hurried down the long hallway and raced down the stairs to the dining room.

"Good morning, Bella," her mom said.

"Morning!" Bella said, sliding into her high-backed chair. She sat across from her parents at the long mahogany table.

Bella swung her legs back and forth under the table. *I don't know how I'm going to make it through breakfast!* she thought.

The glass pitcher of orange juice hovered over Bella's empty glass.

"Yes, please," Bella said.

The pitcher lowered itself closer to Bella's glass and tipped, and a stream of orange juice flowed into the glass. When it was nearly full, the pitcher righted itself and floated over to Queen Katherine. Bella's mom shook her head at the OJ pitcher and nodded at the silver coffeepot instead. The queen's dark-blond hair was in loose waves around her shoulders. She sat at the head of the table next to King Phillip. King Phillip, his brown hair almost the same shade as Bella's, sipped his cup of steaming coffee and smiled at her.

"Looks like you're dressed for something special," King Phillip said. His green eyes settled on Bella.

Bella, orange juice glass in hand, nodded her head so hard that juice almost sloshed over the rim. "Lyssa helped me," she said. "Ben said I needed to wear these special pants—breeches—if I was going to ride today."

"Ride, huh?" Queen Katherine asked. A hint of a smile curled on her lips.

"Yes!" Bella said, bouncing in her chair. "I didn't say anything last night because I was sure if I started talking about it, then I'd never stop. Lyssa drew me a bath with some kind of powder. . . ." Bella raised her eyes to the ceiling, thinking. "Oh! Lavender! She said it would help me sleep. I went straight to bed and tried not to think about Glimmer all night."

Both of her parents laughed. Bella gulped her OJ, finishing the glass in seconds.

"Did you manage to sleep?" her dad asked.

"Until five this morning," Bella said. "It felt like forever until Lyssa came."

"It's just a motherly guess," the queen said, "but you downed that glass of OJ in under a minute. Are you in a hurry to get to the stable?"

"Um . . . *yes*!" Bella said. "Plus, Ivy and Clara will be here soon. I'd already invited them over before Ben told me that I'd get to ride Glimmer today. They're going to be so surprised! All I told Ivy and Clara was to wear boots."

"Don't let us keep you," King Phillip teased. "But you must eat something for breakfast."

Bella stared down at her big empty plate. Eating was the last thing she wanted to do. Her toes wiggled in her new riding boots, and she rubbed her palms over her breeches. She sneaked a glance at her parents and let out a teensy sigh. They wouldn't let her leave without eating—not a chance.

The table, like every morning, was full from end to end with food cooked by the castle's chef. Platters that stayed heated were full of pancakes and waffles. Dishes were piled high with eggs and fruit. A stack of toast floated through the air and stopped in front of King Phillip.

"Two slices of honey wheat toast, please," the king said.

Two pieces of toast landed next to the scrambled eggs already on his plate.

Bella eyed the rest of the breakfast foods, deciding what would be the fastest to eat. "I'd like fruit," she said finally, staring at the bowl of mixed fruit.

The crystal bowl lifted into the air and floated toward Bella. "One scoop, please," the princess said. The silver spoon dug into the bowl of diced fruit and heaped a pile onto her plate.

Bella picked up her fork and speared a chunk of pineapple. She ate honeydew melon, watermelon, apple slices, purple grapes, cantaloupe, raspberries, and blueberries. In record time, the fruit was in her tummy.

The princess looked up at her parents. "Breakfast eaten," Bella said. "Can I go now? Please?"

Both of her parents eyed Bella's plate.

"Who's supervising your lesson today?" King Phillip asked.

"Ben," Bella said. "Frederick trusts him. Ben has tons of experience with unicorns."

"If Frederick thinks his nephew is capable of teaching you how to ride safely, then I'm not going to worry," Queen Katherine said, smiling. "Well, only a little bit."

King Phillip reached over and took one of Queen Katherine's hands in his own. "Don't forget that Glimmer isn't just any unicorn. She is Bella's protector and lifelong guardian. There's nothing in the entire kingdom that could make Glimmer hurt Bella."

The queen nodded. "You're right. I must remind myself of my first time riding Kiwi. He treated me like glass."

Bella pictured her mom's unicorn with green-washed mane and tail. Her father's unicorn, Scorpio, had a yellow mane and tail to match his yellow aura. Bella couldn't be happier to have a purple-washed unicorn to add to the royal family of guardian unicorns.

"Go ahead," King Phillip said. "Have fun and listen to Ben."

Bella pushed back her chair, the wooden legs making a scraping sound on the black-and-white marble tile. "I will! Thank you, thank you!"

She darted out of the dining room and hurried to the castle's front door. She pulled open the heavy wooden door and let out a tiny shriek.

"Sorry!" Ivy said, her hand raised to knock on the door.

"Great timing, Bells," Clara added, giggling.

"I'm so glad you're here!" Bella said. She threw an arm around each of her best friends.

The three besties balanced each other out. Quiet Ivy was a great listener. She had silky, straight blond hair that was cropped close to her chin. She was the one who often asked that Bella and Clara think about a plan before jumping into it. It had saved them from getting into trouble more times than Bella wanted to count!

Clara, taller than her two friends, had long, strawberry-blond hair. She had more energy than anyone Bella had ever met. In fact, Bella wondered sometimes if Clara secretly drank sugar water—gross!—in the mornings. Neither Clara nor Ivy cared about Bella's princess status, and that was exactly what Bella wanted.

"We wore boots like you told us," Ivy said, sticking out her foot. She had on ankle-high black boots with jeans and a T-shirt with a yellow butterfly.

"Good. Ben said it was for safety," Bella said, "in case Glimmer steps on our toes by accident. It would hurt a lot if we had on flip-flops."

The three girls hurried down the castle steps and started down the stone driveway. It was the time of morning where the weed zap spell was at work. The castle gardener cast a spell over Crystal Castle's driveway when night fell. The next morning any weeds that had poked up around the fountain or through the cobblestone driveway began to shrivel and shrink. When she was little, Bella used to sit on the driveway and watch the weeds pout and grumble as they disappeared back into the soil.

"I can't wait for you both to see Glimmer again," Bella said. "And to see me take her for a ride for the first time!"

Clara bounced as she speed-walked beside Bella and Ivy. "Me neither! Ivy and I just saw her last week, but it feels like forever."

"Are you sure you want us there when you ride Glimmer for the first time?" Ivy asked.

"Of course!" Bella said. "Why not?"

"Because it's a *huge* thing," Ivy explained. "I would understand if you wanted privacy. The bond you have with Glimmer is . . ." She paused, tilting her head. "It's so strong. I knew you were going to be linked through your aura match, but I've never seen anything love someone like Glimmer cares for you. It's like she's your best friend, guard, and very cool parent all in one purple package!"

The girls giggled, and Bella felt pride build up inside her from Ivy's words.

"That means so much, Ivy," Bella said, slinging an arm across her friend's shoulders. "I *do* want you and Clara with me today. It's a special day that I want to share with my best friends. Trust me, you're not the only one who is surprised by how fast Glimmer and I bonded. It sounds silly, but it feels as though she's been in my life forever!"

Clara and Ivy shook their heads.

"It's not silly!" Clara said.

"Now Glimmer *is* going to be in your life forever," Ivy added.

Ivy's words sent Bella into a sprint across the

stable yard. Suddenly she couldn't wait another second to be away from Glimmer. Ivy and Clara chased after her, and they skidded to a stop at the stable's entrance.

Bella forced herself to walk—no running allowed in the royal stables—and barely noticed the other unicorns' heads over their stall doors. The stalls had three high, glossy wooden walls that formed a box, and clean straw was spread over the floor. A single dazzling silver rope hung across each entrance. They were enchanted—only Crystal Kingdom royals or those who worked in the stable could remove the ropes and enter.

"Glimmer!" Bella called, as she reached the stall. "I'm here!"

But something was wrong. Bella blinked. And blinked again.

Glimmer's stall was empty!

3

Disappearing Act

"Where is she?" Bella wondered to Ivy and Clara. Her friends peered over the princess's shoulder into the empty stall. "Ben obviously already took her out."

But as she said that, she noticed Glimmer's magical rainbow-colored rope hanging limply on the stall wall.

"C'mon," Bella said. "Let's find them."

Bella turned away from Glimmer's stall, and her friends followed her back down the aisle. She ducked down a side hallway and headed for the storage area. The princess twisted the golden knob on the door and sighed with relief. The dark-haired boy had a white, comfy-looking cushion hanging over his arm.

"Hi, Bella," Ben said with a smile.

"Hey, Ben," Bella said. "These are my friends Ivy and Clara."

Both girls smiled and gave little waves.

"We went to say hi to Glimmer," Bella continued, "but she wasn't there. Did you already take her out?"

Ben frowned. "Bella, I was here getting Glimmer's stuff. I haven't taken her out yet."

"You haven't?" Bella tried to swallow the panic that was rising in her throat. "Someone else must have. Glimmer's not in her stall! Where's your uncle?"

"Uncle Frederick took your dad's unicorn out for a ride," Ben said. "The other stable hands haven't arrived yet."

A small whimper escaped Bella's lips. The giant room seemed as if it was tilting. Bella felt as though she had eaten way too many pieces of chocolate cake and might throw up. If Frederick wasn't here and neither were the other stable hands . . .

"Glimmer's gone," Bella said in a whisper.

Ben's face paled. He put down the cushion, sidestepped around the girls, and headed into the hallway. "No," he said. "I saw Glimmer a few minutes ago. She can't be missing."

Ben, with the girls right behind him, hurried to Glimmer's stall. He stood before the stall entrance, mouth slightly open. His brown eyes seemed to darken as he picked up the rainbow rope and held it in his hand.

"Princess Bella," Ben said, bowing his head. "I must alert my uncle and the royal guards at once. Glimmer must have been kidnapped somehow. She was under my watch, and this is all my fault."

"No!" Bella said. She blinked back tears. "No one could have taken her! The magic rope won't allow it."

But what if Queen Fire somehow—No! Bella pushed the thought out of her mind.

"You and your friends should return to the castle," Ben said. "We will find whoever took Glimmer, Bella. I promise."

"I'm not leaving," Bella said. "Glimmer is my unicorn. I'm going to help find her."

Ben opened his mouth, as if he was about to argue, then closed it. "All right," he said. "When I go tell my uncle, he's probably not going to let me to come back."

"Why?" Clara asked. Her voice jolted Bella. She'd almost forgotten her friends were there.

"Because the princess's unicorn was captured under my watch," Ben said. "I'll likely be banished from Crystal Castle and sent home."

Ben started away from Glimmer's stall. His shoulders slumped, and he hunched forward as he walked. Bella squeezed her eyes shut, pressing her fingertips to her temples. Glimmer missing was too awful to think about, but she couldn't abandon Ben. He had been nothing but kind and helpful to her since his arrival. Bella couldn't stand the thought of him getting in such huge trouble that he would be *banished* from Crystal Castle forever.

"Ben, wait!" Bella called. "The monitors! We didn't watch them."

Slowly Ben turned back to Bella. "Monitors?"

"Frederick didn't teach you?" Bella asked, a flutter of hope in her chest. "Come back. Look." She pointed to a pearly button on the stall wall. "This will show us everything that's happened in Glimmer's stall in the last day."

"Wow," Ivy said. "Press it! Press it!"

"If we find out who took Glimmer," Bella said, "maybe we don't have to tell anyone. Ben, you don't deserve to get in trouble."

"But Bella, I do," Ben said. "Thank you for trying to help me, but I have to tell Frederick."

"Stop, you two!" Clara said. "We're wasting time! Bella, pull princess rank this *one* time and Ben has to listen to you. But only once."

Bella looked at Ben and shook her head. "I don't have to. Please, Ben? Try it my way first,

35

and if we can't find Glimmer soon, you can tell your uncle."

Ben finally nodded. "Okay. But we only have until Wednesday morning's debut."

Without another word to Ben, Clara, or Ivy, Bella reached above her head and pressed the pearl button with her pointer finger.

"Royal monitor of unicorn Glimmer," Bella commanded. "Use your shine and use your shimmer. Show us the past, a day sped up fast. So we can see where Glimmer might be."

Instantly an image projected onto the wood. As if they were looking into a mirror, Bella and her friends gazed into the monitor's screen. It showed the previous morning, speeding through Ben feeding and watering Glimmer, taking her out of her stall to meet with Bella, tucking her in for the night, and then Glimmer eating dinner and falling asleep. But soon Glimmer woke and paced back and forth in her stall. Hours flew by of the pacing unicorn, who only stopped when Ben visited her this morning.

Then it happened. Everyone gasped.

"Monitor, rewind and slow down, please!" Bella commanded.

The screen faded to black. Then a clear image of Glimmer appeared on the wall. The purple unicorn poked her head out of the stall and looked from side to side, up and down the aisle. She put her muzzle over the snap-lock of the enchanted rope, and several moments later, the rope fell to the side of the stall.

Glimmer took in a deep breath, her nostrils flaring. She walked slowly out of the stall and down the aisle, and headed for the back exit. With a push against the wooden door, Glimmer squeezed through, and strands of her silky tail were the last of her caught on camera.

Bella dropped her hand from the button. She put her hand over her mouth, stifling a sob.

"Oh, Bells," Ivy said, grabbing her friend into a hug.

Bella started crying. Giant tears splashed onto Ivy, and sobs made Bella's stomach hurt. Clara rubbed the princess's back, and Bella fought to get her emotions under control. She was so upset that she wasn't even embarrassed to be crying in front of a boy.

"I—I'm so glad no one took Glimmer," Bella managed to get out a few minutes later. "I was afraid Queen Fire or someone had captured her. But—" A fresh wave of tears fell from Bella's eyes. "Glimmer *ran away*. She doesn't want to be my unicorn. All of this time I thought that she was happy, but she wasn't. Glimmer left to get away from me."

"Bella, that can't be true," Ben said. His voice was soft. "I've spent so much time with you and

Glimmer. She loves you as much as you love her. She would *never* leave you willingly."

"She did," Bella cried. "The monitors don't lie."

She slumped against Glimmer's stall. Clara, Ivy, and Ben sat around her.

"I think Ben's right," Ivy said. "Bella, think about how Glimmer acted last night. She was pacing and up almost all night."

Clara nodded, patting Bella's hand. "Something was wrong or upsetting Glimmer."

"*I* must have done something yesterday to upset her," Bella said. "Or maybe Glimmer's felt this way since we've been Paired, and she finally couldn't take it anymore."

"It *has* to be something else," Ben said. "We have to find Glimmer and figure out what's going on."

"I'll be worried until she's back in the stable," Bella said. "I want to start looking right away and keep it a secret. But once we find Glimmer—if we find her—I want her to be able to be free of being my unicorn if that's what she wants."

"Bella, let's find Glimmer first," Clara said. "Once she's safe and Ben's clear from getting into trouble, then we'll find out why she left."

Bella stood on shaky legs. Her heart actually hurt from fear for Glimmer's safety and the pain that her own unicorn didn't want her. *Just because Glimmer might not love me doesn't mean I don't love her,* Bella thought. *I'm so scared for her, and I won't sleep until I find her. I wish Glimmer knew how much I love her.*

"If we're going to keep this a secret," Ben said, "we have to act as though everything is normal. If my uncle comes to Glimmer's stall and asks where she is, I'll tell him that she's with you, Bella."

"I'll tell my parents and Frederick that Glimmer's with *you* if they ask," Bella replied.

Planning to return Glimmer to safety helped to

dash away some of her sadness. Instead of focusing on Glimmer's decision to leave, Bella decided to put everything she had into finding her unicorn. Once Glimmer was safe, then Bella would deal with letting go.

"I want to help," Ivy said.

"Me too," Clara added. "What can we do?"

"We have to start looking without appearing to anyone as if we're searching for anything," Bella said. "What if we all take sections of the castle grounds and search until it gets dark? If Glimmer escaped the grounds, then tomorrow we can map out sections of the kingdom to search."

"Don't forget school," Ivy said, frowning.

Bella groaned. "I forgot that tomorrow is Monday. Okay, *after* school we'll all meet up at the Snapdragon Garden."

"Are you sure no grown-ups will be there?" Clara asked.

41

"Positive," Bella said. "Yesterday I heard one of the gardeners tell my mom that the snapdragon flowers were especially mean this week. She told my mom to be extra careful if she walked through the garden, and Mom said she wasn't going to chance it."

"Oh," Clara said, her voice squeaky. "Okay."

Clara must have been picturing the towering flowers that filled Snapdragon Garden. They were beautiful, but their looks were deceiving. The flowers used their petals to nip at anything that got too close. The flowers couldn't breathe fire like real dragons, but smoke did come out of their mouths when they opened them if they were in a bad mood.

"We only have to go there if we don't find Glimmer today," Ben said. "She might be wandering close by."

Despite her churning stomach, Bella gave Ben a tiny smile. "I hope so."

"We need to get in touch with each other if we find her," Ben said. "Did everyone bring their crystal?"

Everyone nodded and reached into their pockets. They all took out smooth, quarter-size clear stones. The stones, nicknamed Chat Crystals, allowed the friends to send messages to each other.

"Let's cast a spell on them to vibrate and change colors depending on our message," Clara said.

"How about purple if someone finds Glimmer," Bella said. "Red if there is trouble and we need to get back to the stables immediately, and yellow if there's a possible trace of Glimmer and we need to help that person follow the lead."

"Perfect," Ivy said.

Bella held her crystal flat on her palm as her friends did the same. "Crystals, until dusk tonight, please change colors according to my words," she said, putting a spell on the crystals. Once she had finished, everyone tucked away their crystals.

The friends mapped out sections of the grounds and agreed to meet at the back of the stables at dusk. Ivy, Clara, and Ben gave Bella encouraging smiles before they all went their separate ways around Crystal Castle. Bella hoped the plan would work!

4

Search Party

Bella had been walking for hours, and there hadn't been a single trace of Glimmer. It was moments before dusk, and soon Bella would have to turn back to meet her friends. The new boots that Bella had so eagerly laced up this morning had rubbed blisters into her heels and big toes. Sweat trickled down her forehead and soaked the collar of her T-shirt.

Bella's crystal hadn't vibrated once. She had even taken it out of her pocket to see if she had missed a vibration, but the crystal remained clear. No one was having any luck.

Glimmer's definitely not in my section of the castle grounds, Bella thought. *But how did she escape the royal guards? Did she just walk across the drawbridge? Surely she could not have swum through the moat without being seen by guards.*

Bella forgot how lucky she and her friends were that none of them had been spotted by the royal security team. They would have to lie about what they were doing, and Bella hated lying. But this was for a good reason.

The princess took a few more steps and stopped as she reached the creek in front of her. Bella had taken the front left quarter of the castle grounds. Ben, Ivy, and Clara had each taken another quarter of Crystal Castle's grounds. Bella's section included a creek that had a small waterfall at the start. Even though her instinct told her that Glimmer couldn't have made it across the moat, she knew she had to try.

This is the last place left to look, Bella thought. *Then I have to get back.*

She sat down on the grass near the creek bed and undid her boots. She tugged off her socks, rolled up her pant legs, and stepped into the cool water. The creek bottom was covered in a bed of smooth brown and black stones—none sharp enough to cut or bruise Bella's feet.

Teensy minnows and tadpoles swam away from Bella as she carefully walked up the creek toward the waterfall. The ankle-deep water felt good on her blisters. The princess squinted and bent down, the setting sun visible in the water's reflection. *Something* had disturbed the rocks. The entire creek had been smooth and now there were—*one, two, three, four*—spots of rocks smushed into the ground. Bella stuck her hand in the water, tracing her finger over a U-shaped imprint.

Glimmer's shoe!

"Glimmer!" Bella called. She forgot that she wasn't supposed to be calling for the unicorn in case someone heard. She dropped her voice to a whisper. "Are you here?"

Bella stayed hunched over and followed the hoofprints as they went along the creek bed, then vanished. Steps away from the loud waterfall, she looked from side to side, trying to pick up the trail.

"The grass!" Bella said out loud. She sprinted through the creek, her footsteps spraying water up her legs. She put her bare feet in the spots of trampled grass—almost like playing hopscotch. The four diagonal prints zigzagged away from the creek and headed for the property line that divided Crystal Castle from the rest of the kingdom.

Bella slipped her fingers around her crystal. She needed to tell her friends to meet her here. The princess took a few more steps, and the hoof-prints became harder and harder to spot. A shiny screen that looked like plastic wrap was inches from Bella's face. The palm-size screen signaled the end of Crystal Castle land. Bella slowly put a foot through the screen spell, causing it to ripple.

"Princess? Princess Bella!"

Bella yanked her foot back as if it had touched scorching lava. She stifled a shriek and turned to the deep voice that had called her name. She released the crystal, leaving it in her pocket, glad she hadn't called her friends.

One of the members of the royal security team approached her. His sword gleamed at his side, and he was dressed in all black with a pin of the castle's seal on his lapel.

"Um, hi!" Bella said. She hurried away from the hoofprint trail and tried to scuff away the rest of the prints with her feet as she approached the guard. *I don't want him to see any of Glimmer's tracks*, she thought.

"Are you all right?" the guard asked after bowing to Bella. "It's not safe for you to cross the property line, Princess. The other guards and I only patrol the castle grounds unless the king instructs us otherwise."

Bella smiled. "I know. I was playing in the creek and then saw a"—she swallowed—"*butterfly*, and I chased it. I'd never seen one like it before. Thank you for calling to me before I went too far over the line."

The guard nodded, smiling back. His green eyes looked around as if searching for evidence of the butterfly. But he didn't seem to pick up on the princess's lie. "Of course, Princess. Do you need an escort back to the castle?"

"Oh no, thank you," Bella said. "I know my way from here. Thanks!"

Before the guard could say another word, Bella gave him a tiny wave and trotted away. She dashed across the creek, put on her boots, and darted across the grounds, hurrying back to the stables.

That was way too close! Bella thought as she jogged. *I have to be more careful.* Her stomach sank as she reached the stables. Ivy and Clara stood empty-handed and were covered in streaks of dirt. Ben came around the other side of the stables, red-faced and sneakers covered in mud.

"I knew that no one had found Glimmer," Bella

said, reaching her friends. "But I'd hoped my crystal had missed a signal."

The four of them plopped onto the floor of the tack room. Bella reached over and pulled a blade of grass from Clara's long hair.

"We don't have much time," Ivy said. "I have to be home really soon or my parents will worry."

"Mine too," Clara said. "I'm sorry, Bella. I looked *everywhere* in my section. I didn't find a thing."

Ivy and Ben nodded, their eyes downcast.

"At least you guys didn't get stopped by guards," Bella said.

"What?" Ben asked, sitting up straight. He'd been slouching against a wooden cabinet.

"I was in the creek and I found hoofprints," Bella said. "I know they're Glimmer's."

"Oh! Why didn't you message us?" Ivy asked. She swiped at sweat on her forehead.

"I started to," Bella said. "I got caught up following the prints. They led me to the castle line. I was halfway through the screen when a guard saw me."

Clara's mouth formed a giant O shape. "What did you do?"

"I had to lie," Bella said. "I told him that I was chasing a butterfly, and I ran off before he could ask me anything else."

Ben's brows knitted together. "Did he believe you?"

"Yes," Bella said. Her chest tightened a little. "I hated lying, but I had to."

"You did the right thing," Ivy said. She stretched her legs out in front of her. The knees of her jeans were grass stained.

"Now we know that Glimmer isn't on the castle grounds," Bella said. "The hoofprints pointed in the direction of the Dark Forest."

The mention of the Dark Forest caused everyone to fall silent.

"Guys," Bella added. "No one has to go in but me. I *have* to go—Glimmer's my unicorn. I understand if you don't want to go."

Ben shook his head. "No way. I'm going too."

Ivy and Clara nodded in solidarity.

"What if we start by searching around the castle after school?" Ivy said. "I'll tell my parents that I'm staying over for a while."

"I'll do the same as Ivy," Clara said. "If we don't find Glimmer tomorrow, then we'll go into the Dark Forest the next day."

Bella thought for a minute. "That's a good idea. Maybe we should be in pairs this time."

"I'll go with you," Ben said, looking at Bella. "If that's all right."

"Sure. Thanks, Ben," Bella said. "Ivy and Clara, are you okay going together?"

The two girls looked at each other and high-fived. "Team Clivy!" Clara said, giggling.

The overhead lights went from dim to bright. Bella looked out of the small window in the tack room. The sun was almost completely gone.

"You and Ivy still have to get home," Bella said. "I missed dinner, and I don't want Frederick to come looking for you, Ben. We will mess up this entire plan if we all get in trouble on the first day."

"You're right," Ben said. "Everyone needs to go."

"Tomorrow," Bella said. "Snapdragon Garden at two thirty."

5

Act "Normal"

After splitting up from her friends, Bella managed to shower and change clothes before running into her mom. The queen found Bella when the princess was drying her hair.

"When did you come inside?" Queen Katherine asked, folding her arms. Bella studied her mom's face. The queen wasn't angry, but she was definitely a little cross.

"I got in a while ago," Bella said. "I was sweaty and gross from being outside, so I took a shower. I didn't want to track dirt everywhere. I'm so sorry that I missed dinner, Mom."

"Did something happen during your riding lesson?" Queen Katherine asked. She raised a you-better-tell-the-truth "Mom" eyebrow.

"Nothing happened," Bella said. She hated lying to her mom. Queen Katherine trusted Bella, and the princess had never given her parents a reason not to trust her.

Until now. But she had to protect Ben and even shield Glimmer from trouble.

Bella had realized in the shower that Glimmer's decision to run away could get her unicorn into trouble. That was the last thing that Bella wanted.

"Everything went great," Bella added. "Ben was a great teacher. He told me to go after the lesson, but I decided to stay. I wanted to learn how to prepare Glimmer for bed after riding her." Bella stretched her arms behind her back. "It's completely my fault that I got in late," she added.

The queen eyed her, and Bella fought the urge to chew her bottom lip.

Please, please believe me, Mom, Bella thought. *I'm sorry I'm lying. I'll never lie again after this is over!*

"Next time, please make sure you send word that you'll be missing dinner," the queen said. "Don't make a habit of it, though, Bella."

"I won't," Bella promised.

Her mom smiled and stepped forward to wrap her arms around her daughter. "I am proud of you, sweetie. I remember my early days of learning to ride Kiwi, and it was quite tiring. I'm so happy you decided to stay at the stables and care for Glimmer."

"You could have just ridden her and left," Queen Katherine continued. "But you showed a true interest in Glimmer's well-being. That's my girl. Your father will be proud too."

The queen's words made Bella's stomach hurt.

* * *

On Monday morning, Bella was awake long before Lyssa arrived. She dressed herself, moving quietly so no one would know that she was awake, and settled onto her window seat. The events from last night ran over and over in her mind.

A swallow chirped outside her window and hopped on the ledge of the fountain. The bird dipped its head into the water, causing droplets to cascade down its neck and back. The little brown bird bathed in the early morning sunlight.

Last night, after the talk with her mom, Bella had eaten dinner and, claiming to be tired, had gone to bed early. She really had climbed under her covers before her usual bedtime, but she had been awake for most of the night. All Bella could think about was getting through school and searching for Glimmer. She would have to make certain that she didn't miss dinner for a second night in a row.

"Bella?" a soft voice called from the other side of the door.

"Come in," Bella replied. She pasted a fake smile on her face as Lyssa walked inside.

Lyssa's eyes swept over the already-dressed Bella. She tilted her head. "I know why you're up early. You can't keep secrets from me!"

What? How did Lyssa find out? Bella thought, panicked.

"Lyssa, you can't—" Bella started.

"Your ride with Glimmer went so amazing that you were going to sneak out before school to see her," Lyssa interrupted, grinning. "That's why you're up so early."

Lyssa's wrong—so wrong—guess made Bella snap her mouth closed. Relief swept over her that Lyssa didn't know the truth.

"You got me," Bella agreed cheerfully. "I was totally planning to see Glimmer. I got lost in a daydream, and now it's too late."

"Aw, Bells," Lyssa said. She smoothed her cheery yellow cap-sleeve dress. "The day will go by faster than you think. You'll be seeing Glimmer before you know it."

Bella managed a smile. "I hope so."

It was the first sentence of truth she'd spoken in a while.

Lyssa picked up a hairbrush and waved it at Bella. "Come over and let me do your hair," she said. "You have to tell me everything about your first ride!"

Slowly Bella uncurled her legs and walked across her bedroom. She sank into the plush pink-velvet-covered stool in front of her mirror.

Lyssa ran the brush through Bella's hair, locking eyes with her in the mirror. "Are you okay?"

Lyssa asked. The older girl frowned at Bella's reflection. "You're awfully quiet. I thought you would be dying to tell me about your day with Glimmer."

"Oh, I am," Bella said. "Yesterday was amazing, Lyss. I'm just a little tired and sore from riding."

Still brushing, Lyssa nodded. "I get it, Bells. I'm sure you were up the night before thinking about what riding Glimmer was going to be like. Then when it was over, I'm sure you felt like an energy zap spell had been cast on you."

"Exactly," Bella agreed. "Glimmer really does mean more to me than anything in my whole life, and I was so, so excited about yesterday." Under the vanity table, she curled her fingers into fists until her fingernails dug into her palms. It was all she could do to keep from crying. "She's the best unicorn in the whole world."

"French braid?" Lyssa asked, Bella's hair entwined around her fingers.

"Yes, please," Bella said.

"I'm so glad you're happy with Glimmer," Lyssa said. Her focus was on braiding Bella's brown locks. "I'll have to watch you ride sometime."

Bella managed a wobbly smile. "Sure."

Lyssa finished Bella's braid and knelt down by her side. "You know you can tell me anything, right? I can tell when something's bothering you. Are you worried about the Crystal Kingdom debut on Wednesday?"

I'm going to tell Lyssa everything, Bella thought. But then Lyssa would be in an awkward position. Enough people were already telling lies and keeping secrets—Bella didn't want Lyssa to be one of them.

"The debut is stressing me out a little," Bella answered honestly. "It's a big moment in front of the entire kingdom."

Lyssa patted Bella's knee. "It *is*. But you'll have

Glimmer there to support you. It's going to be so different from your birthday, when it was just you."

Bella tried to smile and nod as Lyssa kept talking about the debut. Not only was she worried sick about Glimmer, but what would happen if the princess of Crystal Kingdom showed up to her unicorn debut—*without* her unicorn?

6

Secrets, Lies, and the Dark Forest

The school day dragged. On and on and *on*. Bella, Ivy, Clara, and Ben all huddled together during lunch at a table on the terrace. Bella and the other students in her third-grade class were all taught at Crystal Castle. The princess's parents hadn't wanted Bella to be lonely, so they had invited children of castle employees to attend school with Bella and her tutor.

Today, however, Bella wanted to avoid everyone. While Ben was in school and away from the stables, he always told Frederick a different story about where Glimmer was. Today's little white lie? Ben had let Glimmer loose in a big field to graze.

"Does everyone have a copy of their map?" she said, whispering to her friends.

Ivy, Clara, and Ben, all seated at the round table, nodded.

"Last night I divided up the outside of the Dark Forest into sections," Bella explained. "Everyone's is marked, and I put a spell on the map to only reveal the ink of castle grounds. Just being extra careful."

"Good idea, Bells," Ivy said. Her short hair was clipped back with blue-and-white polka-dot barrettes. Ivy, preparing for the outdoor adventure, had paired sneakers with jeans and a dark-gray T-shirt. Ben, Clara, and Bella were in jeans and dark tees too.

"One question," Clara said. "How do we get past the royal guards?"

Bella rubbed her sweaty palms on her thighs. "I have an idea. What do you guys think about going to my mom after class and telling her that we would like to take Glimmer out in the giant field alongside the road to town?"

Ben rubbed his forehead. "I like it. We don't have to worry about the guards."

"Sounds like a plan," Ivy declared.

"Do you know more about the Dark Forest since the first time we talked about it?" Bella asked Ben.

He shook his head. "I didn't get a chance to read about it yet. Are there big spiders?"

"I wish," Bella said. "We might run into bigger problems than those eight-legged creepers. The forest is Queen Fire's territory. Her guards might be patrolling to keep us out."

Ben's eyes widened, and he nodded slowly, as if remembering Bella's confession about her relationship to Queen Fire.

"My aunt has been stealing unicorns for years," Bella said. "She uses her evil black aura to make all of the good unicorns become bad. And dangerous!"

"Will we be able to recognize them?" Ben asked.

"Easily," Bella answered. "They are red with black eyes." She stopped, her throat suddenly desert dry. She couldn't even begin to imagine what she would do if Queen Fire had captured Glimmer. Bella's sweet purple unicorn being turned evil . . .

"Hey," Ben said, nudging Bella's ribs with his elbow. "Queen Fire doesn't have Glimmer. I know it. Think about the way that Glimmer escaped her stall. She's too smart to be caught by Queen Fire."

"I hope so," Bella said. She picked up her silver fork and stabbed at a pile of macaroni-and-cheese noodles. The food tasted like nothing, and Bella put down her fork, pushing her tray away.

The four unicorn detectives spent the rest of lunch talking in hushed tones about how they were going to track Glimmer, play it cool with Queen Katherine, and most of all, avoid the dangers that could pull them into the Dark Forest.

"Hi, Mom," Bella said. After school had ended, Ivy and Clara had waited for Bella to change into riding clothes. Then they found Queen Katherine in the downstairs library.

"Hello, sweetie," the queen said, looking up from the book in her lap. Queen Katherine smiled at Ivy, Clara, and Ben.

"Mom, is it all right if we cross the drawbridge and go into the field across from the castle?" Bella asked. She saw a frown begin to form on her mother's face. "It's Ben's idea," she added quickly. "He said taking Glimmer to a different setting to ride would be good for her. It will help prepare her for Wednesday, so she won't be so shy or frightened when we take her into town."

"Ben," the queen said, "is Glimmer comfortable enough with Bella to be riding so far away?"

"Yes, Your Highness," Ben answered. "I spoke to my uncle Frederick about it, and he said okay. I *promise* that Bella will be safe."

"Please, Mom?" Bella asked. She tried not to notice Ben wringing his hands behind his back. "We'll be very careful. If I need you or Dad, I promise that I'll send for help via a spell." The queen looked from Bella, to Clara, to Ivy, to Ben. Her face gave away nothing. The queen placed her hands on her lap and smoothed her gold-and-rose-colored dress.

"Have fun," Queen Katherine said. "Be safe and come back in time for dinner."

"Thank you, Mom!" Bella said. "Bye!"

Before the queen could say another word, the friends dashed out of the library, through the castle front door, and toward the Dark Forest.

The guards shot Bella confused looks when

72

she reached the drawbridge, but she waved as she speed-walked by. "My mom knows we're going to the field," Bella explained.

The men and women dipped their heads and resumed walking back and forth across the draw-bridge entrance.

"See you guys in two hours," Bella said, checking her watch. "We'll meet at the Snapdragon Garden unless someone messages the other with their crystal."

"Got it," Clara said. "That will give us plenty of time to get home for dinner."

"Hopefully, we'll be feeding Glimmer dinner tonight, Bells," Ivy said, squeezing her friend's arm.

With that, the friends split into pairs, and Bella and Ben headed for the part of the forest farthest from Crystal Castle. Neither of them spoke. They glued their eyes to the ground, searching for hoof-prints, and walked to the edge of the forest.

It was a cloudless day in Crystal Kingdom, and sunlight fell on their backs. One look inside the Dark Forest made Queen Fire's territory live up to its name. Bella stopped, carefully keeping her toes in the grassy field, and squinted into the forest. It was as if the sunlight didn't extend to the wooded land.

"I can't see anything in the forest," Bella said. "Can you?"

Ben stopped walking and looked into the woods. "Just shadows," he said. "I don't want to think much about what's in there."

"What if Glimmer is?" Bella's voice shook a little. She couldn't stand the thought of her sweet unicorn in the scary Dark Forest.

Ben tilted his head, swiping hair out of his eye. "Let's just search our section. In a couple of hours, if no one's found anything, then we'll think about the Dark Forest."

"It's the only place left," Bella said, looking away from the forest. She started to walk again. The short grass grew tall and weedy. She stepped around a patch of burrs, and the prickly round seeds stretched their spikes as far as they could, trying to latch onto Bella's pants. "If Glimmer was loose in the kingdom, someone would have seen her and reported a royal unicorn sighting. The Dark Forest is *it*."

Bella bit down on the inside of her cheek to keep from crying. She had to stay strong for Glimmer and put her whole heart into searching for her.

And for the next two hours that's exactly what she did.

"Are you all right, Bella?" King Phillip asked. "You're so quiet lately."

Bella couldn't help but slump in her chair at dinner. The chef, Joseph, had prepared a delicious-smelling roasted chicken with plenty of yummy sides, but nothing sounded good to Bella. Not even her favorite mac 'n' cheese!

She and her friends had searched for two hours and met back at Snapdragon Garden. Not even one purple, sparkly hair had been found. Bella's friends promised they would be back tomorrow and they would go with her into the Dark Forest.

"I've been busy with school," Bella said. "I've been spending a lot of time at the stables with Glimmer, too. You know, getting ready for the debut."

Where I debut myself *alone!*

King Phillip peered at his daughter with kind eyes. "This society debut is nothing more than a royal formality. Please don't put too much pressure on yourself."

"I won't, Dad," Bella said. She speared a green bean and forced herself to eat it. "I promise."

"It's going to be nothing as grand as your birthday celebration," Queen Katherine said. "You'll ride Glimmer into town, and Dad and I will be behind you in the Royal Carriage. At the town square, you and Glimmer will stand next to the platform. You won't have to do anything, sweetie, if you're worried about that. This is a *very* informal event. It's just to let the townspeople see their princess and her new unicorn."

"That helps, Mom," Bella said. "Thank you."

Unless the event is canceled, the town is going to be staring at me, Bella thought. She tried to shake away the thoughts. *We are going to find Glimmer. We will.* She repeated the last sentence to herself over and over.

For the rest of dinner, Bella did her best to chat like normal. It felt like hours before the table was cleared and the princess was excused to go to her room. When her door was shut safely behind her, Bella crawled under her covers and cried.

7

Does Glimmer
Want to Be Found?

"We can do this," Clara said. It was just after school on Tuesday, and the girls had gathered to continue their search for Glimmer.

"I wish Ben could be here," Bella said. "He did the right thing, though, by not asking his uncle to let him skip chores and come with us."

Ivy nodded. "It's better that he didn't ask. We need zero suspicion on us."

Bella's gaze wandered ahead to the Dark Forest. The girls were only feet away from the edge of the forest.

"So let's stick with the plan we came up with,"

Bella said, looking back at her friends. "Ivy, you and Clara stick together, and I'll go alone." It was Bella's unicorn they were searching for, so the princess wanted her friends to be as safe as possible. If it weren't for Bella, they wouldn't be going into the Dark Forest.

Both of her friends frowned. They were not thrilled with Bella's plan. Clara and Ivy had both argued with Bella about the princess going alone into the Dark Forest.

"Please don't fight with me about it anymore," Bella pleaded. "I know you're both worried about me being alone, but I'll be okay. We all have our crystals in case we need to get in touch with each other."

Ivy and Clara exchanged looks.

"Just so you know—I'm not happy about this," Clara fretted. She pulled her long hair into a ponytail. "But I'm with you, Bella."

"Me too," Ivy said. She patted the pocket of her

jeans. "Promise us that you'll use the crystal if you even *think* you might get into trouble."

"Promise," Bella said. She took a long, deep breath. "Today is it." She didn't need to remind Ivy and Clara what was at stake. Glimmer's safety. Ben's future as an apprentice at Crystal Castle. Bella's debut tomorrow morning.

"Group hug for luck," Ivy said.

The three best friends squeezed each other tight.

"Let's go," Bella said.

Bella led the way to the edge of the Dark Forest. Light peeked through the tall, leafless trees that stretched into the sky. Before she could think about it, Bella veered away from Ivy and Clara. Immediately, the temperature dropped a few degrees. Bella, glad for her cardigan, pulled the gray sleeves down to her knuckles. Ivy's and Clara's footsteps soon disappeared, and the only sounds in the dim forest were Bella's sneakers crunching on twigs and dead leaves.

Mushrooms—red-and-white spotted—bloomed along the base of a massive tree. Roots as big as Bella swirled into the ground. The princess stepped closer to the tree, in awe of the roots, and movement made her jump back.

The tree roots inflated before her eyes, getting thicker and longer. It was as if they were protecting the tree. Bella took a few steps backward and found a semi-path to walk on. Ravens cawed overhead, and their wings fluttered.

Bella swatted at a bug that whined in her ear. Another one of the annoying insects flew in front of her eyes, and she broke into a run. *That was the creepiest bug ever!* she thought. Not only had the insect been the size of her hand, but it had a red body and four hairy, gross legs. Bella had never seen that bug outside of the Dark Forest.

Bella licked her dry lips, wanting to call for Glimmer, but she was too afraid of alerting Queen Fire's spies. The princess wanted to get in and out of the forest as fast as possible. Her parents had forbidden her to enter the dangerous woods ever since she'd been old enough to talk. Now, not only was she in the Dark Forest, but she was without the protection of her unicorn.

Bella's heart thudded so hard in her chest that she was sure the forest creatures could hear her heartbeat. *Please, please don't let me run into one of Queen Fire's unicorns,* she thought. *Let me find Glimmer and take her home.*

Bella stopped, bending down to look at a marking in the dirt. A hoofprint! The sight of it sent the princess's pulse racing. She was on the right track. Or—Bella gulped—she was on the trail of one of Queen Fire's dangerous unicorns. Bella stood, and a rustling noise filtered into her ears. She saw a flash of something—she couldn't even make out the color—and that was all she needed.

Bella broke into a run, ignoring the squawking birds, the ribbiting frogs, and the scary shadows that covered a lot of the trail. Bella reached a line of hedges and halted, peering over the top.

She gasped. "Glimmer!" Bella cried.

The unicorn lifted her purple-tinted head from the ground and pointed her ears in Bella's direction.

Tears started falling from Bella's eyes. "Glimmer, please don't run away. Please let me talk to you."

Bella swiped at the tears on her cheeks as she took slow steps around the hedge. Glimmer stood like a statue—not a flick of her tail or a blink at the princess.

Bella held out her hand and, reaching Glimmer, placed it gently on the unicorn's shoulder.

Glimmer's muscles rippled, and she let out a huge sigh.

"I know you don't want to be my unicorn anymore," Bella said, choking back tears. "Glimmer, I don't want you to be unhappy. I just want you to be safe. Please come home with me. You can stay at the stables and I promise—you'll be released from your duties as my royal unicorn."

Glimmer craned her neck to face Bella. She blinked her giant liquid-brown eyes and stared into Bella's. Bella didn't break eye contact with Glimmer as she moved her hand to the unicorn's muzzle.

Something was happening. Something Bella had never experienced.

"I must be crazy," Bella said to Glimmer. "I must want you to stay my unicorn so bad that I can tell you want that too."

Glimmer nudged Bella's hand with her muzzle.

She let out a quiet, soft snort. Bella's eyes swept over Glimmer's face, and the unicorn's thoughts rushed into her brain. She could read Glimmer's body language. Glimmer was telling Bella exactly what she was thinking.

"Oh, Glimmer," Bella said, shaking her head. "You *want* to be my unicorn? You didn't run away because you didn't like me?"

Again, Glimmer touched Bella. This time she rested her cheek in the princess's palm and looked back into Bella's eyes.

"You were scared of the debut? Oh, Glimmer! You'd never be a disappointment to me or anyone! You're the only unicorn that I want. I've been so worried about you and missing you since you left."

Bella threw her arms around Glimmer. "I understand that you got nervous. Being a royal can be scary. But you'll always have me. We have each other."

Glimmer stretched her neck around so that it rested lightly on Bella's shoulder as she gave her a unicorn hug.

Bella let go and looked into Glimmer's eyes. "Do you really want to come back to the castle and be my unicorn? That really will make you happy?"

Glimmer blinked, and a sweet look flashed in her eyes.

"Hurray!" Bella said. Happy tears pricked her eyes. "Let's get out of this creepy forest and go home."

Glimmer bobbed her head. Bella picked up her crystal from her pocket and squeezed it in her palm. "I need to tell Ivy and Clara to get out of here right away," Bella explained to Glimmer. "We'll meet them outside of the forest."

Bella couldn't resist hugging Glimmer again. She began to speak the words to summon Ivy's and Clara's crystals. "Crystal I hold in my hand," Bella started. As she spoke, Glimmer's head went high into the air. Her nostrils flared, and her tail began to whip back and forth.

Bella lowered the hand that held the crystal. "Glimmer, what's wrong?"

The princess followed Glimmer's gaze into a line of trees just ahead of them. What Bella saw wasn't easy to miss. Out of the trees, a bright-red unicorn with black eyes and a black horn stepped into the clearing. Its head was lowered—and its horn was pointed right at Glimmer.

8

Most Unusual Rescue

"Glimmer," Bella said in a whisper. "Let's just back away. Maybe it won't fight us."

The words had no sooner left Bella's mouth than the red unicorn swept its ears back and let out a thundering neigh. It had to have been heard throughout the entire forest.

Glimmer nudged Bella beside her, and the princess shrank into her unicorn's coat.

They had no way out.

The red unicorn's black eyes narrowed on Glimmer, and Bella's unicorn bared her teeth. Bella knew Glimmer would fight as hard as necessary to protect her. But she didn't want Glimmer getting hurt. Queen Fire's unicorns were unusually strong and filled with rage. The enemy unicorn struck the earth with a front hoof and lowered its head to charge.

"Enough!"

A familiar voice echoed through the forest.

The red unicorn lifted its head, relaxing its ears, and began backing out of the clearing.

Bella almost fell as she witnessed the unicorn disappearing back into the Dark Forest. Glimmer maintained alert mode, and both she and Bella watched as their unexpected rescuer strode into the clearing.

"Queen Fire," Bella said, trying to keep her voice from shaking.

"You and your precious unicorn are in *my* woods, darling niece," the evil queen said.

Queen Fire looked exactly as she had when

she'd made an unwelcome appearance at Bella's eighth birthday. Red lipstick stained her lips. Long, wavy black hair flowed past her shoulders, and the ends were dyed bright red. She looked nothing like her sister, Bella's mother. Queen Fire's eyes were an endless pit of black.

Her long black dress dragged along the ground, and a red cape was tied across the queen's shoulders. She stopped where her unicorn had pawed the ground and smiled at Bella.

The smile held no warmth. It didn't reach her eyes.

"Why did you save us?" Bella asked. "You stopped your unicorn from attacking."

The queen laughed. "It was not out of sheer devotion and love for you, Princess." The queen tapped a long red fingernail against her cheek. "You haven't spent enough time around your aunt to know how my world—the real world—works.

I saved you and your precious unicorn not just because you are my family, but because it will benefit *me*."

Queen Fire's words made Bella's stomach drop. Being around this woman was almost scarier than facing one of her unicorns. Glimmer shared Bella's thinking, and Bella felt Glimmer's muscles tighten under her hand.

"What do you want?" Bella asked. She summoned every ounce of courage left in her body. "I owe you for your protection. *I* want to repay the debt. If you even think Glimmer is part of any deal, you're wrong."

The queen stared. The forest was silent. Bella felt as though she'd stopped breathing. Then Queen Fire burst into laughter.

"Oh, my Bella!" Queen Fire said, grinning. "You may have a purple aura, dear, but you have the courage of your black-auraed aunt."

"I told you the first time we met," Bella said. "I'm nothing like you!"

Queen Fire's smile left her face. "Time will tell, Princess. You can't control what's inside of you. There may be untapped evil you've yet to even imagine."

Bella gritted her teeth. She had to get Glimmer out of here. It wasn't going to do any good to keep arguing with Queen Fire.

"Please just tell me what you want," Bella said.

The queen folded her arms. "I don't know when I'll want something from you or what that may be. But I agree that you, Princess Bella, are in my debt. When I am ready for you to fulfill my favor, you will know."

The queen smiled again, making Bella's knees shake even harder.

"I—," Bella started.

A loud *crack!* cut her off, and black smoke rose

from the spot where Queen Fire had just stood.

"Let's go! Right now!" Bella said to Glimmer. Glimmer turned in the direction Bella had entered the clearing, clearly beckoning Bella to follow.

Without a look back, the two raced out of the Dark Forest and into the waiting open arms of Ivy and Clara.

9

Not-So-Secret Plan Anymore

"I can't believe Queen Fire saved you!" Ivy said.

"I'm just glad we found you, Glimmer," Clara said, patting the unicorn's neck. The three friends and Glimmer walked over the castle's drawbridge. On the walk back to the castle, Bella had told them about her run-in with Queen Fire in the woods. Both girls had been scared and worried about what happened—and Bella's debt to the queen—but at the end of the talk, they had been grateful Bella's aunt had chosen to stop the unicorn fight.

"Uh-oh," Bella said.

Her parents, Frederick, and Ben stood in front

of the stables. Ben's head was down, and Queen Katherine's arms were crossed.

"Bella, how long were you planning to keep it a secret that your unicorn had gone missing?" King Phillip asked. His voice was low and very serious.

"I'm sorry," Bella said. "But please don't send Ben away! This wasn't his fault. I made him promise not to tell anyone."

"Ben should have come to me," Frederick said. "However, I am the stable manager. It is my responsibility to make sure that all the royal unicorns are safe. I should have asked Ben about Glimmer the moment I began to feel it was odd that I hadn't seen her in a while."

Bella's stomach twisted and turned. Ben couldn't leave because of her!

"How did you find out?" Bella asked, her voice quiet.

"Frederick came to your father and me," Queen Katherine said. "He hadn't seen Glimmer, and with Ben at the stables and both you and Glimmer gone, Frederick was worried that you were out riding alone."

"We came down to the stables immediately," King Phillip continued. "Ben was so worried about you and your friends being in the Dark Forest that he told us the truth. We were moments away from sending out every guard at the castle."

Bella glanced at Ben. He mouthed, "I'm sorry." She shook her head at him.

"Mom, Dad," Bella said. "I'm sorry that I've been lying to you. I should have told you the second that I realized Glimmer had escaped. I know you must have been really worried about me, Ivy, and Clara in the Dark Forest."

"Yes, we were," Queen Katherine said. "Bella, your father and I will discuss this with you tonight.

It's quite serious that you lied and went to a place we forbade you from going."

Bella nodded. "Okay," she said in a whisper.

"Ivy and Clara," King Phillip said, "please go with Ben. He'll ready a carriage to take you both home."

The girls quietly thanked the king and queen and disappeared into the stables with Ben.

"I know you're mad," Bella said. "But please don't make Ben leave Crystal Castle."

The grown-ups exchanged looks. Bella's hand that was tangled in Glimmer's mane was sweaty.

"We are grateful to Ben for telling the truth," King Phillip said. "He also helped keep you safe." The king looked at Frederick. "Ben is welcome to stay as your apprentice if that's what you wish."

Bella held her breath as she watched Frederick.

"He may stay," Frederick finally answered.

"Thank you, Frederick!" Bella cheered.

"Go get Glimmer settled in," Queen Katherine said. "Then come straight inside."

"I will, Mom," Bella said. "Thank you."

A few minutes later she hugged Glimmer again, never wanting to let go. The royal unicorn was safe and secure in her stall. It was just Bella, Glimmer, and Ben.

"Are you ever going to let go of Glimmer?" Ben asked. He smiled and leaned against the stall door jamb. Bella had told Ben about running into Queen Fire. Like Ivy and Clara, he had been upset. But he was beyond relieved that Bella and Glimmer were home safe.

"Nah, I think I'll hold on to Glimmer until I'm fifteen," Bella said, only half-teasing.

"Only until you're *fifteen*?" Ben asked. "Jeez, Bella. That's giving up pretty early. I thought you'd at least hang on until forty."

They both laughed. Glimmer seemed to sense

the lift in mood. She threw up her head and shook her mane. The purple-tinted strands swished against the top of Bella's shoulder and tickled her cheek.

"Fine, fine," Bella said, pretend-sighing. "I guess I can do forty."

Ben grinned and looked down, swirling his boot on the concrete aisle. "Seriously," he started. "I have to thank you again for everything you did for me."

"You don't have to keep thanking me," Bella said. "Really. You've been so great to Glimmer and me since you got here. It wouldn't have been fair for you to get in trouble."

Ben slowly shook his head and let out a breath. "I almost can't believe Glimmer is back and that we pulled it off." He turned his gaze to the unicorn. "I'm going to set up twenty more cameras and cast a dozen spells to make sure you sleep tight, Glimmer."

Glimmer nudged Bella's shoulder. Bella looked into Glimmer's eyes, and what she saw made her feel warm from head to toe.

"I don't think Glimmer's going anywhere," Bella said. She lightly kissed Glimmer's cheek, and the unicorn let out a soft *whoosh* of breath.

"I think it's time we both got some rest," Bella said to Glimmer. "We've got a big day tomorrow."

Glimmer rested her soft muzzle in Bella's hands. She looked into the princess's eyes, and Bella knew that she would be able to sleep well tonight—Glimmer was happy to be home.

10

Glimmer's Big Debut

"Glimmer!" Bella cried, waking and sitting up in bed. Her heart thudded against her chest, as if she had just run laps around the castle's moat.

Glimmer's home, Bella reminded herself. She let out a breath as if trying to exhale the nightmare. She'd been dreaming that Glimmer had been captured by Queen Fire. Goose bumps ran up and down her arms as she remembered the queen's promise to collect on Bella's debt. *But Glimmer's safe from my deal,* the princess reminded herself. *It could be six days or six years before Queen Fire wants something from me.* She took a long, deep breath through her nose. When she exhaled, she pushed all of the thoughts of Queen Fire from her mind. Bella was going to try her hardest not to think about her aunt. At least not today.

Bella yanked back the purple-and-white-striped sheets and comforter and ran to her window. She undid the latch and pushed it open. Her view from the tower was perfect. She could see the stables, pastures, and barnyard. Ben and Frederick emerged from the stables with a gorgeous purple-splashed unicorn in tow. The view instantly made her happy.

Glimmer! Bella thought. *You really are home and safe.*

Through her window, Bella watched as Ben turned Glimmer in a circle and tied her to one of the white fence rails. Frederick carried over a bucket filled with brushes, and Ben began to ready Glimmer for her debut. Bella closed her eyes, trying to clear her mind of anything but her connection to Glimmer. The princess felt happiness, excitement, and a touch of nerves. Bella opened her eyes, grinning. Glimmer's feelings matched her own!

"Good morning, Bella!" Lyssa entered Bella's room. She had a garment bag in one hand.

Bella eyed the bag. "Jeez, Lyss. I thought you were never going to get here."

"Ha, ha," Lyssa said, winking. "That's talk, coming from someone still in her pj's."

"Didn't you hear?" Bella asked, putting a hand on her hip. "Pajamas are *so* in this season. Everyone is wearing them all the time."

Lyssa grinned. "Oh, well then, you won't want the clothes your mom gave me for your debut." She took the black garment bag and started to put it in Bella's closet.

"Um, wait!" Bella said, hurrying over to Lyssa. "The pj's all day is totally a fad. I'm going to stay fashion forward and wear real clothes during the day."

Lyssa laughed. "Wow! What perfect timing, since I brought this!"

Bella watched as Lyssa unzipped the clothing bag. Carefully Lyssa took out a pair of shimmery gold leggings, a plum-purple tee with lace-edged sleeves and hem, and black riding boots. A gold chain with a prancing unicorn pendant hung from the hanger.

"You like?" Lyssa asked.

"I love!" Bella said. "These clothes are perfect for today."

Lyssa helped her change. The castle was quiet when Bella left and headed for the stables to meet her parents.

The king and queen had spoken to Bella for a *long* time last night about the Glimmer situation. Bella had realized that if she had told her parents from the start, she would have probably found Glimmer faster. King Phillip had reminded Bella that what happened wasn't Ben's fault, and if he and Bella had told the truth earlier, then they wouldn't have had to worry about Ben's future at the castle. Most of all, though, the king and queen were relieved that their daughter and Glimmer were home safe.

"Ben!" Bella called, spotting him in the stable yard.

"Hi, Bella," he said, smiling. "My uncle's holding Glimmer. He asked me to keep an eye out for you."

"There's one *huge* problem!" Bella said. She looked over her shoulder to make sure no one else was around. "I haven't actually ridden Glimmer before. Now I have to ride her to the town square and be in front of the entire kingdom!"

Ben tapped his index finger against one of his temples. "One step ahead of you, Princess."

Bella clutched her hands together. "Really?"

"Really. Frederick knows that you haven't had riding lessons, so I asked him if I could lead Glimmer for the debut."

"Ben!" Bella hugged him quickly. "That's only the best plan *ever*! You're a genius!"

Ben shook his head. "Just a *very* smart apprentice." He grinned. "So, Princess Bella, may I assist you during your debut?"

"Hmmm." Bella rolled her eyes to the sky, pretending to think. "*Yes!* Thank you, Ben!"

Ben bowed his head. He waved a hand in the direction of the stable yard. "This way, Princess Bella. It's time for your first ride." He whispered the last sentence, and he and Bella exchanged secret smiles.

Bella half skipped after Ben. She wanted the kingdom to love Glimmer as much as she did. But right now, what she wanted more than anything was to *finally* ride her unicorn. Bella's boots crunched on gravel, and Glimmer turned her head in Bella's direction. Two pricked ears pointed toward Bella, and Glimmer let out a soft whinny.

Bella hurried over, and Frederick laughed and he moved out of the way as the princess threw her arms around Glimmer's neck. The unicorn smelled like sweet hay and daisies. Superfine strands of clear wire had been twisted throughout Glimmer's mane and tail. The wires shimmered and slowly changed from pink to green to purple—they ran through *every* color that Bella had ever seen in Crystal Kingdom! Glimmer's white coat glittered in the sun, and it reminded Bella of pixie dust.

"You look *so* pretty!" Bella told Glimmer. The princess looked into Glimmer's eyes and saw love and happiness. The princess knew *she* would do anything to protect her unicorn in return.

Bella perched on her tiptoes and leaned close

to Glimmer's right ear. "Nothing's ever made me feel more like a princess."

"May I help you up?" Frederick asked.

"Please!" Bella said. *I get to finally ride!* she thought.

Frederick motioned for Bella to follow him as he led Glimmer over to a set of three wooden stairs.

"Climb on up and put your left foot here," Frederick said. He held a triangle-shaped iron with a rubber grip at the bottom. The triangle's bottom supported Bella's weight. Bella followed the stable manager's instructions and lowered herself onto the leather saddle.

Frederick quickly explained how Bella would use her hands and feet to guide Glimmer.

"That's a lot to remember," Bella said. Her heart beat a little faster.

"Ben will be right there, so don't worry,"

Frederick said. He patted her knee, smiling as he waved to Ben.

Ben hurried over and took the rainbow-striped rope from Frederick.

"Oh, Bella!" Queen Katherine, arm in arm with King Phillip, beamed at her daughter. "You look perfect with Glimmer. Phillip, take a photo!"

Bella's dad already had the camera lens pointed at the princess and Glimmer. Bella grinned into the camera. "Unicorn!" she said, giggling.

After a few more photos, the king and queen climbed into the Royal Carriage. The beautiful carriage, powered by the sun, glowed bright despite the sun being out in full force.

With a smile at Bella, Ben led Glimmer forward through the stable yard, across the drawbridge, and out onto the private winding Royal Road to town.

The shimmering purple strands in Glimmer's

mane and tail complemented the crystal-flecked path under her hooves. Glimmer pranced toward town, and Bella couldn't stop grinning.

"Ben?" Bella asked. "What if the crowds scare Glimmer? She's never been around so many people before."

"Again," Ben said, smiling, "got you covered."

Soon they were in town. Ben led Glimmer down a path secured by a few Royal Guards and into the town square. High in the air, a giant red sign flashed QUIET, PLEASE! and NEW ROYAL UNI-CORN! CAUTION!

"My uncle came here before we got here," Ben explained, looking up at the signs. "He asked the crowd not to wave any signs or make any noise that might scare Glimmer. She's new to everything. But soon the people won't even faze her."

Dozens of people, held back by a shield spell, smiled, held up cameras, or whispered to each other as Ben halted Glimmer. Bella looked over her shoulder for her parents. The king and queen emerged from the Royal Carriage and greeted the people of Crystal Kingdom with waves and smiles.

Bella recognized a few reporters from the local newspaper as they scribbled in notepads and had cameras on tripods that recorded the event. She looked over the crowd, and two hands shot into the air. Clara and Ivy! Bella waved at her besties.

The king and queen stood on the podium that towered above the crowd. Bella couldn't help but flash back to her dad standing there, sword at his side, when Queen Fire had scared the crowd on her birthday. The evil queen's words from yesterday made Bella shiver.

Immediately, Glimmer's ears swept back toward Bella, and she struck the ground with a front hoof.

"Easy, girl," Ben said, petting Glimmer. "You okay?" he asked Bella.

"Totally fine. Just thought about yesterday for a second," Bella said.

Ben half smiled. "Look around. Maybe the fact that, oh, a *few* people showed up will distract you."

Bella laughed. "That helps! Plus, we're here on a school day."

"I'm not exactly sad about school being canceled," Ben said. He led Glimmer toward the crowd and turned her in a big circle so everyone could see.

"People of Crystal Kingdom," King Phillip's voice came through a microphone.

Everyone's heads swiveled in his direction. Even Glimmer's!

"Thank you all for joining my family on this beautiful day," the king said. "Queen Katherine

115

and I are thrilled to introduce you to our daughter's unicorn. Princess Bella is now paired with Glimmer."

Chills ran up and down Bella's arms. She leaned forward and patted Glimmer's shoulder. The unicorn bowed her neck in appreciation, letting out a soft whicker.

"Together, let us all welcome Glimmer as a member of the royal family and of Crystal Kingdom," King Phillip said.

The crowd raised their hands in the air as Bella's smile grew. The overhead red sign flashed green to GENTLE APPLAUSE, and cheers broke out across the square.

"See what you would have missed?" Bella asked Glimmer.

The princess leaned forward, hugging Glimmer. Cameras clicked, and the crowd clapped harder.

"Welcome home," Bella said.

Glimmer craned her neck around, a twinkle in her eyes, and bumped Bella's boot with her nose. Bella's heart soared higher than the podium. Glimmer was definitely here to stay!

Green with Envy

"Next Friday is going to be the best day *ever*!" Princess Bella said to her two best friends. Ivy and Clara walked beside Bella as the three girls left their classroom on Friday afternoon. The girls had school every day at Crystal Castle—Bella's home—and shared the classroom with six other third-grade students. Most of them, like Ivy, had parents who worked at Crystal Castle. Another student, older by a year, was Ben. His uncle ran the royal stables. Bella's closest friends weren't official "royals," but they were princesses to her!

"I know! I love spring break!" Ivy said. "No

school for an entire week!" She slung her pink shimmery backpack over one shoulder. Pieces of her white-blond hair were twisted and held off her face by several rhinestone butterfly hair clips. The enchanted butterfly wings fluttered open and shut, making the gemstones sparkle.

"That's *so* exciting, but I'm with Bella," Clara said. "Friday is huge!" Clara, the most outgoing of the three friends, skipped ahead a couple of steps, then turned around and walked backward so she faced her friends. Clara's backpack, covered in teensy blue lights that flashed on when the bag moved, rolled beside her on wheels over the castle's marble floor.

Bella and Ivy giggled at Clara as she almost tripped over her own feet.

"My parents didn't even tell me that they were going to throw a party for our class," Bella said. "We get the whole week off, and on Friday is the party, with a movie in the garden, desserts, and music. And we all get to hang out."

Bella smiled at the thought of spending more time with her classmates. Lately, the princess had barely enough time to see her besties and her new friend, Ben. Ben had just joined Bella's class when he had come to Crystal Castle to be an apprentice for his uncle Frederick. Frederick was the royal stable manager, and he had put Ben to work helping care for the castle's prized unicorns, including Bella's own unicorn, Glimmer.

"Plus, there's an *extra* surprise that I didn't tell you about yet," Bella said mysteriously.

Clara stopped so suddenly that Bella and Ivy almost plowed into her.

"Spill!" Clara said, her long honey-blond waves swishing around her shoulders.

"Tell us!" Ivy added, making wide eyes and pouting.

Bella laughed. "Okay. Want to go to the stables? We could sit with Glimmer and talk. We already got the okay from your parents for you to stay after school for a while."

"Stables. Yes! Let's go! I want to know the extra surprise!" Clara said, grabbing the hands of Ivy and Bella and pulling them forward.

They ran, laughing, down a long hallway in the castle. The girls stopped in front of the giant wooden front door, and Clara told her backpack to "stay." Ivy put hers beside Clara's, and Bella dropped her own purple one on the pile.

A castle security guard, gleaming sword at his side, opened the door for them. Bright sunlight almost blinded Bella for a moment as she skipped with her friends across the Crystal Castle lawn toward the stables.

Bella carefully looked over the grounds. She wanted everything to be perfect for her surprise.

But there wasn't a thing she would change. Royal unicorns, white as fresh snow, munched on emerald-colored grass in pastures on both sides of the castle's driveway. A few unicorns were napping—flat out on their sides—and soaking up the sun. The weather was perfect—warm but not too hot. It was Bella's favorite time of year.

The girls reached the stables and slowed to a walk so they didn't scare any of the unicorns. The royal stables had a mint-green exterior and a black roof.

Inside, a large main aisle had a row of stalls on either side. Since it was so nice out, most of the stalls were empty, as the unicorns were outside. But at the end of the left aisle, a closed stall door held one *very* special unicorn. Bella craned her neck, looking for Ben,

"Glimmer!" Bella called. "We're here!"

She couldn't help but smile when her beautiful

unicorn stuck her head over the stall door. The purple tinted unicorn neighed excitedly when she saw Bella.

Bella slid the giant bolt on the stall door and opened it. Ivy and Clara followed her inside, shutting the door behind them.

"Hi, Glimmer," Bella said softly. "Pretty girl." The princess hugged Glimmer's neck while Ivy and Clara petted her.

Glimmer bumped her velvet-soft nose against Bella's hands, making the princess laugh.

Bella and Glimmer shared a very special bond. Just under a week ago, Glimmer had disappeared from the royal stables. At first Bella had been certain her unicorn had been uni-napped, until she got help from Ben, Ivy, and Clara. They learned that Glimmer had run away, and after days of searching, Bella had found Glimmer deep in the scary Dark Forest. The princess had pleaded with Glimmer to follow her out the dangerous woods. She wanted Glimmer to be safe, even if Glimmer didn't want to be her unicorn.

As Glimmer had nudged Bella's hands just now, it was something the unicorn had done in the woods. When Glimmer touched Bella, something magical happened between them. Bella was able to read Glimmer's body language and, almost like mind reading, be able to tell what Glimmer was thinking or how she was feeling.

That day, surrounded by the Dark Forest, Glimmer had told Bella that she was scared to be the princess's unicorn. Glimmer loved Bella more than anything, but worried she wouldn't be good enough.

Bella assured Glimmer that the unicorn was perfect and everything she wanted.

Princess Bella jumped, startled, as Glimmer bumped her hands a little harder.

"It's like Glimmer's saying, 'Earth to Bella,'" Ivy said with a smile.

"True. She's also saying, 'Get me a treat, please,'" Bella said.

She ran a hand down Glimmer's white neck with her light-purple-tinged mane. "I'll get you one before we leave, okay?"

Glimmer bobbed her head.

The girls settled onto the clean straw and Glimmer, not wanting to be left out, folded her legs under her and delicately lowered herself to the stall floor.

"Aw! I *have* to take a picture of this even though I don't have my camera," Clara said. She made a rectangle shape with her fingers, touching her pointer fingers to her thumbs. Photos were always better with a camera, but magic worked in a pinch. "Photograph," she commanded. She closed one eye and moved her hands closer to Glimmer. "Take picture now."

Click!

A small burst of sparkles shimmered into the air. The photo appeared in the air and Ivy and Clara tilted their heads to see it.

"Aw!" Bella said. "Send me that picture."

Clara nodded. "I will. Camera, I'm finished." The image of Glimmer vanished.

"So do you guys remember my cousin Violet?" Bella asked.

"She's a princess in Foris Kingdom, right?" Ivy asked. "A few months younger than us?"

Foris Kingdom was on one of four sky islands—pieces of land that floated way above the clouds. A person could only reach another island if a rainbow or moonbow was cast. Then, the sky island was in walking distance.

"Right," Bella said. "Violet's dad is my uncle, King Alexander—my dad's brother. You guys know how close Violet and I are. Even though she lives in

Foris, we've been like best friends since we could walk."

"You've talked a lot about her," Clara said. "She sounds so nice."

Bella smiled. "She is. We have bonded even more since my pair to Glimmer."

"That makes sense," Ivy said. "Did Violet want to know all about your pairing? I know I would."

Bella nodded. "I told her most of it over the phone." Bella sighed. "I really wish you could meet her."

Ivy and Clara both frowned, sticking out their bottom lips.

"We would have so much fun together," Bella said. "And we will, because . . .Violet's coming to visit! Surprise!"

Mermaid Tales

Exciting under-the-sea adventures
with Shelly and her mermaid friends!

Trouble at Trident Academy
Battle of the Best Friends
A Whale of a Tale
Danger in the Deep Blue Sea

The Lost Princess
The Secret Sea Horse
Dream of the Blue Turtle
Treasure in Trident City
A Royal Tea

Candy Fairies

Chocolate Dreams

Rainbow Swirl

Caramel Moon

Cool Mint

Magic Heart

Gooey Goblins

The Sugar Ball

A Valentine's Surprise

Bubble Gum Rescue

Double Dip

Jelly Bean Jumble

The Chocolate Rose

A Royal Wedding

Marshmallow Mystery

Visit
candyfairies.c
for more delic
fun with you
favorite fairi

Play games, download activities, and so much more!

EBOOK EDITIONS ALSO AVAILABLE
FROM ALADDIN · KIDS.SimonandSchuster.com

Green with Envy

Don't miss any of Bella
and Glimmer's adventures!

Unicorn Magic

Coming soon

Unicorn Magic

- BOOK 3 -

Green with Envy

BY JESSICA BURKHART

Illustrated by Victoria Ying

Aladdin

NEW YORK   LONDON   TORONTO   SYDNEY   NEW DELHI

This book is a work of fiction. Any references to historical events, real people,
or real places are used fictitiously. Other names, characters, places, and events
are products of the author's imagination, and any resemblance to actual
events or places or persons, living or dead, is entirely coincidental.

ALADDIN

An imprint of Simon & Schuster Children's Publishing Division
1230 Avenue of the Americas, New York, NY 10020
This Aladdin paperback edition December 2014
Text copyright © 2014 by Jessica Burkhart
Cover illustrations copyright © 2014 by Victoria Ying
Interior illustrations by Victoria Ying
All rights reserved, including the right of reproduction in whole or in part in any form.
ALADDIN is a trademark of Simon & Schuster, Inc., and related logo
is a registered trademark of Simon & Schuster, Inc.
Also available in an Aladdin hardcover edition.
For information about special discounts for bulk purchases, please contact
Simon & Schuster Special Sales at 1-866-506-1949
or business@simonandschuster.com.
The Simon & Schuster Speakers Bureau can bring authors to your live event.
For more information or to book an event contact the
Simon & Schuster Speakers Bureau at 1-866-248-3049 or
visit our website at www.simonspeakers.com.
Cover designed by Jessica Handelman
Interior designed by Mike Rosamilia
The text of this book was set in Arno Pro.
Manufactured in the United States of America 0518 OFF
4 6 8 10 9 7 5 3
Library of Congress Control Number 2014952850
ISBN 978-1-4814-1107-3 (hc)
ISBN 978-1-4424-9826-6 (pbk)
ISBN 978-1-4424-9827-3 (eBook)

Contents

1

Spilling Secrets

"Next Friday is going to be the best day *ever*!" Princess Bella said to her two best friends. Ivy and Clara walked beside Bella as the three girls left their classroom on Friday afternoon. The girls had school every day at Crystal Castle—Bella's home—and shared the classroom with six other third-grade students. Most of them, like Ivy, had parents who worked at Crystal Castle. Another student, older by a year, was Ben.

Ben had just joined Bella's class when he had come to Crystal Castle to be an apprentice for his uncle Frederick. Frederick was the royal stable manager, and he had put Ben to work helping care for the castle's prized unicorns, including Bella's own unicorn, Glimmer.

Bella's closest friends weren't official "royals," but they were princesses to her!

"I know!" Ivy said. "No school for an entire week! I love spring break!" She slung her pink shimmery backpack over one shoulder. Pieces of her white-blond hair were twisted and held off her face by several rhinestone butterfly hair clips. The enchanted butterfly wings fluttered open and shut, making the gemstones sparkle.

"That's *so* exciting, but I'm with Bella," Clara said. "Friday is huge!" Clara, the most outgoing of the three friends, skipped ahead a couple of steps, then turned around and walked backward so she faced her friends. Clara's backpack, covered in teensy blue lights that flashed on when the bag moved, rolled beside her on wheels over the castle's marble floor.

Bella and Ivy giggled at Clara as she almost tripped over her own feet.

"My parents didn't even tell me that they were going to throw a party for our class," Bella said. "We get the whole week off, and on Friday is the party, with a movie in the garden, desserts, and music. And we all get to hang out."

Bella smiled at the thought of spending more time with her classmates. Lately, the princess had barely enough time to see her besties.

"Plus, there's an *extra* surprise that I didn't tell you about yet," Bella said mysteriously.

Clara stopped so suddenly that Bella and Ivy almost plowed into her.

"Spill!" Clara said, her long strawberry-blond waves swishing around her shoulders.

"Tell us!" Ivy added, making wide eyes and pouting.

Bella laughed. "Okay. Want to go to the stables? We could sit with Glimmer and talk. We already got the okay from your parents for you to stay after school for a while."

"Stables. Yes! Let's go! I want to know the extra surprise!" Clara said, grabbing the hands of Ivy and Bella and pulling them forward.

They ran, laughing, down a long hallway in the castle. The girls stopped in front of the giant wooden front door, and Clara told her backpack to "stay." Ivy put hers beside Clara's, and Bella dropped her own purple one on the pile.

A castle security guard, gleaming sword at his side, opened the door for them. Bright sunlight almost blinded Bella for a moment as she skipped with her friends across the Crystal Castle lawn toward the stable.

Bella carefully looked over the grounds. She wanted everything to be perfect for her surprise. But there wasn't a thing she would change. Royal unicorns, white as fresh snow, munched on emerald-colored grass in pastures on both sides of the castle's driveway. A few unicorns were napping—flat out on their sides—and soaking up the sun. The weather was perfect—warm but not too hot. It was Bella's favorite time of year.

The girls reached the stables and slowed to a walk so they didn't scare any of the unicorns. The royal stables had a mint-green exterior and a black roof.

Inside, a large main aisle had a row of stalls on either side. Since it was so nice out, most of the stalls were empty, as the unicorns were outside. But at the end of the left aisle, a closed stall door held one *very* special unicorn. Bella craned her neck, looking for Ben.

"Glimmer!" Bella called. "We're here!"

She couldn't help but smile when her beautiful unicorn stuck her head over the stall door. The purple tinted unicorn neighed excitedly when she saw Bella.

Bella slid the giant bolt on the stall door and opened it. Ivy and Clara followed her inside, shutting the door behind them.

"Hi, Glimmer," Bella said softly. "Pretty girl." The princess hugged Glimmer's neck while Ivy and Clara petted her.

Glimmer bumped her velvet-soft nose against Bella's hands, making the princess laugh.

Bella and Glimmer shared a very special bond. Just under a week ago, Glimmer had disappeared from the royal stables. At first Bella had been certain her unicorn had been uni-napped, until she got help from Ben, Ivy, and Clara. They learned that Glimmer had run away, and after days of searching,

Bella had found Glimmer deep in the scary Dark Forest. The princess had pleaded with Glimmer to follow her out of the dangerous woods. She wanted Glimmer to be safe, even if Glimmer didn't want to be her unicorn.

As Glimmer had nudged Bella's hands just now, it was something the unicorn had done in the woods. When Glimmer touched Bella, something magical happened between them. Bella was able to read Glimmer's body language and, almost like mind reading, be able to tell what Glimmer was thinking or how she was feeling.

That day, surrounded by the Dark Forest, Glimmer had told Bella that she was scared to be the princess's unicorn. Glimmer loved Bella more than anything, but worried she wouldn't be good enough.

Bella assured Glimmer that the unicorn was perfect and everything she wanted.

Princess Bella jumped, startled, as Glimmer bumped her hands a little harder.

"It's like Glimmer's saying, 'Earth to Bella,'" Ivy said with a smile.

"True. She's also saying, 'Get me a treat, please,'" Bella said.

She ran a hand down Glimmer's white neck with her light-purple-tinged mane. "I'll get you one before we leave, okay?"

Glimmer bobbed her head.

The girls settled onto the clean straw and Glimmer, not wanting to be left out, folded her legs under her and delicately lowered herself to the stall floor.

"Aw! I *have* to take a picture of this, even though I don't have my camera," Clara said. She made a rectangle shape with her fingers, touching her pointer fingers to her thumbs. Photos were always better with a camera, but magic worked in a pinch. "Photograph," she commanded. She closed one eye and moved her hands closer to Glimmer. "Take picture now."

Click!

A small burst of sparkles shimmered into the air. The photo appeared in the air, and Ivy and Clara tilted their heads to see it.

"Ooh!" Bella exclaimed. "Send me that picture!"

Clara nodded. "I will. Camera, I'm finished." The image of Glimmer vanished.

"So do you guys remember my cousin Violet?" Bella asked.

"She's a princess in Foris Kingdom, right?" Ivy asked. "A few months younger than us?"

Foris Kingdom was on one of four sky islands—pieces of land that floated way above the clouds. A person could only reach another island if a rainbow or moonbow was cast. Then the sky island was in walking distance.

"Right," Bella said. "Violet's dad is my uncle,

King Alexander—my dad's brother. You guys know how close Violet and I are. Even though she lives in Foris, we've been like best friends since we could walk."

"You've talked a lot about her," Clara said. "She sounds so nice."

Bella smiled. "She is. We've bonded even more since my Pair to Glimmer."

"That makes sense," Ivy said. "Did Violet want to know all about your Pairing? I know I would."

Bella nodded. "I told her most of it over the phone." She sighed. "I really wish you could meet her."

Ivy and Clara both frowned, sticking out their bottom lips.

"We would have so much fun together," Bella said. "And we will because . . . Violet's coming to visit! Surprise!"

2

Two Princesses + One Celebration = Awesome!

"BELLA!" Ivy and Clara shrieked.

Bella giggled at her friends' faces. They were pink from shouting, and even Glimmer looked as if she was almost smiling.

"You sneak!" Ivy said. "When is she coming?"

"Tomorrow!" Bella said. "Violet's staying at the castle all week, and she's coming to our class party on Friday."

"Ooh, yay!" Clara said. She clasped her hands together.

"My mom, dad, and I are meeting her at the

end of the rainbow from the Foris Kingdom exit," Bella said.

"Just when I thought next week couldn't get any better," Ivy said. She twirled a stalk of straw around her finger. "I can't wait for Violet to get here."

Glimmer added a soft whicker as if stating her opinion.

"This is going to be so much fun! You said you

told Violet about your Pairing Ceremony," Clara said. "Have you talked about auras yet? Does Violet know about Queen Fire?"

Bella shook her head. "Not yet. I told Violet the basics: that the aura appears on your eighth birthday. When the aura appears, you get to walk down a line of royal unicorns, watching each unicorn glow a different color until you both have the same aura glow color. I told Violet that mine is purple and, of course, sent her a million photos of Glimmer, but I haven't told her about Queen Fire."

Just saying the words "Queen Fire" left a bad taste in Bella's mouth.

"Are you going to tell her?" Ivy asked, her voice soft.

It hadn't been even a week since Bella had been up against the evil queen who ruled the Blacklands—a dangerous place that no one went near—and the Dark Forest.

"I think I have to," Bella said. "Violet is family. Queen Fire is my"—she swallowed—"my mom's twin sister. My aunt. I don't want to keep a secret that big from her."

Bella shook her head hard, trying to send thoughts of Queen Fire away. She knew she had to tell Violet—her younger cousin was three weeks away from her own Pairing Ceremony.

"No more talk of You Know Who today," Clara declared. "We have lots of things to be excited about."

Bella smiled. "We so do! A sleepover is a must this week. I want you both here as much as possible all week long."

Just the thought of Violet visiting made Bella want to do cartwheels. Violet was one of her best friends, and they hadn't had a week together in years. Usually they only saw each other during holidays or vacations. They had *so* much to talk about!

Violet's parents had agreed to let the princess have a week off from her private tutor to spend time at Crystal Castle. Bella's dad, King Phillip, had assured Violet's parents that his niece needed to come spend time with kids her own age and the party would be good for her. The king and queen hadn't wanted Bella to grow up lonely or without interaction with kids her own age, so that was why they had decided to have a small classroom in Crystal Castle.

"Did I mention how *amazing* this week is going to be?" Bella asked. She grinned, and they all cracked up. Laughing, the three friends high-fived.

3

Instant Besties

"Mom! Dad! We're going to be late!" Bella called up the winding staircase. She shook her head, sending her wavy brown hair across her shoulders.

"Bells, don't worry," Lyssa said. "You'll make it in plenty of time to pick up Violet."

Lyssa was Bella's handmaiden. But that sounded like a stuffy title.

Lyssa, who was fourteen years old, was really more like an older sister. Since last year, Lyssa had helped Bella with getting dressed, doing home-work, and, today, carefully curling Bella's straight brown hair into waves.

"Are you sure?" Bella asked. "What if the Rainbow Rail Express gets here early?"

The Rainbow Rail Express was a fairly new mode of transportation. It allowed passengers to travel to the other sky islands. Each morning someone important at the station had to cast a spell to connect one island to the next. Rainbow Rail was so new that even Bella hadn't been on it yet.

Lyssa smiled. "If it does, I'm sure Violet will call or message you."

Bella walked away from the staircase. "Mirror," she said, snapping her fingers.

A mirror appeared in front of Bella. The princess eyed her hair and clothes. Lyssa, who usually took weekends off, had come to Crystal Castle this morning to help Bella get ready for Violet's arrival.

"Do you think this dress is right, Lys?" Bella asked. The princess scanned her reflection in the mirror. The sleeveless soft-pink dress had a full tulle skirt and a rosette at the waist. Bella turned and looked over her shoulder. A satin tie was looped in a pretty bow at the back, which buttoned up.

"I think it's *perfect*," Lyssa said. "You tried on four other dresses before deciding on this one, remember?" The older girl walked over to Bella and hugged her.

Bella squeezed Lyssa back, glad that she had Lyssa's help to choose today's outfit. "I'm so nervous!" Bella admitted. "Isn't that silly?"

She walked over to a red velvet-covered bench and sat down. Lyssa sat beside her, turning so she faced Bella.

"It's not silly at all," Lyssa said. She tucked a strand of shoulder-length honey-blond hair behind her ear. Her green eyes were kind as she looked at Bella.

"It *feels* silly," Bella said. "Violet's my cousin.

We talk all of the time. I want to make this week the best for her. I don't want Violet wishing she had stayed home."

"Hosting a houseguest makes *anyone* nervous," Lyssa said. "You're a little scared because you care so much. Like you said, you want to make this visit great for Violet. If you didn't care, you wouldn't be nervous."

"Really?" Bella looked up at Lyssa. The older girl somehow always knew what to say to make Bella feel better.

Lyssa nodded. "Really. I bet Violet's nervous too. She probably wants to be a good guest and not make *you* wish she had stayed in Foris."

"Never!" Bella said. "I wish she could stay here forever."

Lyssa and Bella laughed, and the prickles of nerves evaporated from Bella's body.

There was the sound of footsteps on the stairs,

and King Phillip and Queen Katherine descended the staircase.

"Thank you, Lys," Bella said, hugging the girl again.

"Anytime! Have fun!" Lyssa said. They stood and Lyssa dipped her head as the king and queen approached, before she exited the room.

"Ready to go, Bells?" King Phillip, smiling, looked down at his daughter. Queen Katherine, in a flowing hunter-green dress, stood next to him.

"Yes! Yes!" Bella exclaimed. "Let's go!"

The guards opened the doors, and the royal family stepped outside and headed for the Royal Carriage. The giant orb-shaped carriage extended stairs and opened its doors so Bella and her parents could climb inside.

The Royal Carriage was solar powered and required no driver. King Phillip and Queen Katherine were the only voices the Royal Carriage listened to for directions. Bella settled herself on the cushy seat across from her parents.

"Please take us to the Rainbow Rail Station at the Foris Kingdom platform," King Phillip commanded the carriage. "At the fastest speed."

Without hesitation, the carriage glided forward. It moved over the gravel driveway and passed the guards who stood like statues on either side of the drawbridge. The guards' armor had the Crystal Kingdom seal: a diamond with two rearing unicorns below. The words CRYSTAL KINGDOM ran under the unicorns.

The carriage turned onto the road and then zipped through the countryside toward the Rainbow Rail Station. Trees, fields, and houses whizzed by. "What are you going to do first with Violet?" Queen Katherine asked Bella.

"Introduce her to Glimmer," Bella said. "I can't wait for them to meet!"

She had barely finished her sentence when the carriage started to slow. Rainbow Rail Station came into view. The station—with signs pointing to different rails to various sky islands and kingdoms—wasn't crowded. A line of five or six people, suitcases trailing behind them, walked away from the platform as one of the silver bullet-shaped trains left the station. It was daylight, so the train followed rainbow paths. When night arrived, moonbows would be cast to take over.

Bella followed her parents out of the carriage. Together, they walked to a concrete platform with a sign above that flashed FORIS. DEPARTURES AND ARRIVALS. As they walked, people who caught their eye bowed their heads or smiled at the royal family. No one snapped photos or gawked. King Phillip and Queen Katherine had worked very hard to make sure their family was approachable and normal— just like every other resident in Crystal Kingdom.

"Violet's train should be arriving at noon," Queen Katherine said. "The schedule says it's on time. See?" The queen pointed to a large board above the platform. It listed all the current train schedules and whether or not a train was delayed. A clock next to the board read 11:59 a.m. Violet would be in Crystal Kingdom any second!

Bella craned her neck and stood on tiptoes, looking down the rainbow for the train. She blinked and a silver train, sunlight glinting off the roof, raced toward the platform.

"Mom! Dad!" Bella said, hopping up and down. "She's here! That's Violet's train!" The speeding train halted silently, and the doors slid open at the front of the train. A handful of people were now standing around the royal family as if they were waiting for someone too. Bella tried to look inside the train through its windows to see if she could spot Violet, but there were too many people moving around. A line of people began exiting the train and spilling onto the platform.

"Do you see her?" Bella asked her dad.

"Not yet," King Phillip said. "Stay still and let Violet find us."

Bella's view of the train exit was blocked as a group of people stopped and gazed around. Where was Violet?

"Uncle Phillip! Aunt Katherine!"

A small figure pushed through the crowd and stopped, grinning, in front of the princess and her parents.

"Violet!" Bella said. "You made it!"

All of Bella's earlier nerves disappeared the second she saw her cousin. Violet dashed toward Bella, her long red curls bouncing, and they hugged. Violet's powder-blue dress looked pretty against her red hair, and she had on silver ballet flats that were almost identical to Bella's.

"Violet, darling, you look beautiful!" Queen Katherine said. She wrapped her arms around Violet, and King Phillip was next in line for a hug.

"I'm *so* happy to be here," Violet said. Her hazel eyes sparkled with excitement. "I was practically counting the seconds on the train ride."

"Let's get off the platform and start the journey home," King Phillip said. He snapped his fingers at Violet's sparkly suitcase. "This way, ladies."

Bella's dad helped his wife, daughter, and niece maneuver through the crowd. The townspeople respectfully stepped aside to allow the royal family to exit. The king and queen got a few paces ahead. Violet grabbed Bella's hand, and the girls grinned at each other. They skipped forward but slowed when they couldn't get by a family that was shuffling along, their luggage floating alongside them.

"*Excuse* me!" Violet said with a huff, then rolled her eyes.

Violet pulled on Bella's hand, pushing them past the group. Bella looked back over her shoulder as the family frowned and watched them walk away, whispering to each other. The princess's face turned bright pink. *That was so rude!* Bella thought. Violet had never done anything like that before.

"Vi," Bella said. "They had a lot of stuff—"

Violet sighed. "I know. I haven't slept much lately! I've been too excited and I guess I'm kind of cranky."

That made sense. Bella smiled at her cousin and kept going toward the carriage.

Once they reached the carriage, everyone settled in, and King Phillip requested that it take them home.

Bella, sitting across from Violet, caught her cousin's eye. There were a few moments of silence. "Omigosh—" Violet started.

"We have—" Bella said at the same time.

They burst into giggles.

"You go," Bella said.

"No, you go!" Violet said.

"Oh, girls. Come on now," Queen Katherine said. "Don't you have anything to talk about? Why all the silence?"

Everyone in the carriage laughed.

"I've been counting the days until you got here," Bella told her cousin. "I was going a little crazy this morning. It felt like noon was never going to come!"

Violet nodded. "I know! I felt the same way. On the train, I asked the conductor *twice* if we were going to arrive on time, because I was sure the train was moving too slow."

"You're here now, and that's all that matters. I have the *best* week planned." Bella smiled. "Friday is going to be so much fun. You'll get to meet everyone in my class."

"I can't wait. But I'm dying to meet Glimmer," Violet said. "I feel like I know her already after everything you've told me."

"She's so excited to meet you, too," Bella agreed. The carriage pulled away from the station and headed home to Crystal Castle.

Bella and Violet chatted the entire way home. They didn't stop as the carriage glided back across the drawbridge and approached the castle. Violet had seen Crystal Castle before. Her attention was on something else: the unicorns.

"Look at them!" Violet pointed, climbing out of the carriage. She shielded her eyes with a hand and looked toward the pastures dotted with grazing unicorns.

"Violet," Queen Katherine said. "Are you tired from traveling? Or hungry? You can come inside and rest for a while if you would like."

"Thank you, Aunt Katherine," Violet said. "But I'm way too excited to be tired! Can Bella show me Glimmer?"

"Please?" Bella added.

"Go have fun," Bella's mom said, smiling.

"Come on! This way!" Bella grabbed Violet's hand. Giggling, they ran to the stable, and skidded to a stop when they reached the entrance.

"Frederick is the stable manager," Bella said. "Don't run in the stable unless you want to get in trouble."

Violet nodded, eyes wide.

As they moved closer, Bella could see a unicorn tied to a stall. But it wasn't just *any* unicorn.

"There she is," Bella said, looking at Violet. "That's Glimmer!"

Someone walked around Glimmer's far side, brush in hand.

"Ben, hi," Bella said.

Ben smiled and waved the brush as the girls walked down the stable aisle.

"Ben is Frederick's nephew," Bella explained to Violet. "He's from Foris too. He goes to school with my friends and me and works at the stable before and after class."

They reached Ben, and Violet shyly shook his hand. "I think every other word I've heard for a week has been 'Violet,'" Ben said, then laughed. "Bella, I hope you don't mind. I took Glimmer out to groom her so she'd be extra shiny for company."

"Mind? Not at all! Thank you," Bella said.

Glimmer wore a lavender-purple headpiece attached to a matching rope so Bella or Ben could lead her. Ben stepped away from Glimmer and stood next to Bella. The unicorn turned her head, looked at Violet, and let out a snort.

"She's saying hi," Bella said. "What do you think?"

Violet didn't move or speak. She just blinked for several seconds.

"She's *beautiful*," Violet finally said. Bella wasn't going to disagree. Every inch of Glimmer's coat sparkled like fresh snow. Her purple-tinged mane and tail were combed straight. Glimmer strained against her rope to reach her muzzle closer to Violet.

Violet's eyes shifted to Bella's.

"It's okay," Bella said. "Glimmer's so friendly. She wouldn't hurt anyone."

Violet took a tiny step forward, and Glimmer slowly lowered her muzzle into Violet's open hands. The princess of Foris laughed.

"Her whiskers are tickly," Violet said. She ran a hand up Glimmer's forehead and petted her cheek. "Wow. She is so soft!"

Glimmer blinked her big brown eyes and leaned into Violet's hand. Bella couldn't help the grin spreading across her face. Her favorite cousin and her favorite unicorn had already become friends.

"I've never seen Glimmer so friendly with anyone new," Ben said. He folded his arms, smiling. "She really likes you, Violet."

Bella's cousin grinned. "I *really* like her. She's perfect, Bella."

Bella reached up and scratched behind Glimmer's left ear. "I know she is. You're going to have so much fun with her all week."

"Can I brush her?" Violet asked. She looked from Ben to Bella.

"Sure," Bella said. "She loves it."

"I'll show you how," Ben said, handing Violet the blue-bristled brush he held. "But be careful of your toes." He picked up another brush and nodded toward Violet's ballet flats.

"We will both wear boots next time," Bella said. "Violet was so excited to meet Glimmer that we came straight from the carriage."

"Bella said you're from Foris," Violet said to Ben. She mimicked him as he stepped up to Glimmer's side and flicked the brush lightly over the unicorn's coat.

"My family is still there," Ben said. "Except for my uncle. He is allowing me to be his apprentice and learn everything about unicorns."

Glimmer blinked slowly and peeked through her big eyelashes. Bella knew that look well. The princess leaned against the stall door.

"You guys are spoiling Glimmer," Bella said in a teasing tone. "She has not one but two grooms. Glimmer's so relaxed she's starting to fall asleep."

Violet threw her arms around Glimmer's neck and hugged the unicorn. "Get your beauty sleep, Glimmer."

Something pulsed inside the right pocket of Bella's dress. She pulled out her Chat Crystal—a quarter-size stone. The stone changed colors and vibrated depending on who contacted Bella. She had cast a spell on the stone to become a vibrant purple when Queen Katherine messaged her.

"It's from my mom," Bella explained, letting the crystal lie flat on her palm. "We better go up to the castle, Violet."

"Oh, fine," Violet sighed, sticking out her bottom lip. "We will come back, right?"

"Only all the time!" Bella said. "We can visit Glimmer after dinner, I bet."

Violet smiled and slid her arms around Glimmer's neck. She squeezed the unicorn tight, and Glimmer leaned into the hug. "I don't know how you ever leave her," Violet said.

Bella stood on her tiptoes and kissed Glimmer's cheek. "I'm only able to leave because I know I can come right back," she replied.

The girls said good-bye to Ben, Violet gave Glimmer a final hug, and the girls left the stable.

"Aren't you *so* excited that you'll have a unicorn just like Glimmer soon?" Bella asked.

Violet nodded. "I can't wait. Glimmer is *so* special—you're lucky, Bella. I want to spend the whole break in the stable!"

"We can do that," Bella said. "But it's even better with Clara and Ivy—my best friends that I've told you about."

"Meeting Glimmer and now your friends—yay!" Violet said. She looped an arm through Bella's. "This is going to be the best vacation ever!"

"It so is!" Bella agreed. "And speaking of Glimmer, I am *so* excited to tell you all about my Pairing Ceremony! It's going to be so much better in person than over Chat Crystals."

"Yeah, me too," Violet said slowly. She looked over at Bella. "Race you!" Violet tore off toward the castle, laughing as she ran. Bella sprinted after her, giggling so hard she could barely walk.

4

Early Princess Gets the Unicorn

Bright sunlight filled Bella's room. She blinked slowly and yawned, stretching in her bed. *I love Saturdays,* she thought. *And Violet's asleep just down the hall!* That made Saturday even better.

On the wall at the end of Bella's bed, a handful of sparkly silver letters read HAPPY WEEKEND! They were Blinkers, and using her voice, Bella was able to change their color and message anytime she wanted. The Blinkers knew her so well that they had already preprogrammed their "Happy Weekend" message to appear every Saturday.

Yesterday Bella had helped Violet unpack and

settle into her guest room. One of the maids hung all of Violet's clothes in the closet. The girls picked out a pair of Bella's riding boots for Violet so her toes would be safe from unicorn hooves.

They'd ended up sitting cross-legged across from each other, talking and swapping stories until Queen Katherine called them for dinner. Bella had asked Violet if she wanted to talk about the Pairing Ceremony, but Violet was too sleepy. She said she wanted to be super awake when she heard the story. Bella's mom wanted to end the night with the family all together, so she and King Phillip had watched a movie with Bella and Violet until bedtime.

After such a full day, and with all of the excitement with Violet's arrival, Bella had fallen asleep as soon as her head hit the pillow.

Bella rolled over onto her side and checked the time on her pink alarm clock. It was barely after eight. *Violet has to be tired from traveling,* Bella thought. *I want to wake her up to hang out with me, but that would be mean. I can wait a little longer.*

Bella sat up, stretching her arms. She slid out from under her covers and plucked a cozy cotton robe off her closet door. The princess went to her favorite spot in the entire castle—her window seat.

She watched the flowers wake up—yawning and stretching like the princess had done moments earlier. Unicorns nibbled at the grass in pastures surrounding the castle. A handful of people whose faces Bella couldn't make out unloaded wood from a large van. Bella followed the workers with her eyes and realized what they were building: a *stage*. What would a stage—?

"Oh!" Bella said. She put her nose against the windowpane. The stage was for Friday's party!

Queen Katherine had mentioned to her last week that workers would be making an outdoor dance floor. Bella had been excited at the time but forgot about it as her cousin's visit got closer and closer.

I didn't even get to explain the class party to Violet last night, Bella thought. Both princesses had gone straight to bed after the movie. King Phillip almost had to carry sleepy Violet up the stairs.

Bella couldn't wait another second. Violet had to see this! The princess hopped off her window seat and sprinted across her room. She lifted a foot, and one of her slippers—purple with pink sequins—lifted off the floor and glided onto her foot. Bella opened her bedroom door and hurried down the hallway. She eased open the door to the guest room.

The large four-poster bed was empty. The bed had been made up with a daisy-patterned quilt, and the blinds were open.

"Violet?" Bella called out, walking into the bedroom. The bathroom door on the right side of the room was open, and no one was inside.

Bella left the guest room and headed down the hallway. She hurried down a black-and-white marble spiral staircase and heard her mom's laugh coming from the kitchen. Bella pushed open the white double doors, and Queen Katherine, sipping something steaming from a mug, smiled when she saw her daughter. Thomas, the chef at Crystal Castle, stood across the kitchen island from the queen and had a pen in hand.

"Morning, sleepyhead," Queen Katherine said.

"Hi, Mom," Bella said. "Good morning, Thomas."

The black-haired chef tipped his head. "Princess Bella."

"Honey," Queen Katherine said, "Thomas

and I are putting together a menu for Friday's party. Do you want to help us with food and drink ideas?"

"Yay! That's exciting!" Bella said. "I'd love to help. But where's Violet? Her room is empty."

The queen put down her mug and waved a hand at a glass pitcher of OJ. The pitcher rose into the air, tipped, and poured orange juice into a short glass. Bella's mom handed it to Bella.

"Violet was up a couple of hours ago," Queen Katherine said. "Thomas made her a lovely breakfast, and we talked for a while."

"Oh, okay," Bella said. She took a gulp of OJ. "Where's Violet now? I have to find her and show her the view from my window. The platform for the party looks so amazing."

Queen Katherine smiled. "I'm glad you think so. Violet headed down to the stables about an hour ago. She talked about Glimmer so much,

Bella. You must be so excited that Violet and your unicorn get along so well."

Bella smiled, nodding. But *something* felt wrong.

"I wonder why Violet didn't wake me up," Bella asked.

"I'm sure she didn't want to disturb you so early in the morning," her mom said. "Have some breakfast, then change and go join her."

"I'm not that hungry," Bella said. "I'll eat a little later."

Before Queen Katherine could question why Bella was skipping breakfast—something she *never* did—Bella walked out of the kitchen and slowly climbed the stairs.

Violet and I have always woken the other person up if we were having a sleepover, Bella thought. *We never wanted to waste any time we could be spending together.*

Once she got to her room, the princess closed her door. She opened her closet door, flipped on the chandelier, and walked inside.

A nagging feeling in her stomach wouldn't go away. Why hadn't Violet asked her if they could go see Glimmer? Did Violet like *Glimmer* more than Bella? That would explain why she hadn't woken up Bella *and* why she'd gotten up so early.

Stop being silly, Bella told herself. *Violet probably wants to be around a newly matched unicorn, since she's having her own ceremony soon.*

Still feeling a little grumpy, Bella changed out of her pj's and into a sky-blue T-shirt with a sequin pocket, black leggings, and riding boots.

She sat down on her bed and dialed Clara's and Ivy's phone numbers on the castle phone in her room. "Leave message," Bella said aloud.

A small, square silver frame appeared in the air. It floated until it found the perfect spot in front of

Bella. A red light started flashing—it was time to record a message.

"Hi!" Bella said. "I wanted to see if you guys wanted to come over and meet Violet and hang out. One of our carriages can pick up both of you whenever you're ready. I'm heading down to the stable, so I'll take my Chat Crystal. Clara, send a pink signal for 'yes' and when you're on your way. Use red for 'no.' Ivy, message me with purple if you can come and blue if you can't. Bye!"

The square folded and disappeared into the air. Bella hopped off her bed, shook out her arms, and rolled her shoulders, trying to shake off her weird mood. She pocketed her Chat Crystal and left the castle.

The sun warmed Bella as she headed to the stable. The closer she got, the worse she felt about how she had reacted to Violet being at the stable. When the princess walked through the stable entrance, she was smiling as she headed for Glimmer's stall.

"Good morning, Princess Bella," Frederick said. The stable manager was fixing a gold nameplate on one of the stall doors.

"Morning," Bella said. "I hope Glimmer was a good girl last night." She stopped near a stall door and peeked inside at one of the royal unicorns.

"Perfect as always," Frederick said.

That made Bella grin.

"But if you're looking for her," Frederick said, "she's not in her stall. Ben took her out for a walk with Princess Violet."

That feeling came back deep in Bella's stomach.

"Oh," she said. "Um, okay. I'll go find them. Thank you."

She turned around and walked out of the stable. Bella walked over to the dark-brown fence that made up the riding arena. She climbed the

46

fence and sat on the top board. Glimmer, Violet, and Ben were nowhere in sight.

I've never cared if Ben took Glimmer out of her stall, Bella thought. *I wouldn't even mind if he rode Glimmer, even though he's not allowed because she's matched to me.*

Bella didn't know why, but she was annoyed that Glimmer wasn't in her stall. It kind of felt like Violet had taken something of Bella's without asking first. Bella sighed. She knew she was being silly, but she couldn't stop how she felt. She wasn't mad at Ben, but she was irritated with Violet. *The walk was probably Violet's idea,* Bella thought. *She put Ben on the spot. He probably felt like he couldn't say no to a princess.*

Bella's shirt pocket vibrated. She reached inside and pulled out her Chat Crystal. It flashed two colors: pink and purple.

The princess let out a tiny sigh of relief. Ivy

and Clara were coming. Having her friends around would get Bella out of her bad mood.

Just relax for a minute, she thought. *It's not like Violet took Glimmer out alone. That* would be a reason to get mad.

Bella tipped her face toward the cloudless sky of Crystal Kingdom. She closed her eyes and took a deep breath in through her nose and a slow exhale out through her mouth. It was something her mom did to relax, and she had shown Bella. The princess took a couple of deep breaths and listened to the tweeting birds, chattering squirrels, and occasional neighs from unicorns talking to each other.

"It's just *so* crazy that you're from Foris! We have lots to talk about."

Bella opened her eyes at the sound of Violet's voice. Her cousin, Ben, and Glimmer headed her way. Ben waved with his free hand—the other held a rainbow rope attached to Glimmer.

"Good morning, Bells!" Violet said. She climbed the fence boards and sat next to Bella.

"You got up really, really early," Bella said. "I went to look for you, and my mom said you had left way before I came downstairs." She gently elbowed her cousin. "Why didn't you wake me?"

"Yeah, Vi," Ben said.

Vi? Bella thought. It had always been *Bella's* nickname for her cousin.

"I didn't want to wake you," Violet explained. "I peeked into your room before I went to breakfast. You were snoring so loud—it sounded like you really needed sleep!"

Ben grinned, looking from Violet to Bella.

Bella felt herself blush. She looked down and stuck out her hands to rub Glimmer's nose. The unicorn walked right up to Bella and thrust her nose into the princess's hands.

"Aww," Violet said, scooting closer to Bella.

"You're blushing. I didn't mean to embarrass you! You snore supercute!"

Bella nodded. "I know!" she finally said with a smile. It was no big deal. Violet didn't have an ounce of meanness in her. She wasn't making fun—right?

Glimmer moved her head out of Bella's hands and craned her neck toward Violet. The unicorn nudged Violet's arm. She squealed, hopped off the fence, and threw her arms around Glimmer.

"You're the cutest! Lucky you, Glimmer. You've got the best match in all of the kingdoms."

Bella smiled at the compliment.

"I hope it's okay that I asked Ben if we could take Glimmer for a walk," Violet said.

"Oh, um . . ." Bella stumbled over her words. "Of course."

Violet looked up at her cousin. "Are you okay? Is that a problem?"

Bella shifted her eyes from Violet to Ben to

Glimmer, then smiled. "Of course not! I'm really happy that Glimmer likes you so much."

The second part of that is true, Bella thought. *But the first kind of isn't.*

"Once Ivy and Clara get here," she said, "do you want to talk about the Pairing Ceremony?"

"Um . . ." Violet's eyes were on the driveway. She hesitated, then looked at Bella. "Maybe later, if that's cool? I'd really just love to hang out with you and your friends."

"Okay, sure," Bella said.

Suddenly a carriage appeared at the driveway of the stable. The doors opened, and Ivy and Clara climbed out. They stopped, looking in different directions for Bella. The princess wanted to shout at them, but she didn't want to scare Glimmer. Ivy spotted Ben, Violet, Glimmer, and Bella, and tapped Clara's shoulder. Both girls waved and hurried toward Bella.

"Hi, Violet!" Clara said when she and Ivy reached Bella and the others. "Finally! You're here!"

Clara gave Violet a huge hug before the princess could even introduce her cousin.

"Welcome to Crystal Kingdom!" Ivy said, hugging Violet next. "I'm Ivy, and this is Clara. We've heard *so* much about you from Bella. It's so great that you're here!"

Violet's fair cheeks flushed. "I'm so happy to meet both of *you*! Bella has told me tons of stories about her best friends."

"I didn't even get to tell you more about the party," Bella interrupted. *Ivy and Clara didn't even say hi to me,* she thought. The princess had thought that bringing Ivy and Clara over would improve her mood. Instead she felt even grumpier.

"Oh my gosh," Ivy said. "Bella! Total fail in the hosting department!"

Everyone laughed. Except Bella.

"We can tell you *everything*," Clara said. "You don't even know about the class sleepover." She clasped her hands together, grinning. "Bells, would you like to do the honors and start telling Violet about the party?"

Bella placed a hand over her stomach. She hadn't planned it, but she needed a break from everyone—even though Ivy and Clara had just arrived. "Um, actually, I'm not feeling very well."

"What's wrong?" Ben asked, his eyes darting back and forth as he looked at Bella and the rest of the girls.

"Nothing major—my stomach is just a little upset. I think I need to go back to the castle and lie down," Bella said.

The princess climbed down from the fence, and Clara put an arm across Bella's shoulders.

"I've got Glimmer," Ben said. "I'll take her back to her stall. Feel better, Bella."

Bella thought she saw a look of annoyance flicker across Violet's face.

Ivy tipped her head in the direction of the castle. "Can you walk? Or do you need to sit down somewhere softer than the fence?"

"You can sit on my jacket," Clara said. She started to shrug out of her dark jean jacket.

"Oh, no!" Bella said. "Thank you, Ivy. That's so sweet, but I can walk. And I want you guys to stay here and have fun in the stable. I'm just going to be lying down and watching TV."

"As long as you're *sure* you're okay," Violet said, "I'd like to hang out at the stable. Plus, it would be awesome to get to know you guys." She looked at Clara and Ivy. "We don't want to bother Bella if she wanted to take a nap or something."

"True . . . ," Clara said. She scrunched her eyebrows together like she always did when she was worried.

"What if we at least walk you back to the castle?" Ivy asked. "Then we'll have our Chat Crystals and we'll be there in two seconds if you message us."

"That's more than enough, guys. Thank you," Bella said. "And I'm okay to walk by myself."

Before her friends could argue any more, Bella gave them a little wave and walked away from the group.

She felt guilty *and* a little sad at the same time. She had never lied to her friends before. She had already lied to Violet about not caring that the Foris princess took Glimmer for a walk. Now Bella had just lied again to Ivy and Clara when she had told them she wanted them to stay behind.

With every step, Bella actually started to *really* feel sick. She had been sure that Violet would come back to the castle with her. Once, Bella had gotten a stomach bug during a spring vacation while her family was visiting Violet and her family.

Violet had refused to stay away from Bella, even though she could have gotten sick too. She helped the kitchen staff bring Bella chicken noodle soup, crackers, and bubbly water.

I have to remember that Vi doesn't have friends like I do, Bella thought. She took in a deep breath, trying to fight back tears. She wished Clara and Ivy wouldn't have stayed back with Violet, but the princess didn't want her friends hanging with her if they didn't want to.

The princess had also guessed that based on how fast Ivy and Clara had bonded with Violet, they, too, would stay behind.

One minute, Violet was the cousin that Bella loved and adored. The cousin that Bella was happy to share Glimmer with. The cousin that she wanted Ivy and Clara to love.

So why did these little flickers of New Violet keep coming up?

* * *

A couple of hours later, Bella woke up on the living room couch. She'd actually fallen asleep not too long after she'd curled herself in a blanket. She blinked, and her cousin and two besties were sitting on the floor in front of her. The girls were surrounded by shopping bags. Bags of every color and shape stretched from the fireplace to the couch.

"How are you feeling?" Violet asked.

"What is all this?" Bella asked at the same time.

"You go," Violet said.

"I feel totally fine," Bella said. "I guess I just needed a nap!"

Queen Katherine walked through the living room toward the kitchen. "How do you feel, sweetie?"

"Perfect, Mom," Bella said.

"Well, I came over to check on you and you looked so peaceful. I cast a sweet dreams spell, so

I hope you had good dreams," Queen Katherine said.

"Mom!" Bella said, yanking up the blanket to cover her face. "Sweet dreams spells are for little kids."

She started giggling, and so did Violet and her friends.

The queen blew Bella a kiss, started laughing, and walked out of the living room.

"So, where did all of this come from? What's inside the bags?" Bella asked, sitting up and stretching.

In the moments before she had fallen asleep, she had thought through everything that had just happened. Bella knew she had to keep reminding herself that her cousin didn't have a unicorn and she didn't have friends like Ivy and Clara.

Plus, knowing Ivy and Clara, they had probably thought they needed to sort of chaperone

Violet, since she was company and Bella was too sick. Bella didn't want to spend another second thinking about what had happened earlier. She was ready for a fresh start with Violet. She owed it to her cousin to give her another chance. Now, she was just excited to be with Violet and her friends.

"We were hanging out at the stable," Clara said. "I was talking to Ivy about the Crystal Kingdom Magic Market, and we both needed new outfits and sparkly jewels for the party. We had heard about a sale. Plus, Violet had never been to our amazing market!"

"You guys went to the market?" Bella asked slowly. Her friends and cousin had gone shopping? Without her?

"We called your mom to ask permission and to see if you were awake," Ivy said. "But Queen Katherine told us that you were still asleep."

"I mean, I'm glad you were able to go," Bella said. "But couldn't you guys have waited until tomorrow so we all could have gone together?"

Clara made an apologetic face. "Sorry, Bells, but there was something I really wanted for the party, and I wanted to make sure it was still there. You really didn't miss anything, so don't feel bad! I bet we can even go back tomorrow if we want."

Bella didn't even want to hear the word "shop." Violet was not making a fresh start very easy!

"Want to go to my room and watch TV?" Bella asked, changing the subject. She got three nods in return. The girls piled their bags out of the way in the living room and dashed up the stairs after Bella.

In Bella's room, Ivy claimed the window seat, curling her legs beneath her. Clara plopped into Bella's brown-and-pink polka-dot beanbag chair. She pushed it next to Bella's bed and sank back into the cozy chair. Violet and Bella sat down on Bella's pink couch.

Just smile, breathe, and don't *get upset. They thought you were sick. They* had *to go today.* Bella turned on the big TV screen and scrolled through her list of recorded shows.

"Ooh, wait a sec!" Clara said. "We need to explain the party to Violet. Can we do that and then start a show?"

Bella and Ivy nodded. This time, Bella really did want to tell her cousin all about Friday's party.

"Yes, let's!" Ivy said.

"Clara, you start," Bella said.

Clara grinned. She did a little dance in her seat. "Violet, you already know that Ivy and I go to school here with Bella, right?"

"Yes," Violet said. "Doesn't your dad work here, Ivy?"

"He is a groundskeeper for the castle," Ivy explained. "I brought Clara to the castle with me one day because I just knew that she and Bella would get along."

"The three of us totally clicked," Bella said. "We were best friends so fast. My mom and dad saw how happy I was once I'd made friends with Ivy and Clara. That's when they got the idea to invite other kids to have school in the castle."

"But I'm the odd one," Clara said, giggling. "My parents work in town at Crystal Bank and Crystal Kingdom Inn. I sneaked in because of Ivy."

They all laughed.

"Ooh, that's right. Your parents don't work here," Bella said, teasing Clara. "I'm kicking you out of our classroom!"

Clara stuck out her tongue at Bella.

Grinning, Ivy rolled her eyes. "So we have

seven other people in our class, including Ben. He's a little older than us, so our tutor, Ms. Barnes, gives him higher-level work. The other six kids are our age—eight."

"My parents didn't even tell *me* about the party," Bella said. "Ivy, Clara, and I all found out at the same time. Ms. Barnes said that we got the entire week off and on Friday, the class was invited to come to the castle." She took one sip of soda and then another.

"Ms. Barnes didn't get *super* specific," Clara added. "All we know is there will be a movie, music, and desserts."

"Oh! Add a giant wooden platform to that list," Bella said. "I watched some construction workers this morning. It looks like they're building a dance floor or something."

Violet's eyes widened. "I would be way too nervous to dance in front of your class. I don't know any of them."

64

"You know Ben," Ivy said. "Everyone in our class is friendly. You'll fit right in."

"Totally," Clara said. "I wish you could go to school with us! Wouldn't that be the best, Bella?"

"The best," Bella echoed, her tone a little flat.

"Bells," Violet said, "is it okay if I go get us some snacks?"

"Sure," the princess replied. "Use my intercom if you want to reach the kitchen staff."

But Violet stood. "That's okay! I'll just run down there and be right back."

"Ooh, I want to pick out snacks!" Clara thrust up her hand for Violet to grab.

"Me too!" Ivy jumped up. "Be right back!" she said over her shoulder to Bella.

Giggling, the girls ran out of the room and down the hallway, leaving Bella sitting alone in her room.

"Ugh," Bella said aloud. She pulled the purple pillow from under her head and placed it over her face. The princess squeezed her eyes shut and tried to block all the *Violet! Violet! Violet! Violet!* thoughts that wouldn't quiet down in her head. Suddenly Friday felt *very* far away.

5

Stable, Dinner, Sleep, Repeat

As the Friday class party got closer, Bella felt as if she and Violet were growing further and further apart.

The same routine played out every day since Violet's first day at Crystal Castle. Violet always managed to be up before Bella. The princess had even set an alarm so she would wake earlier, but over the past four mornings, this one included, Violet had been awake and dressed, and had either eaten breakfast or been in the process of eating when Bella had reached the kitchen.

Every time Bella asked Violet what she wanted

to do, Violet had the same answer: Go to the royal stables and visit Glimmer. Not that Bella *ever* wanted to stay away from Glimmer, but she was starting to feel as though Glimmer was Violet's unicorn and not hers.

Ben always helped Violet groom or feed Glimmer when Bella's cousin came to the stable without Bella.

And, as if that wasn't enough, Ivy and Clara *adored* Violet. Bella had started to come up with more excuses not to hang with the three girls because she felt like an outsider with her own best friends. She didn't know what her cousin was up to at the moment. Actually, she hadn't seen Violet for a couple of hours.

"Five more minutes," Bella said to Glimmer.

Bella had taken Glimmer from her stall and released her into one of the castle's grassy pastures. Gentle sunlight beamed down on them, and it was a cloudless day in Crystal Kingdom. A light, warm breeze blew back Glimmer's mane as the white unicorn nibbled on grass. Bella wanted—no, *needed*—to talk to someone, so she had taken Glimmer outside where no one was around to hear her talk. She was sitting in the pasture, knees drawn up to her chest.

"The very last thing I want to tell you is about yesterday morning," Bella said. "I got up and, of course, Violet was already up. I went into the back room of the castle that leads to one of the patios."

Glimmer took a step closer to Bella and munched the long green stalks of grass.

"I peered through the glass, and Violet was sitting in a lawn chair, using her Chat Crystal. I blinked, like, fifty times to make sure what I was seeing was real."

Glimmer's big brown eyes stared into Bella's as the unicorn listened.

"Violet was talking to *Clara*. As in, *my* best friend Clara. Without me!" Bella let out a giant sigh and ripped up the stalks of grass that she had been twisting around her fingers.

"I'm so confused, Glimmer. Before Violet got here, all I wanted was for her to make friends with Ivy and Clara and for you to bond with her. All that has happened, and it's not what I was expecting, I guess. I feel like somebody crashing their party."

Glimmer cocked her head as she looked at Bella.

"They haven't really left me out of anything, but I don't think they'd miss me."

It was true—all of the girls had taken a carriage ride through the Crystal Kingdom countryside, played hide-and-seek in the lush gardens, and spent hours petting all the royal unicorns. But Bella could barely get in a sentence among Ivy, Clara, and Violet.

"Bye, Glimmer," Bella said, hugging her unicorn. "I'm going to find Violet." She kissed Glimmer's check and went back to the castle.

Violet's room was empty, so Bella went back to her own room. She climbed onto the window seat and pulled out her Chat Crystal.

Bella desperately wanted to talk to Lyssa, but her older friend had the week off, and she didn't want to call Lyssa on her break and bother her. Bella had thought about talking to her mom, but her mom loved Violet and just wouldn't understand.

The class party was two days away. Some of Bella's classmates had sent her messages, saying how excited they were about Friday. Queen Katherine and King Phillip had spent hours each day working on different aspects of the party—most of which were kept secret from Bella.

The princess had thought that the class party would be practically the only thing Violet, Ivy, and Clara would want to talk about. That and Violet's upcoming ceremony. Bella had brought those up in conversation every day up until this morning, and her besties and cousin weren't nearly as into it as Bella had imagined. Violet, especially. She shut down *any* talk about the Pairing Ceremony. Bella didn't even bother to try to talk to her cousin about it anymore. The only topic that seemed to hold Violet's attention was unicorns. And more unicorns.

And *more* unicorns. It was almost like Violet was skipping over the ceremony in her head and going straight to the unicorn part.

Talking about unicorns was *far* from boring for Bella. But Violet was so bubbly every time they talked—and she seemed to only want to discuss the awesome parts of having a unicorn. No mentions of the birthday ceremony, fear about not finding Violet's perfect match—anything! Bella couldn't believe that Violet hadn't come to her yet with questions about the Pairing Ceremony.

But, despite Violet's always cheery attitude, Bella made a promise to herself that she would find the right time to sit Violet down and explain all about red auras and Queen Fire's presence in her life. She didn't want to rain on her cousin's Pairing Ceremony, but she did want Violet to be prepared for anything.

Bella, sitting with her legs stretched in front of her, looked out her window at the party preparations. Queen Katherine stood in the center of the now-finished wooden stage, gesturing as she talked to one of the party planners. Tiny pinpricks of excitement covered Bella's arms. Her first-*ever* school party! It would have been a little scary if Bella's class was huge and if she didn't know everyone. But all of her classmates knew each other—and were all friends.

Bella tried to put herself in Violet's place. *I would feel nervous,* she thought. *Meeting new people is always a little scary. But she knows Ivy, Clara, and me.*

Bella still didn't understand why Ivy and Clara suddenly didn't seem excited about Friday anymore. BV (Before Violet) the princess's besties hadn't stopped talking about the party. Now, AV (After Violet) it was only a topic of conversation if Bella brought it up.

Bella rubbed her eyes. Nothing about this vacation was going as she had imagined. Not as though it had been bad or anything, but it was weird somehow, in some way Bella couldn't quite put her finger on.

She sighed. Ivy and Clara were going to be at Crystal Castle in a few hours. They'd planned a sleepover tonight. Each girl was supposed to bring a different color nail polish. Bella had so many bottles of Sunray Sweets polishes in reds, pinks, purples—even a yellow one! The best part of a mani-pedi was after the color and applying a coat of Sunray Sweets Shine-On top coat. The polish, packed with sunray berries, glowed when it was applied. As it dried, the polish began to shine brighter and brighter. Nails looked as if they had their own tiny spotlight. The polish's glow turned off at night and recharged when back in the sun.

Bella stretched and stood. It was just after noon. Maybe Violet was in her room now. It had been at least half an hour since Bella had last checked. *You need to stop acting like you're five and just call Ivy and Clara,* Bella told herself. *They're not mind readers. How can they know something's wrong if you don't tell them?*

Bella walked down the hall, slowing when she heard Vi's voice.

Bella tiptoed to her cousin's door and leaned toward the cracked opening.

". . . Dad, really! Glimmer is . . . wish . . ."

Bella stepped away from the door. If Violet's conversation with her dad were anything like the ones she had with Bella and her friends, Violet was going to be on the phone for a while.

Bella picked up her Chat Crystal. Suddenly she needed to talk to Ivy and Clara more than anything.

Bella placed the round crystal flat on her palm. She stared at it. "Ivy, Clara, can I call you?" She paused. "Send message, please."

The crystal blinked its silver I'M WORKING ON IT message.

While she waited to hear back from her friends, Bella sifted through some of the outfits she had narrowed down for the party. *I wish I knew what my friends were thinking of wearing,* she thought. *We could be choosing our clothes together.*

Bella shut the closet door. Hard. She reached for the clear Chat Crystal, and it blinked purple and pink the second her fingertips touched it.

Ivy and Clara were able to talk. Bella ran honey gloss over her lips, trying to decide how to approach her friends with her feelings about Violet.

Both of the princess's friends seemed to have gotten close to Violet. Fast. Bella looked up at the photographs of her and her friends that practically covered the wall space above her desk.

She placed her Chat Crystal on a cloud-shaped pillow in front of her. "Please call Ivy and Clara," Bella commanded. A bright silver flash, then beams of pink light fanned in front of Bella. Purple shot up next to the pink so the colors were side by side. This was a new feature designers had recently added to the Chat Crystals.

The colors faded as images of Ivy and Clara appeared in their places. Ivy, cross-legged in her desk chair, waved at Bella before turning her head in Clara's direction. Ivy smiled at Clara, who did the same and, teasingly, stuck out her tongue at Bella.

"What's up, Princess?" Clara asked. "Or, excuse me. Let me try again. What matter do you, erm, wish to talk—no, *speak*—of, Your Highness?"

Ivy and Clara giggled, but they stopped short when they saw Bella's serious expression. Both girls sat up a little straighter, and Ivy clutched her hands in her lap.

The princess chewed on the inside of her cheek. "Something's kind of bothering me. You guys are going to think I'm being dumb," she said.

"Don't say that," Ivy said. "We've never said that and we never would."

Clara bobbed her head in agreement. "Exactly. Bella, we're your best friends. Nothing that's upsetting you is *ever* going to be small or dumb to us."

Bella gave her friends a tiny smile. She took a deep breath. "This is really hard for me to say, but I want to be honest with you because you're my best friends. It feels like you guys and Violet became friends so fast. Which I'm *happy about*." Bella added the last sentence really fast. "I love that my favorite cousin and my favorite friends like each other so much. I just feel left out. Like you guys wouldn't notice if I wasn't there."

"What are you talking about?" Ivy said. "We would *so* notice if you weren't with us. Bella, if you think we're being extra nice or something to Violet, it's because she's your cousin."

"Ivy's right," Clara said. "I was kind of nervous about Violet visiting, because I really wanted to like her and get along with her because of how close you guys are. Ivy and I are your best friends! We'd never, ever want to hurt your feelings. You and Ivy are so important to me—like family!"

"We didn't choose Violet over you," Ivy added. "I was only trying to be nice to your cousin—I promise. I'm so sorry you felt left out."

"Me too," Clara said. "Maybe Ivy and I sort of treated Violet like a shiny new toy. I'm sorry I made you feel like you weren't included, Bella."

The knots in Bella's stomach loosened a little.

"Thank you both for saying what you did," the princess said. "I—I also wanted to talk to you without Violet around to see if you were still as excited about the class party as you were before Violet got here."

"Are you kidding?" Ivy asked. "I get more excited every day!"

"Me too!" Clara said, smiling at Ivy and then at Bella.

"But we're not talking about it. Ever," Bella said. "I've tried to bring it up, and the conversation always goes back to unicorns."

"Violet seems more comfortable talking about stuff other than the party," Clara said. She shrugged. "Maybe she's a little nervous?"

"I don't know," Bella said.

"Have you talked to Violet about this?" Ivy asked.

"Not yet," Bella said. "I wanted to talk to each of you first."

"What do you guys talk about when Ivy and I aren't there?" Clara asked. "Have you talked to her about your Pairing Ceremony and Queen Fire?"

Bella shook her head so hard it almost made her dizzy. "Violet's being so annoying!" she complained. "I barely see her. If I do, she's always at the stable with Glimmer. We haven't talked for one second about my ceremony. I thought she would want to know more, since her ceremony is soon."

82

"It sounds like you two need to sit down and talk," Ivy said. "You've got to tell Violet how you feel."

"I feel like Violet wants to steal Glimmer or something," Bella said, only half joking. "She must think that her Pairing Ceremony is going to be so perfect that she doesn't need any advice from her cousin. She hadn't been acting like the Violet that I remembered."

"Definitely talk to her," Clara said. "Sooner rather than later."

"Okay," Bella said. "I'll go see if she's done talking to Dad. Thanks for putting up with me, guys."

The friends blew kisses to each other, and Ivy and Clara signed off.

Bella put the Chat Crystal beside her bed and went back to the guest room. Once again, she leaned close to the door. Silence.

"Violet?" Bella called, knocking on the door. "You still on the phone?"

After a few seconds with no response, Bella opened the door. The guest room was empty. She went back to her room and pulled on boots. At least she knew where to find Violet: the stable.

6

Glimmer's Gone Green

Minutes later Bella reached the stable. Ben wasn't in front of Glimmer's stall like he had been so often over the past few days. *Maybe they're inside the stall with Glimmer,* she thought. She could see the stall door was bolted tight.

"Violet? Ben?" Bella said, reaching Glimmer's stall. "Are you—"

She stopped midsentence.

"Ben! HELP!" Bella yelled. "Frederick! Help! Please!"

Her fingers felt clumsy as she unbolted the stall door and stepped in. She blinked furiously.

Gone were any traces of Glimmer's usual purple color. Instead Bella's unicorn was a vibrant emerald green from nose to tail!

Oh NO!

"Bella?" Ben called down the stable aisle.

"In Glimmer's stall!" Bella yelled back. "Glimmer's sick!"

The princess reached a hand out to Glimmer's cheek. Glimmer didn't feel hot.

Ben skidded to a stop and entered the stall. Immediately he began feeling Glimmer's muzzle, looking into her eyes and ears, and lifting up her lip.

"What's wrong with her?" Bella said, trying not to cry. If she cried, she would probably scare Glimmer.

"Glimmer, tell me what's wrong," she said.

"Bella."

Bella turned at the sound of her father's voice.

King Phillip stood outside Glimmer's stall with Frederick.

"Ben," Frederick said. "Come."

Ben bowed his head to King Phillip and did as he was told. The king nodded at Ben.

"Dad, we need Frederick!" Bella said. "Where is he going?"

"He's going to explain to Ben why Glimmer changed color," her dad said. "Glimmer isn't sick, sweetie."

"She's not?" Bella's knees almost crumpled under her from relief. "Then what's wrong?"

"Let's take a walk together," King Phillip said. He held out a hand to Bella. She took her dad's warm hand and stepped out of the stall. She latched Glimmer's stall door and followed her dad out of the stable.

Sunlight beamed down on them and made the castle seal on King Phillip's shirt sparkle. He turned his kind green eyes to Bella. "How have things been going with Violet?" the king asked.

Bella looked up at her dad. "Good," she said. Then she frowned. "Okay, not so great. But Dad, what's wrong with Glimmer?"

"Glimmer will be just fine," King Phillip said. "Tell me what's going on." He and Bella started down a pebble-lined path to one of the ponds. Bella wanted to know right now why her beautiful, sweet unicorn was green, but it seemed like her dad wouldn't tell her without Bella answering his question.

"I guess things aren't going exactly as I expected," Bella said. "I was feeling a little left out because Violet, Ivy, and Clara became friends like that." She snapped her fingers. "Plus, Glimmer loved Violet from the moment they met. I promise, Dad, I'm so happy that everyone likes Violet so much. That's why it's so confusing, I guess, that I keep having these weird moments of being annoyed at her."

The king nodded. "Have you told Violet any of this?"

"Not yet," Bella said. "I talked to Ivy and Clara before I came to the stable. I told them how I felt, and they understood. They told me I should talk to Violet, and I was looking for her at the stable."

The princess and her father walked the rest of the way down the path in silence and reached a wooden dock. Bella walked to the far end and sat down, swinging her legs above the water. King Phillip sat beside her. The water turned clear as Bella glanced at the pond. When Bella was little, she always wished she could see the creatures at the bottom of the pond, so King Phillip had applied a crystal clear spell to the water. Whenever Bella visited and glanced at the water, it would become crystal clear and the princess would be able to see the life at the bottom of the pond.

A small boat tied to the dock bobbed in the water. It had a glass bottom so Bella could watch crabs, fish, and other creatures whenever she floated around in the boat.

"There's more," King Phillip said. "I can tell. I happen to know my daughter very well." The king touched Bella's arm with his hand. "What else is wrong, Bells? You can always talk to me."

"I know I can," the princess said. "It's hard. I don't know what I'm feeling! This whole week was supposed to be about the party on Friday. But all Violet wants to talk about is unicorns, and she hasn't even asked me how my ceremony went. Every time I bring it up, she doesn't want to talk about it. It's like she thinks her Pairing Ceremony is going to be easy and perfect. Or maybe she thinks the ceremony part will be boring. I don't know."

King Phillip reached over and put an arm across Bella's shoulders. Bella leaned against her dad, feeling relieved to have told him what had been going on all week.

"You and Glimmer share a bond that no one else has with you," King Phillip explained. "She is very in tune with all of your emotions and feelings. Glimmer is green, Bella, because you are feeling one emotion *very* strongly."

Bella sat up so she could look at her dad's face. "What? *I* turned Glimmer green?"

"Your feeling of envy or jealousy toward Violet," King Phillip said.

Bella was quiet for a moment. "That's the weird feeling I've had. The thing I didn't know how to explain. It was jealousy all along."

"Jealousy is a powerful emotion," King Phillip explained. "It can motivate people to do things they otherwise wouldn't, make them feel things that possibly aren't true, and it can be a consuming emotion."

"I've been jealous of Violet this whole time," Bella said. "Dad, I was jealous that she and Ivy and

Clara became friends so fast. Same with her and Glimmer. I guess I'm a little hurt, too, that Violet's here and I could have told her every detail about my ceremony, but she doesn't want to hear it."

The king stayed quiet, nodding and listening to his daughter.

"Dad, how do I get Glimmer back to normal?"

The king smiled. "You might want to start with talking to Violet."

Bella wrapped her arms around her dad. The king hugged her back. "I love you, sweetheart," her dad said. "I know you'll have Glimmer back to purple in no time."

Bella scrambled to her feet. "I've got to find Violet right now!"

7

Let's Talk

Almost an hour had passed since Bella had talked to her dad. She still hadn't found Violet. The princess had looked everywhere and asked everyone, but no one had seen her cousin.

Bella finally went back to the castle, deciding to look for Violet inside.

She entered through a side door in the kitchen and almost smacked right into Violet.

"I've been looking everywhere for you!" Bella said. She looked at her cousin. Violet's eyes were pink and her nose was red. "Have you been crying? What's wrong?"

Bella reached out a hand toward Violet, but her cousin yanked her arm away from Bella. "You don't have to be nice," Violet said softly, her chin wobbly as she talked. "I heard you talking to Ivy and Clara. I'm sorry I ruined your entire week. I'm going upstairs to pack and am going home tonight."

Violet turned away from Bella and darted out of the kitchen.

"Violet! Wait!" Bella called after her. But Violet didn't stop. Bella followed her to the guest bedroom and watched as Violet yanked her suitcase on top of the bed and began pulling clothes off hangers and tossing them into the suitcase.

"Violet, please," Bella said. "Please just let me explain. Give me ten minutes, and if you still want to leave after, then I'll help you pack. Okay?"

Violet swiped at her nose with her hand. She plopped on the bed, hanger in hand. "Ten minutes. Go."

"I am so sorry you heard me talking to Ivy and Clara," Bella apologized. "I should have talked to you first. Have you seen Glimmer this afternoon?"

Violet glared at her. "No. I didn't go anywhere near the stable, since I'm trying to steal your unicorn, apparently."

"I'm sorry that I said that, too," Bella said. "But if you had seen Glimmer, you would have been pretty surprised. Because of me being so jealous of you, Glimmer turned green!"

Violet blinked. "She's *green*?"

Bella nodded. "It's all my fault. Glimmer won't go back to normal until I stop feeling so jealous of you."

"Jealous of what?" Violet asked.

So Violet hadn't heard that part of the conversation with Ivy and Clara.

"I'm . . ." Bella paused, taking a deep breath.

"I'm jealous that you got here and everyone instantly wanted to be your friend. Ivy and Clara never make a new friend this fast. You and Ben can talk about Foris all the time. Even Glimmer loves you like crazy!"

Bella took a breath.

"There's just one more thing," the princess

said. "I'm not sure why, but you don't want to talk about the Pairing Ceremony. Ever. I've tried to talk to you about it, and you always stop me. Vi, I was so scared before my ceremony. If you had already done yours, I would have asked you a million questions. You haven't asked me any. It hurt my feelings, too, because my ceremony was the biggest night of my life, and you don't want to hear about it in person."

Bella watched as Violet dropped her head.

"I haven't asked you because it reminds me too much of home," Violet said in a whisper. "Once I go back, it's all that I'll hear about or have to think about. I've been having so much fun with you, Ben, Ivy, and Clara. I don't have one friend at home."

"Oh, Violet," Bella said. Her cousin's lower lip trembled.

"It's so amazing being around friends! On the train ride here I was so scared that I wouldn't fit in and that your friends would think I was weird or something. But they've been so nice. Friday's party is coming up so fast—I don't want this visit to end."

"My friends are the best," Bella agreed. "And there's nothing 'weird' about you, Violet. You'll have to come over more often to be around us. Maybe your parents would consider letting kids of castle employees go to school with you or something."

Violet gave Bella a tiny smile. "That sounds cool and scary at the same time. I feel so lucky to already have made friends here with your help. I'd be really scared to have kids I don't know in a room at my castle."

"They would love you," Bella promised. "Really, Vi. You'd make friends at home just as fast as you did here."

"I'm sorry, Bella," Violet said. "I came here to

be on vacation with you. I was so excited to have *your* friends like *me*. You kind of have to like me because we're family."

"I was jealous because it seemed like all of my friends liked you better than me," Bella replied. "And I didn't feel like we were spending enough cousin time together. I've missed you!"

"I missed you, too!"

Bella pointed at Violet's suitcase. "Ten minutes are probably up. Do you want help packing?"

Violet nodded. "Yes."

Bella felt as though her heart plummeted to her feet.

"With unpacking," Violet said, smiling.

"Ahhh! You totally scared me!" Bella said with a laugh. "Are we okay?"

"More than okay," Violet said. "I know that you, Ivy, and Clara will be at the party. It's not going to be as scary as I thought."

"It's going to be way more fun than you can imagine," Bella said. "Trust me."

"Bella, I would really love to hear about your ceremony, if you still want to tell me about it," Violet said. "Being scared of my own ceremony was the reason I spent so much time with Glimmer. I thought if I spent time with a happily matched unicorn that it would help me somehow at my ceremony. I'm sorry that I kind of treated Glimmer like my own unicorn."

"It's okay," Bella said. "I understand now. Of course I'll tell you about my ceremony. There's so much you don't know. And after that, maybe we can pick outfits for the party?"

Violet nodded. "I'd like that. I definitely need help choosing the perfect outfit."

"Me too. That's why I'm glad you're here. Sparkling grape juice toast please," Bella declared. "Hold your hand like mine," she told Violet.

A glass appeared in each of their hands. Bubbly grape juice filled each of their glasses.

"Too cool," Violet said, grinning. "So remembering that trick at home."

Bella raised her glass. "Here's to starting over, to being good best friends, and being the best cousins ever!"

"Yay to that!" Ivy grinned.

The girls clinked their glasses together, then took a sip of their juice. They finished their small glasses quickly.

After a final squeeze, they left the guest room and headed for the stables.

Crossing her fingers for luck, Bella peered into Glimmer's stall.

Purple!

Glimmer let out a soft whine and walked up to the stall door. She nuzzled Bella and Violet.

"Oh, Glimmer!" Bella exclaimed. "I'm so glad

you're purple again! I promise never to let that happen again."

"Let's talk inside her stall," Bella said to Violet. The girls went into the stall and sat down on clean straw. Glimmer circled once, then lowered herself onto the straw next to the girls.

"So," Bella started, "there's a *lot* that happened at my ceremony. Some of it is amazing and some of it not so much."

"I want to hear all of it," Violet said.

And so Bella told Violet all about her ceremony, red auras, Queen Fire's scary appearance on Bella's birthday, and details about the nasty, evil queen of the Blacklands.

The cousins talked for hours—so long that Glimmer fell asleep. By the end of the conversation, Violet was super excited for her own ceremony—exactly what Bella had hoped for. The girls decided not to spend another second talking about Queen Fire, and instead they left a sleeping Glimmer in her stall and headed up to the castle. Lightning bugs flashed across the castle property—the girls had talked until the sun had started to set.

That night Bella went to bed in a better mood than she had been in all week. The girls stayed up talking and giggling, just like Bella had always wanted for the visit. Bella drifted off to sleep, glad to have her cousin by her side, and vowing to make sure the rest of Violet's visit was magical.

8

Lyssa to the Rescue

Bella blinked, staring up at her ceiling. An excited tingle ran through her body. She looked at her clock. Just after nine in the morning.

"Violet," Bella whispered. Her cousin was sound asleep next to her, clutching one of Bella's stuffed unicorns.

"Violet!" Bella said, louder this time. "It's party day!"

Violet turned on her side, facing Bella. Strands of red hair had escaped from the French braid she had done last night.

"Oh! It's Friday!" Violet sat up, hugging the

unicorn. "Omigosh! I'm so nervous and excited at the same time!"

Bella grinned. "No nerves necessary! You know four people already—Ben, Ivy, Clara, and me. You won't be alone for a second. Let's go have breakfast!"

They both climbed out of Bella's bed and put on matching fluffy light-blue cotton robes. Thursday had passed in a blur. Ivy and Clara had come over, and everyone had done mani pedis. The girls pooled their collections of Sunray Sweets nail polishes.

"You said Lyssa is coming today, right?" Violet asked as the cousins walked down the hallway together.

"Yes. She might even be here now. I asked her to help get our outfits ready."

"Ooh, I can't wait to meet her," Violet said.

The girls reached the breakfast table, and

Bella's parents stood to hug each of the girls.

"How did you sleep?" Queen Katherine asked. She raised an eyebrow at Bella. "You *did* sleep a little, right?"

"We did, Aunt Katherine," Violet said. "I fell asleep instantly."

"Me too," Bella added. "I thought I'd be awake all night thinking about the party, but I think my body knew I needed to rest up for today."

Queen Katherine smiled. "Good girls," she said. She and King Phillip remained standing as Bella and Violet sat in front of empty plates.

"We have a few last-minute details to attend to," Queen Katherine said. "Enjoy your breakfast."

Violet and Bella smiled as the king and queen left the dining room. Silver trays reached from one end of the table to another. The clear lids revealed eggs, pancakes, sausages, bacon—so many yummy options!

Bella and Violet filled their plates, and Bella was on her last chocolate chip pancake when she heard footsteps behind her.

"Morning!" a cheery voice called.

"Lyssa!" Bella said. "I'm so happy you're here! Thank you for coming. Violet, this is Lyssa."

"I've heard so much about you from Bella," Lyssa said, smiling at Violet. "I'm so glad to finally meet you."

"Me too," Violet said. "Bella said you can put together perfect party outfits. I so need your help!"

Lyssa grinned. "Aw, I'm glad Bella says nice things about me. She usually tells everyone how I mismatch her socks and try to dress her in stripes and polka dots at the same time."

Bella dropped her jaw. "I do not!"

Lyssa winked at her, and all three girls burst into laughter. Bella said a silent *thank you* for Lyssa being there. The older girl was sure to help Bella and Violet look amazing and help with Violet's nerves, too.

"It's my pleasure to come over," Lyssa said cheerfully. "I stopped by yesterday, too."

"You did?" Bella asked. "I didn't even see you."

Lyssa smiled. "I peeked in on you two and Ivy and Clara. You were *very* serious about the right nail polish." Everyone laughed.

"I'm finished with breakfast if you are," Bella said to Violet. Her cousin nodded.

"Then let the party makeovers begin, ladies!" Lyssa said.

Bella and Violet clapped. Giggling, the three of them headed upstairs.

"Even though the party is, like, eight hours away, I feel like I won't be ready in time," Bella said.

"We have *plenty* of time," Lyssa assured her.

"We're going to do hair and face masks and a little spa time before we really start getting ready."

In Bella's room, Lyssa pulled the dresses she had selected the day before. She spread the four choices across the bed.

"Did you bring dresses for tonight?" Lyssa asked Violet.

"They're in the guest room," Violet said. "I brought a few and went shopping here. It would be so great if you helped me choose."

"Of course," Lyssa said. "All right. Bella, hop in the shower and wash your hair. While you're showering, I'm going to help Violet settle on a dress. Then Violet, you'll shower while I help Bella. Then I'll do hair masks for deep conditioning, okay?"

"Yes!" Bella and Violet chorused.

Violet grinned at Bella. Seeing her cousin smile like that made Bella even more excited for tonight. It was going to be the best party ever!

9

Social Butterfly

Lyssa had just finished curling Bella's hair when Ivy and Clara, both in Crystal Castle carriages, arrived. Each classmate of theirs was being picked up by a carriage.

"Wow!" Clara said, stepping back to look at Bella and Violet. "You both look amazing!"

Bella blushed and saw color flushing Violet's cheeks too.

"Lyssa helped us pick out the outfits," Bella said. "She was with us all morning and afternoon."

Bella wore a teal scoop-neck dress with a tulle skirt covered in petal appliqués. The dress had a bow at her right hip, and it zipped up the back. Bella's feet were comfy in black peep-toe ballet flats. Lyssa had curled Bella's naturally straight brown hair, and it fell in waves around her shoulders.

Violet sparkled in a hunter-green dress. The color made her red hair pop. The dress had three layers of ruffles along the bottom, and it was dotted with light-catching green sequins. Violet wore a pair of Bella's rhinestone-dotted black velvet ballet flats. Lyssa had flat-ironed Violet's curls into straight, shiny curtains of red hair.

Violet and Bella had hugged Lyssa and thanked her over and over as they left Bella's room. Once outside, the girls followed a smooth path that had been placed over the grass and led to the stage. Each time Bella put a foot on the path, it changed colors.

A carriage came to a smooth stop in the driveway and Todd, a boy in Bella's class, jumped out of the carriage. Todd followed the light-path and climbed the stairs to the platform.

"Hey," he said to the girls. He had bright-green eyes and freckles sprinkled across his nose.

"Hey, Todd," Bella said. "This is my cousin, Violet."

Todd smiled. "Hi."

Bella leaned close to Violet. "See? It's not so bad, right?"

Violet nodded. "I think this is going to be fun!"

Upbeat music played through big music crystals that rotated around the platform. The sun was just about to set, and rainbow-colored spotlights flickered on and off.

More carriages arrived, and each time, Bella made sure to introduce Violet until she had met each person in Bella's class.

"Ben!" Bella stuck her arm in the air and waved

at the dark-haired boy who stood on the platform's edge. Clara, next to Bella, waved at Ben too.

Smiling, Ben nodded at the other people, who were in groups chatting and swaying to the music.

"You look nice," Bella said to Ben. Ben had on a black shirt with black pants instead of his usual stable uniform.

"Thanks. You all look nice too," Ben said. "This is going to be fun! It was so nice of your parents to do this."

"I know. We all see each other every day, but really never get a chance to hang out," Bella said. "Tonight we can!"

"May I have your attention, everyone?"

All the kids turned their heads in the direction of the front of the stage. Queen Katherine, in a sunny yellow dress, smiled at them from atop a small podium.

"I'm so excited to have all of Bella's classmates

here tonight," Queen Katherine said. "A party was long overdue! I read progress reports for each of you and know how hard you work at school. I'm so proud to have you as students at Crystal Castle."

Everyone started clapping.

"There are some yummy treats under the red tent," Queen Katherine said once the applause died down. "The party ends at nine, but if you would like to go home sooner, come find me or King Phillip and we'll get a carriage ready. This isn't the last party, by the way. I am already planning an end-of-spring party, and I hope you'll all come!"

Cheers rang out across the platform.

"Thank you, Queen Katherine!" Todd shouted from his spot next to Bella.

"Thank you!" the rest of the class added.

"You're welcome, and have fun!" the queen said.

Music began flowing through the speakers again. Bella almost hopped up and down when she glanced around and spotted Violet chatting away with a few kids from the class.

Bella, Ivy, Clara, and Ben started dancing and talking as they moved around the floor. The platform lit up under their feet just as the walkway had done.

No one was on the sidelines—every person in Bella's class was dancing on the floor. "Are you having fun?" Bella asked Violet as she sidled up next to her cousin.

"So much fun!" Violet threw an arm around Bella. "Thank you for inviting me! This is one of the best nights ever!"

"Aw, I'm so glad!" Bella said, hugging her cousin back.

Bella accepted an empty plastic cup from Ben and peered at the bottom. "Sunray and cranberry juice with ice, please," she said. Immediately two ice cubes appeared in her cup, and it slowly filled with orange-red liquid until it was just full enough. Bella took one sip and then another. Sunray juice was so good! It was sour and sweet and unlike any other fruit in Crystal Kingdom.

Ben and Bella chatted about Glimmer's green transformation.

"Uncle Frederick explained it to me," Ben said. "That's so amazing, Bella. I can't even imagine having a unicorn so in tune with me that she changes colors if I'm feeling something so strong."

"In this case, it was kind of a curse," Bella said, shaking her head. "But I hope if Glimmer ever changes colors again that it will be from a good emotion that I'm having."

"Hey," Ben said, touching Bella's arm. "No one's perfect. You must have worked it out, because the last time I saw Glimmer, she was purple."

"I had a little help from my dad," Bella said. "I finally did the right thing and I learned my lesson."

After dancing for a while, everyone headed
to the Bamboo Garden. A giant movie screen
appeared in the air as the students plopped down
onto lounge chairs, blankets spread on the soft
ground. During the movie, trays with dozens of
delicious desserts floated to everyone. At the end
of the movie, the credits rolled and the music
began again.

Soon the sun had set, but everyone was going strong. Violet, a new social butterfly, flitted from group to group, and Bella couldn't help but grin as she watched her cousin. Violet and Adrienne, a cheery girl in a tangerine-colored dress, were off to the side of the floor talking.

The party was perfect. Bella couldn't have asked for anything more. She hoped that Violet would go home with new friends and maybe convince her parents to invite kids of Foris's castle workers to school at the castle.

"Bella," Ivy called out, almost having to shout to be heard over the music. "Some lady in a Crystal Castle uniform wants to talk to you. I feel like I've seen her before, but I don't know why."

"I bet she's one of the party planners. She probably can't find my mom or dad," Bella said.

"She said she would be waiting for you by the food tent," Ivy said.

"Thanks, Ivy," Bella said. "Be right back."

Bella hurried down the platform steps and peered inside the massive tent. The red canvas covered the banquet tables full of food and drinks.

"Hello?" Bella called.

"Over here," a pleasant voice replied. Bella spotted a blond woman waving and smiling.

Bella walked over to the woman. "If you're looking for my parents, they're around here somewhere," Bella said.

"Oh, no, dear," the woman said. Her blond hair started turning black at the roots, and her rosy cheeks paled. Ruby-red lips and eyes that glittered black stared at Bella.

"I'm not looking for your parents." The woman continued to change in front of Bella's eyes. The princess gulped. Goose bumps covered her arms. It felt as though the temperature had dropped fifty degrees!

Black hair cascaded down the woman's back, and the ends were red. The Crystal Castle uniform was replaced with a black cape and a long black dress that touched the ground.

The sweetness was gone from the woman's voice. A hard edge with a rough tone was in its place.

"I'm looking for *you*."

Queen Fire was here.

10

IOU

"What are you doing?" Bella asked the evil queen, heart thumping. "My father forbid you from ever setting food on our land again. The second guards see you, they'll take you right to a jail cell."

Even as she said the words, Bella knew that she couldn't call security. If she did, Queen Fire would certainly tell Bella's parents about their encounter in the Dark Forest. The king and queen would be beyond furious if they ever learned of Bella's trip onto the forbidden land.

Queen Fire laughed. It was an eerie cackle that sent shivers down Bella's spine. Bella glanced around, worried that someone might have heard, but the tent was empty. Everyone was dancing onstage or talking on the sidelines. Bella was grateful that none of them were near Queen Fire. She hated that her aunt had just spoken to Ivy.

"No one can see or hear us," Queen Fire said. "See the black ring?" She nodded toward the ground. There was a circle of black powder around them.

"What is it?" Bella asked.

"Just a little privacy wall spell," the queen said. "I would have hated for security to come. I know my dear twin sister doesn't want to see me. Pity that I must cast a spell to be allowed to speak to my niece."

Queen Fire had Bella cornered and she knew it. Bella clenched her hands into fists, willing herself to stay calm. "You did this to yourself," Bella said. "It's not my parents' fault that you aren't part of our family."

"Oh, Bella," Queen Fire said. "You have so much to learn about the truth behind my exile from Crystal Castle. But that is a story for another day. I have another matter that brought me here to speak with you."

Bella's mouth went dry. Her thoughts raced back to that day in the Dark Forest. She knew why Queen Fire was here. The only thing Bella wanted was to make Queen Fire happy so she would leave without anyone ever knowing she had been there.

"I want you to leave," Bella commanded. "This party is important to all of my friends. What do you want?"

The queen smiled at the princess, her lips coated in red lipstick. "I'm here to collect, Bella. You did promise me a favor, after all."

Bella tried to slow her speeding heart rate. "What is it?" She couldn't think of anything the

queen didn't already have or couldn't get on her own.

Queen Fire laughed. She took a step closer to Bella. "No, not money or jewels."

Bella's eyes widened.

Queen Fire pointed an index finger at her. The long nail, painted bloodred, matched her lipstick. "Silly girl. I want *you*."

Here's a sneak peek at Bella and Glimmer's next adventure:

The Hidden Treasure

Princess Bella stared at her evil aunt, Queen Fire, trying to look brave. Bella had been having a great time with the rest of her classmates at a fun dance that her parents, King Frederick and Queen Katherine, had planned to celebrate the end of the year. But Queen Fire had been a not-so-fun party surprise.

"How long does this"—Bella pointed to the black powder that hid them both from the other guests—"last?"

"Dear niece, don't worry about our privacy," Queen Fire said in a sugar-sweet tone. Bella's aunt had raven-black hair that hung down her back, glittering eyes, and matching ruby-red lips and nails.

"Did you have to come during my party?" Bella asked.

"I can come and go whenever I please," Queen Fire said. She glanced away from Bella, taking in the happy chatter and fun as Bella's classmates danced nearby.

Bella started to say something, but she bit her lip to keep quiet. Had she imagined the flicker of sadness on Queen Fire's face?

"Please let me go," Bella begged. "This is the last day I can spend with my cousin before she goes home. I know I owe you a favor, though, and I am not going back on my promise."

Images flashed through Bella's mind—picture after picture of that horrible time when Glimmer, her unicorn, had run away to the Dark Forest. Bella and Glimmer had just started to get to know each other after Bella had been matched with Glimmer on her eighth birthday. But Glimmer had run away, and when Bella had found her in the scary Dark Forest, they were suddenly in the path of Queen Fire's dangerous unicorns. Bella and Glimmer had been seconds away from serious trouble before Queen Fire saved them. In turn, Bella had pledged to help her aunt if she ever needed. And if she did not help her aunt, her aunt was going to take Glimmer away.

Queen Fire crossed her arms. "I had a feeling you would back out of our deal."

Bella felt like she was underwater—like someone had stuffed cotton balls in her ears. The class party felt very far away, and Bella did not know what to say to her aunt.

"Fine," Queen Fire sighed, waving a pale hand in the air. "Go back to your party, dear. I'm getting rather tired of hiding, though. I want you at *my* castle tomorrow by noon."

Bella chewed on the inside of her cheek. She didn't want to ask more questions that would keep the queen here longer, but . . .

"Can I come on Sunday? Please? Tomorrow is my last day with my cousin before she goes home to Foris."

Queen Fire stared, unblinking, at Bella. "Sunday. Noon. Or I'll have my guards begin to ready a stall at my stables for Glimmer."

"Not a cha—"

Queen Fire vanished before Bella could finish her sentence. Bella looked down, and all the black powder had disappeared too.

Okay, pull yourself together, Bella. You can't let anyone see that you're upset.

Bella glanced down at her shaking hands. She

walked over to a crystal punch bowl floating in the air.

"One cup, please," she said, testing out her voice. She thought she sounded like her usual self.

A ladle dipped into the bowl, filling a cup with red punch. The cup lowered itself in front of Bella.

"Thank you." Bella took the cup and sipped, trying to shake off Queen Fire's visit. She smoothed her sparkly teal dress with her free hand.

"Bella?"

A familiar voice called her name.

"Over here," Bella said as she forced a smile onto her face.

Her best friends, Ivy and Clara, along with her cousin, Violet, surrounded her.

"Did you help that lady who was looking for you?" Ivy asked.

Bella nodded, grabbing Ivy's hand and tugging her forward. "Yes. Let's go back to the party."

The princess accompanied her friends out of the tent and made a silent vow never to let Queen Fire that close to her friends ever again.

Candy Fairies

Chocolate Dreams

Rainbow Swirl

Caramel Moon

Cool Mint

Magic Hearts

Gooey Goblins

The Sugar Ball

A Valentine's Surprise

Bubble Gum Rescue

Double Dip

Jelly Bean Jumble

The Chocolate Rose

A Royal Wedding

Marshmallow Mystery

Frozen Treats

The Sugar Cup

Sweet Secrets

Taffy Trouble

Visit candyfairies.com for games, recipes, and more!

Making friends one Sparkly nail at a time!

Break out your sleeping bag and best pajamas. . . . You're invited!

Sleepover Squad

❀ Collect them all! ❀

The Hidden Treasure

Don't miss any of Bella
and Glimmer's adventures!

Unicorn Magic

Unicorn Magic

- BOOK 4 -

The Hidden Treasure

By Jessica Burkhart

Illustrated by Victoria Ying

Aladdin

NEW YORK   LONDON   TORONTO   SYDNEY   NEW DELHI

To Lex and Grace Carson.
You both fill my life with such
love and beauty! <3

This book is a work of fiction. Any references to historical events, real people,
or real places are used fictitiously. Other names, characters, places, and events
are products of the author's imagination, and any resemblance to actual
events or places or persons, living or dead, is entirely coincidental.

ALADDIN

An imprint of Simon & Schuster Children's Publishing Division
1230 Avenue of the Americas, New York, NY 10020
This Aladdin paperback edition March 2015
Text copyright © 2015 by Jessica Burkhart
Cover illustrations copyright © 2015 by Victoria Ying
Interior illustrations by Victoria Ying
All rights reserved, including the right of reproduction in whole or in part in any form.
ALADDIN is a trademark of Simon & Schuster, Inc., and related logo
is a registered trademark of Simon & Schuster, Inc.
Also available in an Aladdin hardcover edition.
For information about special discounts for bulk purchases, please contact
Simon & Schuster Special Sales at 1-866-506-1949
or business@simonandschuster.com.
The Simon & Schuster Speakers Bureau can bring authors to your live event.
For more information or to book an event contact the
Simon & Schuster Speakers Bureau at 1-866-248-3049 or
visit our website at www.simonspeakers.com.
Cover designed by Jessica Handelman
Interior designed by Mike Rosamilia
The text of this book was set in Arno Pro.
Manufactured in the United States of America 0319 OFF
6 8 10 9 7 5
Library of Congress Control Number 2014958803
ISBN 978-1-4814-1108-0 (hc)
ISBN 978-1-4424-9829-7 (pbk)
ISBN 978-1-4424-9831-0 (eBook)

Contents

1

Party Crasher

Princess Bella stared at her evil aunt, Queen Fire, trying to look brave. Bella had been having a great time with the rest of her classmates at a fun dance that her parents, King Phillip and Queen Katherine, had planned to celebrate the end of the year. But Queen Fire had been a not-so-fun party surprise.

"How long does this"—Bella pointed to the black powder that hid them both from the other guests—"last?"

"Dear niece, don't worry about our privacy," Queen Fire said in a sugar-sweet tone. Bella's aunt had raven-black hair that hung down her back,

1

glittering eyes, and matching ruby-red lips and nails.

"Did you have to come during my party?" Bella asked.

"I can come and go whenever I please," Queen Fire said. She glanced away from Bella, taking in the happy chatter and fun as Bella's classmates danced nearby.

Bella started to say something, but she bit her lip to keep quiet. Had she imagined the flicker of sadness on Queen Fire's face?

"Please let me go," Bella begged. "Today and tomorrow are the last days I can spend with my cousin before she goes home. I know I owe you a favor, though, and I am not going back on my promise."

Images flashed through Bella's mind—picture after picture of that horrible time when Glimmer, Bella's unicorn, had run away to the Dark Forest. Bella and Glimmer had just started to get to know each other after the two had been matched on Bella's eighth birthday. But Glimmer had run away, and when Bella had found her in the scary Dark Forest, they were suddenly in the path of Queen Fire's dangerous unicorns. Bella and Glimmer had been seconds away from serious trouble before Queen Fire saved them. In turn, Bella had pledged to help her aunt if she ever needed it. And if she did not help Queen Fire, her aunt was going to take Glimmer away.

Queen Fire crossed her arms. "I had a feeling you would back out of our deal."

"I'm not letting you have Glimmer!" Bella said.

"Then I suggest you listen very carefully. There is a crystal hidden in your castle. It has, let's say, *sentimental* value to me."

"Where is it?"

Queen Fire laughed. "Niece, if I knew the answer, I would have told you. I'm not *that* evil."

"So that's what I have to do?" Bella asked. "I have to find this crystal?" She paused. "Is it hidden away for a reason? Am I going to get in trouble for finding the crystal and giving it to you?"

Queen Fire leaned close to Bella. "If you're worried about getting in trouble, then don't get caught."

Bella felt like she was underwater—like someone had stuffed cotton balls in her ears. The class party felt very far away, and she did not know what to say to her aunt.

Bella swallowed. "Is that all? Because I really need to get back and—"

"Fine." Queen Fire sighed, waving a pale hand in the air. "Go back to your party, dear. I'm getting rather tired of hiding, though. I want you at *my* castle tomorrow. We need to talk. I need to make sure you understand the importance of your task."

Bella chewed on the inside of her cheek. She

didn't want to ask more questions to keep the queen here longer, but . . .

"Can I come on Sunday? Please?"

Queen Fire stared, unblinking, at Bella. "Sunday. Before sunset, or I'll have my guards begin to ready a stall at my stables for Glimmer."

"Not a cha—"

Queen Fire vanished before Bella could finish her sentence. Bella looked down, and all the black powder had disappeared too.

Okay, pull yourself together, Bella. You can't let anyone see that you're upset.

She glanced down at her shaking hands. She walked over to a crystal punch bowl floating in the air.

"One cup, please," she said, testing out her voice. She thought she sounded like her usual self.

A ladle dipped into the bowl, filling a cup with red punch. The cup lowered itself in front of Bella.

"Thank you." Bella took the cup and sipped, trying to shake off Queen Fire's visit. She smoothed her sparkly teal dress with her free hand.

"Bella?" A familiar voice called her name.

"Over here," Bella said as she forced a smile onto her face.

Her best friends, Ivy and Clara, along with her cousin, Violet, surrounded her.

"Did you help that lady who was looking for you?" Ivy asked.

Bella nodded, grabbing Ivy's hand and tugging her forward. "Yes. Let's go back to the party."

The princess accompanied her friends and her cousin out of the tent and made a silent vow to never let Queen Fire that close to her friends ever again.

2

Swimming in Secrets

"I can't believe it's your last day here!" Bella said, sticking out her bottom lip.

"I know," Violet replied as she twirled the ends of her red hair, which was in two braids. "I begged my parents to let me stay longer, but they said I had to come home for school."

Both princesses frowned. They were each lying on a giant raft—Bella's pink and Violet's frosty white. The rafts hovered above the pool water as the girls soaked up some sun. Bella pushed the down button, and her raft lowered until it touched the water. It was a very warm day in Crystal Kingdom, and Bella was ready for a swim in one of the royal pools. Violet, Princess of Foris Kingdom, was Bella's cousin. She was a little younger than Bella.

"I can't wait till Ivy and Clara get here," Violet said, slipping off her raft and into the crystal-clear pool water. The bottom and sides of the pool were covered in clear pea-size crystals that made the water look sparkly. "I feel like I've known them forever—not less than a week!"

"They are such good friends like that," Bella agreed.

Violet climbed up the pool stairs, walked the length of the pool, and stopped in front of the diving board.

"Higher, please," Violet commanded. The white board lifted off the ground and rose a few inches into the air.

"Go, Vi!" Bella cheered.

"Cannnnnonnnnbaaaallll!" Violet yelled as

she jumped off the board, wrapping her arms around her legs.

Bella giggled as her cousin caused waves in the pool and splashed her.

Queen Katherine had spelled the pool to be just deep enough for cannonballs, but no diving was allowed. They were only allowed to jump off of it or do cannonballs when someone else was in or around the pool.

For the few seconds that Violet was underwater, Bella let out a giant sigh that she felt she had been holding inside since Queen Fire had talked to her.

Keeping secrets is so hard, Bella thought. *Where do I even begin to look for the crystal?*

There was zero chance she would tell her mom and dad, but as Bella watched Violet break the surface of the water, grinning, Bella *knew.* She had to tell her friends and her cousin. If she didn't, it would go against their rules of BFFs. Queen Katherine appeared with a basket of flowers resting in the crook of her arm. She waved at Bella, and Bella's stomach felt all flip-floppy when she waved back at the queen.

"Awesome cannonball!" Queen Katherine called out.

Violet smiled. "Thanks!" she said as she crooked her finger at her raft and it sailed through the air, stopping inches before her.

Bella rolled off her raft and slipped underwater. As she sank down a few inches, the princess rubbed her temples. She had almost fallen asleep twice on her pool float because she had been up most of the night trying to figure out every spot the crystal could be hidden. As Bella had mapped late into the night, she got more and more nervous, because she wasn't just retrieving a crystal for Queen Fire—the princess was *stealing*. Queen Fire hadn't said a word about "borrowing," so Bella didn't think Crystal

Castle would be getting the magical sparkler back. She felt like a unicorn was sitting on her chest.

Bella surfaced, swimming toward the ladder. She walked up to the diving board.

"Let me set the height," Violet said. "Okay, Bella? Or are you scared?"

Bella stuck out her tongue at her cousin. "Raise the board as high as you want!"

Violet lifted a hand out of the water. "Up, please."

The board rose and rose and *rose*.

Was Vi ever going to tell the board to stop? Bella wondered, feeling like there were teensy butterflies in her stomach.

"Please stop!" Violet called out. "That's perfect."

Silvery shimmery stairs—which glittered in the sunlight—appeared. Without thinking, Bella grasped the cool bars of the ladder and climbed to the top. The princess was afraid that if she stopped, she might back out.

11

"Okay! I'm doing it!" Bella said. "Here I gooo!" She ran a few steps forward, then pushed off of the board with the tips of her toes. She hugged her knees to her chest and hit the water.

She kicked to the surface and blinked through the water in her eyes. "I dare you," she said, looking at Violet. "Let me raise the board."

"Up, please," Bella said as her cousin climbed out of the pool and headed for the diving board. "Stop."

The board halted—hovering close to the area where Bella had jumped.

Violet's steps slowed as she neared the board's stairs.

"Ooh, that's pretty high," Bella called, grinning.

"Stop it!" Violet said. "You can't scare me." She climbed the stairs.

Bella raised her hands in the air. "I wasn't trying to. I was just telling the truth—you set the diving board *pretty* high." Bella kicked her feet, splashing, as she swam to her raft and climbed on top.

The princess's cousin frowned, taking a step back from the end of the board.

"I guess I could lower it," Vi muttered to herself. She shook her head. "No! Cannonball!"

Violet reached the end of the diving board in two steps. She pushed off the high dive, bringing her knees to her chest and wrapping her arms around them. Then all Bella could see was a pink blur of Vi's swimsuit and two red braids sticking up in the air just before Violet crashed into the pool, sending water everywhere.

Bella laughed. Her raft bobbed a little from the small waves that rippled across the water after Vi jumped in. Violet popped up and raised a fist in the air.

"Yes!" Violet said, grinning. "I'm the all-star champion of Crystal Castle cannonballs. I think I deserve a ribbon or, no, a *trophy*."

"Ha, ha," Bella said, sliding off her raft and into the water. "You must be joking. I have held the all-time record for the most awesome cannonballs in any of the four sky islands!"

Violet scrambled atop her raft. "Prove it."

"Who's proving what?" a voice called out.

"Yeah! Spill, because I want to play!"

Ivy and Clara, both in their swimsuits, waved from the entrance by the pool. A wide-brimmed floppy hat shielded Clara's eyes from the sun. Clara's long, strawberry-blond-colored hair was up in a pretty ponytail. Ivy's chin-length blond hair had rainbow clips holding her hair away from her face.

"Yay, we're all together!" Bella cheered.

"Get in!" Violet said, motioning toward the water. "We're trying to decide who can do a better cannonball."

"That's easy," Ivy said. "I can." Smiling, she kicked off her flip-flops and ran toward the water.

"Cannonball!" She hit the water and it sprayed everywhere. All of the girls burst into laughter.

After each girl showed off her cannonball skills, they kept on playing and swimming in the water until their fingers and toes were all shriveled up. They all shook out their beach towels and sat by the pool, waiting to dry off.

Bella rolled onto her stomach, propping her chin up on her hands. "There is something that I need to tell you guys."

The other three girls all looked at Bella.

"But you can't get too worried, okay?" Bella asked. "Promise?"

Ivy shifted her eyes to meet Clara's. Violet stared at Bella as if she was trying to determine what Bella was going to say before she said it.

"Promise," Violet finally said.

"Guys?" Bella asked, looking at Ivy and Clara.

"Promise," they said in unison.

Bella took a deep breath. "Queen Fire kind of showed up at our party yesterday."

3

A Super-Secret Mission

"What?!" Ivy, Clara, and Violet chorused.

"Queen Fire?" Ivy said. "When was she at the party? And why?"

"Why did you wait until now to tell us?" Clara asked. She sat up and crossed her arms.

"Because of this!" Bella said. "I knew you guys would be upset, and can you try to keep it down a little? I don't want my parents or anyone else to walk by and hear this."

"We have to tell Uncle Phillip and Aunt Katherine right now," Violet insisted. "You can't keep this a secret, Bella."

"Vi, please at least listen to what I have to say, okay? I didn't have to tell you guys, but I did. I told you because I know you'll all be able to help me."

Violet, Clara, and Ivy were silent.

"Okay," Clara said as Ivy and Violet nodded.

"Thank you," Bella said, sitting up on her beach towel. "Ivy, you actually met Queen Fire."

"I did? When?" Ivy asked, her mouth hanging open in surprise.

"Do you remember when you came and got me during the party? There was a woman in the food tent who wanted to see me."

"Oh, yes!" Ivy said, nodding.

"That was Queen Fire," Bella said.

She glanced around and listened. But she didn't see anyone, and all she heard was an occasional unicorn hoofbeat as they went around for a walk. Bella was also on the lookout for any Busy Bees. Busy Bees lived in Crystal Kingdom and had a *super*-annoying habit. They were very nosy! The bees searched for gossip and talk around the town and the castle. Once a Busy Bee had locked in on gossip, it would release its stinger. The stinger recorded the gossip for as long as the bee could fly near the gossiper without getting caught. Once the bee had finished, it would fly into one of the Busy Bee Boxes that were scattered throughout the kingdom. The bee would share the gossip with other bees and would some-times—if asked nicely—share random gossip to someone collecting honey from the box.

"Once we were alone, she dropped her disguise," the princess continued. "She wanted me to help her out and make sure I paid her back for her help."

"What do you mean?" Violet asked.

"Queen Fire saved Glimmer and Bella when they were lost in the Dark Forest," Ivy said. "As thanks, Bella promised to help Queen Fire."

"If Bella doesn't keep her promise . . ." Clara let her sentence trail off.

"If I don't keep my promise," Bella picked up, her voice wobbly, "Queen Fire will take Glimmer away for good." The princess's shoulders slumped and she sniffed, wiping her eyes with the back of her hand.

Violet gasped. "Bella! Now we *really* have to tell your parents!"

20

Bella shook her head. "No way. I'm not telling them, Vi. I'm trusting all of you because you're my best friends."

"What do you think she wants?" Ivy asked.

"She wants a crystal that's hidden inside the castle. I'll give her whatever she wants. Not even the biggest crystal in the world means more than Glimmer."

The other girls were quiet.

"I would do the same thing," Clara declared. Bella shot her friend a grateful smile.

"How can we help?" Clara asked.

"I'm with Clara," Ivy said. "I don't like it, but I'm in. What does the crystal do, anyway?"

"I don't know," Bella said. "I'm sure I'll find out tomorrow."

Bella, Ivy, and Clara looked at the Princess of Foris Kingdom. Violet was staring down at her toes, which were painted a cheerful yellow. Except no one was in a cheerful mood anymore.

"I *have* to leave tomorrow," Violet said. "But that doesn't mean I can't or don't want to help. Count me in."

"Thank you so much," Bella said. "There has never been anything more important to me than Glimmer. So I have to do whatever Queen Fire says. No matter what."

"I say that we don't waste another second," Violet said. "We may not have all the details, but we *do* know that Bella has to find this crystal somewhere within the castle, right?"

Bella and the other girls nodded.

"I say we start making lists and a map of places to check. I don't think we should leave out a single room," Violet added.

"Great idea!" Bella said.

"Let's get some Secret Scribble notebooks," Clara said. "I nominate Vi to draw the map. It will take a lot of work, so maybe you can finish them on the train

22

tomorrow and send it to us with your Chat Crystal?"

Secret Scribble notebooks were the *best*. They only revealed the page's contents to the first person to open the notebook. The pages appeared blank to everyone else unless the owner wrote names in the notebook of other people who could see the pages.

"Of course, yes," Violet said. "But it's Bella's home. Don't you think . . . *oh*, right." The Foris princess grinned, and her smile seemed contagious to everyone except Bella.

"Why are you all smiling?" Bella asked. "Vi, what did that 'oh, right' mean?"

"Um, well," Violet started. "Bells, I'm sorry. I love you, but your drawing skills . . . let's just say that Clara asked the right person for this particular job."

"Hey!" Bella said. She sat up and reached for an outdoor pillow on the nearest lounge chair. She lightly tossed it at Violet, then picked up another and tossed it at Clara.

Ivy cracked up.

Bella smiled. At least they could laugh about the whole secret, scary mission! The news about Queen Fire hadn't exactly been the kind of news that the princess liked to share with her friends. It made her sad when she made *them* upset.

"Oh, so you agree with them?" Bella asked Ivy, trying to keep a fake frown on her face. "Then you can have a pillow too!"

"Nooo!" Ivy managed to say as she continued to giggle.

But there wasn't another pillow in Bella's reach. She darted to the next lounge chair and grabbed a pillow from there.

Bella launched the pillow into the air as the other girls shrieked and jumped. As they giggled and jumped into the pool, Bella was happy that she wasn't in this alone.

4

Unicorn Sparks

"That's an hour!" Ivy said, reaching over to shut off the timer. She, Bella, and Clara were on the princess's bed with vocab flash cards spread all around them.

Earlier that morning, Bella had come home from the Rainbow Rail Express Station, where she and her parents had dropped off Violet. The cousins had shared a fierce hug, and Violet had whispered that Bella had to keep her updated about Queen Fire. After Bella and her parents got back, Clara and Ivy came over to study and start on Operation: Find the Crystal.

"I'm so glad your parents let us come over," Clara said. "Studying for an hour wasn't too bad."

Queen Katherine had allowed Bella to have friends come over today only if they studied for the upcoming week's vocabulary quiz.

"An *hour* was okay," Bella said. "But being stuck in school starting tomorrow is going to take up lots of time. Time that we could be using to search for the crystal."

"I know," Ivy said. "But if we don't get good grades, then you know our parents will only let us see each other in class. And then we would really be in a big pickle!"

Bella nodded, putting a rubber band around the flash cards. "That *is* true," she agreed. "This is so the wrong week for us to be kept apart!" She leaned close to her friends. "I want to make a list of places to search for the crystal, but let me see where my parents are. Did you guys bring your notebooks?"

Ivy and Clara nodded, and each girl reached for her backpack.

Bella hopped off her bed and pressed the button next to her intercom. Long before she had even been born, cameras had been put in all over the castle and its grounds. They helped keep everyone safe.

"Where are Mom and Dad?" Bella asked, letting go of the blue button. Immediately, two screens appeared on the wall. Queen Katherine was in the living room, smiling and laughing with two of her own best friends. "Mom: check," Bella said in a whisper. King Phillip, seated at his giant desk, rubbed his chin and frowned at whatever was on the papers in front of him. "Dad: check."

"Clear?" Ivy asked.

Nodding, Bella turned off the cameras and climbed back onto her bed. "We don't have to whisper—just keep our ears open. Mom's got

27

friends downstairs, and Dad's in the opposite wing in his office."

The princess picked up a pen she'd been using and grabbed her Secret Scribble notebook from her nightstand.

"Let me see if Violet can hang with us," Bella said, picking up her Chat Crystal. "She should be home by now." Bella put the clear, smooth stone on her palm. "Chat Crystal, please ask Violet if she can talk to me and my friends. She has to be alone."

The crystal swirled pink, purple, and yellow while it relayed Bella's message to her cousin. Within a few seconds, a light began to project up from the stone.

"Yay, she's free!" Bella said. She put the Chat Crystal on a pillow at the front of her bed. The light switched to a fuzzy outline of a person, and then Violet popped into view. Just like Bella, Ivy, and

Clara, Violet sat on her bed with her pink Secret Scribble notebook on her lap.

"Hi!" Violet said, waving. Her bright-yellow comforter covered in white daisies matched her bubbly personality.

"Hi!" Bella and her friends chorused back.

"You messaged me at the perfect time," Violet said. "I got home a few hours ago, and my parents are out at some kind of grown-up event."

"I miss you already," Bella said. "But I'm glad you're 'here' to help."

Violet stuck out her lower lip. "I miss all of you, too! I'm sorry I can't be there, Bells, but I'll do everything I can from here. Oh!" Vi held up a folded piece of paper. "This is the map I promised to draw. Hold on a second."

Violet put down the paper and placed her Chat Crystal on top. "Please send this to Princess Bella of Crystal Kingdom," she said.

The Foris princess had no sooner finished her sentence when a paper floated down from the ceiling and landed in Bella's lap.

"Got it," Bella said, smiling and holding it up so Violet could see.

"I hope it's helpful," Vi said. "I did the best I could."

"I'm sure it will be," Bella said as she unfolded the paper. "Violet!" she exclaimed.

The map was easily four times as big as Bella's notebook. Violet had managed to draw all of the sparkly and important details of the Crystal Castle. She even included the lush and beautiful gardens that were on the grounds of the castle—some of Bella's favorite places!

"Um, *wow*," Clara said.

Ivy's eyes were wide. "How did you do this?! This is amazing!"

Violet's cheeks blushed almost as red as her

hair. "Thank you! I started to draw the castle but realized that I didn't know *every* room, even though I've visited a lot."

"I live here, and *I* don't even know every room!" Bella said. All of the girls laughed.

"I virtually visited Foris Kingdom's library, and because I'm a princess, I was able to see really old maps of the castle," Violet said. "It was the perfect thing to do on the train. So I used those to help me. That map *should* have every single room of Crystal Castle on it."

"Every one is labeled," Bella said, touching the headings for KITCHEN and FIRST-FLOOR GREAT ROOM.

"Violet, thank you," Bella said. "This is going to help so much. I'm holding on to this map to use next time I'm half-asleep and my mom is calling me to breakfast!"

The cousins smiled at each other. A clock chimed in Violet's room, and Bella was soon reminded of the reason that she and her friends were all gathered.

"Is it okay if we all start throwing out ideas and I'll write them down in this notebook?" Bella asked. "Tomorrow after school, we can start with the ones that seem like the best guesses and check them off as we go. Today, after we make the list, I'll go to Queen Fire's castle."

"We'll have your back," Ivy said.

"Ivy and Clara, you won't be able to cover for Bella every second while she's searching for the crystal or with Queen Fire," Violet said. "What if you covered for them, Bella? You could assign different rooms of the castle to each other. Bella, you would know the castle the best, so maybe you can search some rooms that aren't used as much after your parents go to sleep or are busy. Rooms that aren't as familiar to Ivy and Clara."

"Smart," Clara said. "Bells, maybe you could also search any rooms—like your parents' bedroom— that would be fine if you were caught in them, but not if Ivy and I were found."

"Brilliant," Bella said.

"Everyone is a million percent sure that their notebook is *totally* secret, right?" Ivy asked, worried.

33

"Yes," Bella said. "I kept testing mine last night to make sure. I must have opened and closed it a dozen times."

"I did the same thing," Clara said.

"Me too," Violet added.

"Okay, so on to the list," Bella said. "Basement and basement storage rooms."

"I'll check off rooms on the map once you write them down," Clara said. She made two tiny pink check marks on Violet's map. "Don't forget—we have to really check each room. Like spies. We have to move paintings, look under rugs—stuff like that. The crystal probably isn't in plain sight."

The other girls nodded.

"How about the library?" Ivy said. She wrinkled her nose. "Oops. Sorry—I meant *libraries*."

Bella wrote that into her notebook.

The four friends worked nonstop until each wing of the castle was divided up. Bella made a big wish on all the stars in Crystal Kingdom that this plan would work.

"Glimmer, I have to tell you a secret," Bella began.

Her unicorn's purple-tinged ears swiveled back and forth—something Glimmer did when she was nervous.

A couple of hours ago, the princess and her friends had finished with their list of rooms. Bella's mom still had guests, thankfully, so the queen had been a little distracted when Bella had told her that she, Ivy, and Clara were going outside to play in the gardens and stables.

Bella had just left her friends in Snapdragon Garden and had collected Glimmer from the Royal Stables.

They were in one of the many large pastures that King Phillip and Queen Katherine kept for the royal unicorns. Bella had taken Glimmer far away from the stables so no one could hear them. She hoped the Busy Bees would stay away.

"You have to trust me and not get scared," Bella said. She smoothed her cheery sky-blue sundress and took a deep breath.

Glimmer's mostly white coat dazzled in the sunlight like thousands of diamonds. Her mane and tail were purple—the color of Bella's aura.

Bella looked into Glimmer's big brown eyes. "I'm going to Queen Fire's castle."

Glimmer snorted and threw up her head.

"Shhh, it's okay," Bella said. "I promise! I owe her a favor, remember?"

Glimmer stared at Bella with scared eyes.

Bella and Glimmer were so close that their bond allowed Bella to read Glimmer's thoughts by watching the unicorn's body language. They had been together since Bella's eighth birthday, when Glimmer had been the one, out of a lineup of royal unicorns, who had matched Bella's aura. Once a royal and a unicorn were paired, they took care of each other for life.

"You want me to take you with me?" Bella asked. "I can't. There's less of a chance that Mom and Dad will notice I'm gone if you're still here."

The unicorn shook her head, and tiny sparks began to crackle all over her body. They were like tiny firecrackers that left itsy-bitsy clouds of smoke.

Bella gasped. She put a hand on Glimmer's forehead. "Oh, Glimmer, don't be so worried about me! Is that why you're . . . *sparking*?"

Glimmer bobbed her head; her purple mane flew everywhere, some hairs staying stuck up after she'd finished moving.

"Oh, poor girl," Bella said, reaching forward and fixing the bits of mane.

She threw her arms around the unicorn's neck.

She hugged Glimmer tight. The sparks slowly stopped until the final poof of smoke disappeared. "Glimmer, please don't be scared. The best thing you can do is be brave and not let Frederick or Ben see you sparking or acting nervous. Okay?"

Frederick was in charge of the royal stables. His nephew, Ben, was his apprentice. Ben and Bella were good friends. Ben had been busy brushing a unicorn when Bella had passed on the way to Glimmer's stall. Besides the need to keep everything tip-top secret, Bella wanted to keep Ben safe, too. It was bad enough that her best friends and cousin knew—and were already so deep into the plan.

Bella swept her fingers over Glimmer's cheek. "You *really* think Queen Fire might hurt me?" She paused. "I don't, sweet girl. I saw a good side of her, *and* she's my aunt. I don't think she would ever do anything like that."

Glimmer snorted, dropping her head.

"I wouldn't go if I didn't owe her," Bella said. "The sooner I pay her back, the sooner we won't ever have to think about Queen Fire again. If I get into any sort of trouble, you'll know. Stay out here," she added with a wave of her arm. "Eat some dandelions and take a nap. That way, I'll be back when you wake up."

She hugged Glimmer, then turned away. *I hope I can keep my promise,* Bella thought. She touched the Chat Crystal in her pocket, comforted by knowing Ivy and Clara had their own Crystals in hand, waiting for any signal of trouble.

"Oof," Bella exclaimed as she jerked to a halt. She twisted around and saw that Glimmer was tugging on the hem of her dress.

Bella couldn't help but laugh. "Glimmer. Please don't worry!"

The unicorn kept her teeth clamped on Bella's dress.

Bella sighed. "Glimmer, if I don't go, then there *will* be trouble. Please."

Glimmer stared at Bella with her big brown eyes and long eyelashes. Finally, she dipped her head and let go of her dress.

"Don't worry, Glimmer. I'll be back in a unicorn minute!" Bella said. She kissed Glimmer's cheek.

Bella broke into a jog as she headed toward the castle's drawbridge. The bridge was always protected by guards and their dogs. Bella slowed to a walk as she neared the guards.

"Good day, Princess Bella," a tall, thin guard greeted the princess.

"Same to you," Bella replied. She smiled at that guard and the one on her other side. He bowed his head as Bella passed.

Bella walked along the drawbridge and let out a huge sigh. The guards were behind her! That meant—

"Princess!"

Bella stopped in her tracks.

"Yes?" Bella said, slowly turning around. Her heart pounded in her chest and her palms sweated. *Keep your cool,* she thought. *Don't let the guards see that you're nervous!*

One of the guards walked up to her, towering over her.

Bella swallowed hard. Was her mission over before it even began?

"This fell out of your pocket," the guard said.

The guard placed a small, folded piece of notebook paper on Bella's waiting hand. She closed her fingers around the paper.

"Thank you," the princess said. "This was a recipe that I needed. I'm going to the sunray berry patch. My friends are staying here to find the other ingredients for sunray pie in my mom's gardens. I'll be back in a bit." Bella forced herself to stop rambling.

With a little wave to the guards, she was off again. Bella hurried—the longer she was gone, the higher the chance that she would get caught. She hoped her mom would be busy with friends the entire time that she was away, so that Ivy and Clara wouldn't be put to the test of covering for the missing princess.

Bella acted as if she was going to take a left and go to the sunray berry patch. She glanced behind her, and the second she was out of sight, she went in the opposite direction toward the Dark Forest. Cutting through the scary woods was the fastest way to Queen Fire's. This was definitely a trip that Bella wanted to make as fast as possible.

She slipped the paper that she'd been clutching into one of her jacket pockets. It was a very important note that she had written and then put a Go Home and Find Parents spell on. In the note, Bella told her parents that she was at Queen

Fire's castle in the Blacklands and needed help.

If anything went wrong while Bella was with Queen Fire, all she had to do was drop the paper onto the ground. It would zip through the air in millions of little pieces and turn back into a readable note only when it reached the king or queen.

A compass was in her other pocket. It would help her find the fastest path to Queen Fire's castle.

Bella stopped at the edge of the Dark Forest. She took a deep breath, trying to calm her nerves. She looked back toward Crystal Castle. The sun was high in the cloudless sky. Knee-high emerald-green grass grew on both sides of the cobblestone path she had just traveled along. Rainbow butter-flies floated through the air, some stopping on pink, purple, and yellow tulips that dotted the fields.

In front of Bella was nothing but darkness.

A crow cawed, and the noise made the hairs on Bella's arms stand up. She shivered even in the warm air. The trees lining the forest entrance were leafless and skinny. The temperature dropped with each step closer to the forest—a place forbidden to Bella and all of her friends and classmates.

"You can do this," Bella said out loud. "This is for Glimmer." She inhaled, saying a silent thank-you to Ivy, Clara, and Violet. The princess had a feeling that it was going to take all of them to pull this off.

5

The Queen's Castle

The Dark Forest swallowed all of the sunlight as Bella took a few steps inside. She pulled the compass crystal from her pocket. She held it in her hand, ready to give it instructions.

"Queen Fire's castle," Bella said. Her voice was shaky—something that she had to fix before she spoke to Queen Fire. She couldn't show the queen how scared she was.

The compass shone a rainbow of light forward on the ground, pointing the way. Bella started to follow its path, then turned around. She could not see Crystal Kingdom anymore. It was as if the trees

that she had passed had grown together to trap her inside the forest. Bella took another deep breath and kept going.

Buzz!

Bella swatted the air with both of her hands. A basketball-size fly that glowed in the dark zoomed toward her. The Hairy-Scary—a fly native to the forest—had bright-yellow wings and bulging green eyes. It was covered in glowing orange fur.

The Dark Forest was full of gross bugs!

"Go away!" Bella shouted as the Hairy-Scary headed toward her. She ducked before it ran into her, then started running, not even looking at the compass.

Bella ran until she couldn't hear the fly's wings. She slowed down, looking behind her. Nothing but darkness and—"Oompf!"

The princess landed on her knees, the compass

flying from her hand and landing facedown just ahead of her.

Bella hurried to her feet even though her knees throbbed. She swiped the compass from the ground, blowing dirt off of it. The princess used the compass as a flashlight to see what had caused her fall. A thin tree root was raised just high enough to catch her foot.

"Please stay here, compass," Bella said. She removed her hand from under the compass, and it stayed in the air while she looked at her knees. Thankfully, the soft forest dirt had prevented her from getting too hurt—there was only a small cut on her left knee.

"Oh, *great!*" Bella said, pulling the compass closer. Her dress was now streaked with dirt, thanks to the fall and where she had wiped her hands, not knowing that they were so dirty.

Ivy and Clara will help me do a cleanup spell,

Bella thought. *I'll worry about Mom or Dad seeing my dress and knees when I'm home safe.*

Bella plucked the compass out of the air and found a semi-clear path. She walked for several minutes before the towering trees began to thin out and she finally saw the sky. It was no longer the brilliant blue that it had been when the princess had left home. Full black clouds rolled across the gray sky. Bella's heartbeat jumped up as fast as a hummingbird's wings because of what she spotted next. Not far in the distance, smoke billowed into the air. Two black towers with triangle-shaped tops stretched into the sky.

Queen Fire's castle.

Bella walked toward the smoke, this time keeping a closer eye on the trail.

It could have been minutes or hours when the princess stopped. Fear—and a tiny bit of curiosity—ran through her. This was it. She was glad, no matter how scared she had been, that she had come alone. She didn't think her aunt would be happy if she brought company—like Ivy or Clara—along on her first visit.

She tried to be brave, but it was hard. Who knew what was in the castle? Knowing her aunt, there could be *anything* beyond those castle doors. The red unicorn that had almost attacked Glimmer was scary enough. She patted the note in her pocket and swallowed hard. Everything would be okay as long as she had that note. Her parents could rescue her. Bella stopped when the entire castle came into view. It was as big as her own, but made of glass instead of stone. Two red unicorns stood guard on either side of the door.

This is it. I have to save Glimmer, Bella thought.

As she walked closer to the castle doors, she watched colors flickering in the glass, first red, then black, finally purple. *Purple—that's my aura,*

Bella thought. Why was that? She didn't have time to think about it, though, because almost all too soon she had reached two unicorns on concrete pedestals standing guard. They had black manes and were more muscular-looking than the royal unicorns.

"My name is Bella. *Princess* Bella. I'm here to see Queen Fire," she announced to the unicorn guards. They sidestepped away from the door, their hooves striking the concrete, as the door swung open.

Bella stepped carefully into the great hall, looking around her. The inside was glass, but without the colors swirling, like the outside. It looked like her own castle with different colors. There was a large painting at the end of the hall that caught her eye. In the painting, Queen Fire stood with her unicorns, with one on each side of her. Red and black rugs covered the floor with dizzying zigzag designs.

Not sure what to do, Bella walked into the

closest room and sat down on a red velvet couch. It faced an empty fireplace. There were no family pictures on the walls of Queen Fire's castle. For a minute, Bella actually felt sad for her mom's sister.

The princess shivered as she looked around the room. Suddenly, with a whoosh of black smoke, a fire appeared in the fireplace and warmed the room up instantly.

"You came after all, dear niece," Queen Fire said. She walked around to face Bella. Her long, black, wavy hair tumbled down her back. She wore red crystal earrings that sparkled in the firelight.

"I promised that I would come," Bella said. "I need you to keep your promise and not hurt Glimmer."

"As long as you hold up your end of the bargain, I will keep my word," Queen Fire said.

"What does this crystal do?" Bella asked. "Why do you need it?"

"That answer comes in due time," Queen Fire

said. A black leather chair shot forward. Sitting down, the queen looked over at Bella. "Do the king and queen know you're here?"

"No—"

"Oh, dear," Queen Fire said. A look of what might have been sadness flickered across her face. "You injured yourself on the journey. Are you hurt?"

"No," Bella said, shaking her head. "I'm fi—"

Before she could finish her sentence, the queen snapped her fingers. A short man in a white coat trotted into the room, stethoscope around his neck and a black bag in hand.

"Your Highness?" the man asked, looking at Queen Fire.

"Dr. Foster, please tend to my niece's injuries," Queen Fire said.

"Really, I'm okay," Bella said. "Thank you, but—"

"I'll return in a moment," Queen Fire interrupted. She disappeared, leaving Bella with the doctor.

The doctor, who had a kind face and thick glasses, placed his bag on the floor.

"I'm Dr. Foster," he said, holding out a hand.

Bella shook his hand. "I'm Bella."

"Do you mind if I take a look at your knees?" he asked. His silver hair and easy manner made Bella feel at ease.

"Okay," she said.

The doctor asked Bella how she had fallen and applied a disinfectant that stung a little. A quiet woman had come with a bowl of steaming-hot water and soap as the doctor treated Bella. She held the bowl while Bella washed dirt and grime from her hands. Then the maid sprayed something that foamed onto the dirty parts of Bella's dress. In seconds, the foam disappeared, and so did the stains. The servant left without uttering a word. Dr. Foster smoothed a small bandage over Bella's cut just as Queen Fire reappeared.

"It was lovely to meet you, Bella," Dr. Foster said. "Safe travels home."

"Thank you, doctor," Bella said, smiling at him.

He bowed to Queen Fire and disappeared.

"Are you hungry?" Queen Fire asked. She didn't wait for an answer from Bella. Two silver plates floated in the air, holding forks and a kind of cake Bella had never seen before. It was a chocolate cake topped with dark-red berries.

Bella was starving after her journey through the Dark Forest—but she was scared to eat it. *What if it's a trick?* She watched as Queen Fire took a plate and fork for herself.

"A Dark Forest specialty," the queen said. "Try it." She dug her fork into the cake.

Bella finally took a bite of the cake. She was relieved when she tasted a rich dark chocolate. She took another small bite. She sneaked a look toward her aunt. This was perfectly normal. A niece and an aunt eating dessert. Bella's mind wandered as she thought about what it would be like to have a *nice* Queen Fire in her life.

"Your castle is really . . . *interesting,*" Bella said. "Um, thank you for inviting me, but I can't stay long. My friends are covering for me at home."

"The fact that this is your first visit to your aunt's castle is sad. How wrong my sister was to keep me a secret from you. It was quite a pleasure to see you on your eighth birthday. I'm not forgetting your dear friends, and unicorn, of course," Queen Fire said. Her eyes were dark as coal.

Whatever "normal" niece-and-aunt-relationship thoughts Bella had vanished.

"My mom wasn't wrong. You're *bad* and you steal unicorns."

Queen Fire smirked.

"Please just tell me anything I need to know about the crystal. The sooner I get home, the faster

I can find it." Bella rested her hands on her lap after her plate and fork floated away. She didn't want Queen Fire to see them shaking.

"Oh yes, the reason I brought you," Queen Fire said.

"The special crystal is hidden in a vault. I'm guessing that vault is inside the castle."

"Guessing?" Bella asked. "Does that mean it could be *anywhere*?" She felt a bit sick with this new piece of information. It was already enough to have an entire castle to search. But if the vault could be on the *grounds* . . .

"Not anywhere," Queen Fire said, scowling. "It's definitely in the castle, and I wouldn't waste your time looking on the grounds. The crystal is very important to me."

"Why?" Bella asked.

"It is"—the queen paused—"personal."

"I can get it for you. I mean, I can try. I'll look

everywhere for it. Once I find it in the vault, I'll bring it to you," Bella promised. *What if she wants to be part of our family again?*

Queen Fire stared blankly at her, tilting her head a little. "No, princess, you must get me into the castle. You can remove it from its hiding place, but only I can take it from Crystal Castle. The crystal will lose all of its worth to me if you try to take it off castle grounds. I'm the only one who can remove it." Queen Fire paused. "Well, so can your mother."

"Only you and Mom?" Bella asked. "Why just you two?"

The queen shot Bella a dark look that made the princess swallow and forget her next question.

"But my dad said that if you ever came to our castle again, he would throw you in jail! We would *never* make it past the guards, and—"

"Bella, remember our agreement," Queen Fire pointed out.

Bella looked at her. A vision of Glimmer's beautiful white coat turning red flashed in front of her eyes.

"I'll get you into the castle. I'll do anything!" Bella said. "But you must promise me that you won't hurt my family, me, or my unicorn."

"All those precious things will be kept safe. You have my word. Hurry home before your parents discover that you're missing. And, darling Bella? You have one week to find the crystal and get me safely inside Crystal Castle. Or Glimmer is mine."

One week?! Bella felt like she had eaten too many pieces of sunray pie. There was no way they could search the castle in just one week. But she had no choice.

"Fine. I'll do it," Bella said.

"So you shall. And to show that I'm a woman of my word, I will create a contract for us," Queen Fire said. She clapped her hands, and with a puff of black smoke, a contract appeared. Bella read the words carefully and saw that Queen Fire hadn't lied. The paper said that if she helped her aunt, Glimmer was safe.

The contract hovered in the air, a dark black *X* marking the spot for Bella's name. Bella grabbed the black pen floating next to the paper. She closed her eyes for a second and then dashed off her name. The ink glowed in red and then turned to gold. The contract disappeared in the same black smoke.

"Excellent," Queen Fire said. She waved her hand. "You may go. I'll look forward to hearing about your progress each day."

Without a look at her aunt, Bella almost stumbled over her own feet as she hurried out of the room. She wanted to be home and pretend this hadn't happened.

"Bella?"

The princess jerked to a halt, slowly spinning to face Queen Fire.

"Don't forget. If you fail, Glimmer is mine."

6

Search Party

Once Bella's feet hit the dirt outside the castle, she bolted for the Dark Forest. She ran so fast that not even the speediest Busy Bee could catch up to her.

She slowed to a jog and made an abrupt U-turn when she realized that she had no berries! Oops! She hurried back to the sunray berry bushes and pulled a few handfuls into the tote that she had hidden at the edge of the berry patch.

I could have blown my cover on the first day! Bella scolded herself. She forced herself to breathe and pasted a smile on her face. She glanced down at her watch—she had been gone for a little over an hour.

The guards tipped their heads. "Greetings, Princess Bella," a different, smiling guard said. "The previous guard informed me of your trip." He tipped his head toward the berry tote. "Hard time finding good, ripe berries?"

"Oh, um, yes," Bella said. She forced herself to laugh. "I did something silly—I lay down on the grass for a minute to watch the clouds, and I fell asleep." She patted the heads of the two nearby guard dogs. She was afraid the words I AM A GIANT FIBBER would pop up with an arrow pointing to her.

But nothing happened. The dogs' wet noses didn't turn red signaling danger or sensing that someone was *very, very* nervous—nervous like they were hiding a secret or about to attempt to smuggle someone onto the castle grounds.

The guard smiled. "I'm just relieved that you're safe."

With a wave to the guards, Bella pulled out her Chat Crystal.

I'M BACK! she wrote to her friends. MEET ME IN MY ROOM? She didn't want to spend time searching the dozens of gardens for her friends.

The Chat Crystal vibrated and turned bubble-gum pink. ON OUR WAY! came from Clara's crystal. Bella put the crystal back in her pocket and looked out to the pasture where she had left Glimmer. She spotted the gorgeous unicorn and whistled to get Glimmer's attention. Glimmer's eyes connected with Bella's, and it made the princess willing to make the trek to Queen Fire's castle every day if it meant coming home to her unicorn.

Bella blew Glimmer a kiss. "I'll come see you later!" she called. Glimmer let out a loud whinny and kicked up her heels, dashing across the grass.

Once inside, Bella dumped the berries into a plastic bowl for Thomas, the main chef. He could whip up something tasty with the berries.

Heading toward her room, the princess felt a little better. The canopy bed with its soft lavender sheets and big fluffy comforter always made her smile. She looked over at the pictures with her friends and then a picture of Glimmer. The picture frames changed colors according to the sunlight. Right now the frame was a soft pink. Bella was glad it wasn't red. She didn't need a reminder of Queen Fire.

"You're safe!" Ivy said as she dashed through the doorway, startling Bella. She ran up to Bella and hugged her hard, with Clara right behind her. The friends group-hugged, and Ivy and Clara hopped onto Bella's bed. Bella typed a quick message to Violet, letting her cousin know that she was home safe and would message her later.

"Tell us everything," Clara said. "Don't leave out *one* detail!"

"What was the castle like?" Ivy asked, her big blue eyes open super wide.

"I'll tell you both everything, but first, did my mom or dad notice that I wasn't with you guys?" Bella asked.

"Queen Katherine found us once," Ivy said. "Clara and I were sitting on one of the benches in the Sunshine Garden."

"We heard someone heading toward us, so we started talking about the sunray pie we were excited to make," Clara said.

"What did my mom say?" Bella asked, feeling like her heart was beating a thousand times a minute.

"She just said that sunray pie sounded good, and before she could ask, we told her that you were out getting berries at a new patch you had found. We told her that we'd stayed behind to look through the gardens for new ingredients that we wanted to try in the pie."

"I'm sorry that you had to lie," Bella apologized. "I should have thought more about that when I asked you to cover for me."

"Ivy and I talked about that while you were gone," Clara said. "We hate lying too, but not when it's for the right reasons. Keeping Glimmer is *definitely* a right reason."

Bella launched into the story of her afternoon, not leaving out a single detail. Then she flashed a grateful smile to the girls. "You guys are the best friends in the world. You covered for me today. I wouldn't have gotten away with it without you. Now I have to start the search for the vault that has the crystal."

"What do you mean '*I* have to start'?" Ivy asked, tucking a lock of hair behind her ear.

"You and Violet have been so amazing, from maps to talking to my mom, but I can't ask you guys to do more. I know what I said before, but I changed my mind. I should do this on my own."

"Um, no, best friend," Clara said. She and Ivy glanced at each other, then looked at Bella.

"We know you so well," Ivy said. "Clara and I knew you'd say all of that stuff. But we're not going to let you change the plan we all agreed to."

Clara touched Bella's arm. "We're going to help you whether you like it or not. But it would be a lot easier if you just liked it already!"

Bella laughed, shaking her head. "You two aren't going to give up, are you?"

"Nope," Ivy said. "So get out Violet's map and let's start checking rooms off that list."

The princess was quiet for a moment as she looked at her friends. Finally she let out a giant sigh. "Okay, okay!" Bella said, smiling. "If you *insist*."

"We do," Clara said. "I have to be home in a couple of hours, so let's go! Where should we start?"

Bella scanned the map. "How about we all start in the great room? We'll be searching for it while totally being out in the open. If someone comes into the room, just pretend we're playing a game."

"Let's go!" Ivy said, hopping off Bella's bed. "We should look on our way."

The search was on! It took the friends five times as long to get to the great room as usual. The hallways from Bella's room to the downstairs were clear. The girls spread out in the great room. Bella slid a giant photograph of herself as a baby to the left and touched the bare wall. After an hour, they found a book that Bella had been looking for, a stale cookie, and a sparkly butterfly barrette. But there was no crystal to be found. At least, not yet.

7

Tick, Tock

Bella's alarm chimed, playing the official Crystal Kingdom anthem to wake her up. She hummed along as she pushed the button on the rainbow-shaped alarm clock to turn it off. Most mornings, if she didn't wake up at the first chirp of the alarm, the clock would shine a light on her bed. The light would turn a rainbow of colors, getting brighter until she got up. Today was different.

The sun was streaming through her window and covering everything in a nice warm light. The North Tower had the best views, and her bedroom was one of her favorite places in the whole world.

She especially loved to watch the unicorns grazing in the pasture. From her window seat she could see Kiwi and Scorpio, her parents' unicorns, and Glimmer. Their soft coats shone under the sun. Everything looked like it was perfect in Crystal Kingdom.

But it isn't, Bella thought. Today was Day Four. Day Four out of the seven that Queen Fire had given her to find the vault containing the crystal. On each of the previous days, Bella, Clara, and Ivy had searched the castle, checking room after room for the vault. Queen Katherine had allowed Bella's friends to stay after school for three days in a row when Bella told her that they had a special project together. They did: finding the vault.

The girls checked in with Violet often with updates and where they had searched. This crystal was harder to find than a piece of a spelled secret note! The number of rooms checked kept going up while the amount of time left kept going down.

Thankfully, Queen Katherine and King Phillip had been busy with a new Crystal Kingdom project—a royal secret, of course. Bella didn't even care what the secret project was—she was grateful that it kept her parents busy. Poor Lyssa—the princess's handmaiden, who was like an older sister—was out with the flu. As much as Bella wanted Lyssa to be well, it made it easier for Bella and her friends to search without her at the castle.

Only today, Friday, and Saturday are left, Bella thought. She buried her head in her pillow, trying not to panic. She took a few deep breaths and remembered that she had Violet, Clara, and Ivy on her side. They would find the vault.

She picked a pretty purple dress that had a dark-purple hem. The effect looked like the edges of one of Crystal Kingdom's beautiful sunsets. It was the perfect dress for Bella, and she was happy because it was the color of her aura. She pulled on her silver shoes and admired how they sparkled.

"Bella! Breakfast," Queen Katherine said on the intercom. Bella's tummy rumbled. She remembered how Queen Fire could seem like a person and not an evil queen for a moment. The smell of pancakes came into her room, and she shook her head free of anything but the thought of her breakfast with her parents for now. Bella hurried over to the intercom and pushed the button before her mom could call again.

"Coming!"

Bella quickly yanked her comforter up to the top of her bed and fluffed her pillows. They were a little sideways and lumpy, but it would have to do.

She darted out of her bedroom and skipped downstairs, ready to fill her belly with the cook's delicious food. Her feet flew across the castle's floors as she hurried into the great dining hall.

She took her place in her favorite chair, which had a big, soft velvet cushion. As Bella sat down, one of the kitchen staff, Rebecca, came in carrying their plates.

"Fresh hot scrambled eggs and berry pancakes for the princess," she said. The cook had drawn a whipped cream smiley face on her pancakes, with berries for eyes. It looked delicious, and Bella was hungry!

"Thanks, Rebecca, this is so cute," Bella said. She took her fork and dug in.

"You keep eating pancakes like that, and you're going to turn into a pancake," King Phillip said. His green eyes twinkled to show Bella he was kidding. Bella rolled her own eyes. It was a joke he made often, but she loved it.

"Dad!" Bella laughed.

She ate everything on her plate, then glanced at the clock on the wall. She wanted to talk to Ivy and Clara before school started about where they needed to look today.

"Can I be excused?" Bella asked.

"You may," Queen Katherine said. Rebecca came over from where she was waiting and took her plate.

Bella thanked her and scooted her chair back. Before the queen could ask where she was going, she ran up the stairs, down the hall, and into her bedroom. She grabbed her book bag and went out the front door, hopping over a shrub and finding Ivy and Clara already waiting near one of the castle's many water fountains.

"What's wrong?" Bella asked Clara. Her friend was frowning, and her arms were across her chest.

"I'm so, so sorry, Bella," Clara said. "My mom told me this morning that I have to come home after school today."

"It's okay," Bella said, feeling her heart race a

little bit. "You've been here every day after school. Ivy and I—"

"I can't stay either," Ivy interrupted. "I tried *everything*, but my parents both said I had to come home this afternoon because I've been staying at your house all this week."

Bella felt panic start to well up inside her, but she didn't want her friends to see. They had been doing *nothing* but helping her, and they already felt bad.

"It's okay," Bella said. "I'm so sorry if I got you in trouble with your parents. You each have searched with me every single day. I'm not mad or upset—I promise."

Bella's promise was real. She wasn't mad the tiniest bit. She was just scared. Scared that she had to try to find the crystal herself with time running out.

"Are you sure?" Ivy asked, chewing her bottom lip.

"Completely sure," Bella said. "It will be the

76

perfect day for me to check some rooms that only I should be in. Come on. Let's get to class." She smiled, wanting her friends to believe that she really was okay.

But the truth was she was anything but okay.

8

Hiding in Plain Sight

Bella fake-smiled her way through the entire school day. Clara and Ivy kept asking her over and over if she was okay, and she said yes every time. For once, Bella had actually been happy when her friends left the castle to go home after school.

The second she closed the front door, the smile slipped from Bella's face. She took the stairs two at a time and threw her backpack on the floor. She bit the inside of her cheek to keep from crying.

Tears are not going to find the vault, she told herself. *You can't fall apart now. You can do this.*

Bella took a few deep breaths and closed her

eyes. All she saw was Glimmer. The unicorn's sweet face made her smile. Bella's smile widened to a grin when she thought about the stubborn patch of Glimmer's mane that was determined to have a permanent curl—no matter how much Bella combed it before finally deciding to leave it alone. It was one of the things that made Glimmer unique, and it was fitting for the sometimes stubborn unicorn!

I'll get my homework out of the way, and then the search is on, Bella thought.

She got off her bed, picked up her backpack, and sat at her desk. She pulled out her books and opened her blue assignments notebook.

"Hi, sweetie."

Bella looked up at her mom, who stood in the doorway. "Hi. You look so pretty!"

Queen Katherine looked elegant in a flowing green dress, and her long blond hair was styled

79

into perfect waves. "Thank you, Bells. Dad and I have a special dinner tonight. Official kingdom business. I'm sorry that we're going to be out late on a school night."

"It's okay, Mom," Bella said. "I'll just be doing homework. You're not going to miss anything that interesting!"

Queen Katherine smiled. "I happen to think *everything* you do is interesting. I just feel especially bad leaving you while Lyssa is out sick again. Are you sure you don't mind? You could come to dinner if you'd like."

"I've got a lot of homework. But thanks, Mom." Bella reached her arms into the air. "Hug."

The queen laughed and walked over to Bella. Standing, the princess snuggled into her mom's arms, smelling the familiar scent of the queen's favorite perfume—Sunray Delight.

Queen Katherine let go of Bella and ran a hand

over her daughter's cheek. "You sure you're okay with your dad and me going out?"

"Positive."

"I'll come and say good night when I get home," Queen Katherine said. "Love you."

"Love you, Mom."

Bella opened her assignment notebook, determined to keep her focus on schoolwork. But her eyes strayed to the Secret Scribble notebook.

"You cannot go looking for the vault until your homework is done," Bella said aloud. "So focus."

She worked through a set of twenty math problems and read the assigned chapter in her history textbook. For English, she had to read the first chapter of the next book her class was reading—*Kingdoms from A to Z*, a collection of essays from people who lived on the four different sky islands.

Oops. Mom ordered that book for me last week,

and I forgot to ask her for it. Hopefully, it's on the bookcase in the great room.

Bella headed downstairs and scanned the books on the brown bookcase. Usually her parents put new books horizontal on the shelves until after they had read them. But the book Bella needed wasn't easy to spot.

"Is that it?" she wondered out loud, reaching upward. Maybe one of the maids had stuck the book in with the rest by mistake. The book's spine was solid black—nothing gave away the title. *Weird,* Bella thought.

Bella touched the book and it *vibrated.* She yanked back her hand as if she had been shocked. Her mouth fell open as the bookcase slid to the left. The princess looked around to see if anyone else in the house—a maid or *anyone*—was passing by and seeing what she was seeing.

Then Bella understood. She knew exactly what

the bookcase had been hiding. She, Ivy, and Clara had been searching the entire castle for the thing that had been hidden in one of the busiest spots in the castle: the vault. *Calm down,* Bella told herself. *You don't even know for sure.* But something in her went against every nagging little thought that she could be wrong. Deep, deep in her gut she knew this bookcase wasn't hiding a secret tea room. The bookcase was hiding the vault.

Bella pulled on the book again, putting the bookcase back in its usual spot. She had to message Ivy and Clara—they deserved to see the crystal when Bella did.

Bella ran up to her room, swiping her Chat Crystal off her desk.

I FOUND IT!!! she messaged to Ivy, Clara, and Violet.

Seconds later, her Chat Crystal lit up with messages.

BELLA!! WHERE?!

WHAT DOES IT LOOK LIKE??

I KNEW YOU'D FIND IT!

For the first time in four days, Bella felt like she could breathe again. She would wait for Ivy and Clara so they could see the crystal together. In this moment, though, there was only one thing on her mind: getting to Glimmer and telling her that she was safe. The vault had been found, and she had nothing to worry about.

Almost.

9

Be Our "Guest"

Princess Bella looked out at Crystal Castle from one of her favorite places: her window seat. She watched two young royal unicorns playfully nip each other, then dash off as they seemed to be playing a game of Unicorn Tag. Bella's eyes were on them, but her mind was somewhere else. She replayed the last few days in her head. Just as she had been doing long before sunup.

The day after she had accidentally discovered the vault, Bella had gone inside with Ivy and Clara. The crystal wasn't in a display case with bright lights shining on it as Bella had expected. Instead the girls had had to go through more books—dozens of them—before finding it. The smallish room had shelves from wall to wall. Every possible inch of shelf space was filled with books. A fake book had a hole cut into it, and inside rested a pearl-colored gem about half the size of Bella's fist. Bella had sent a photo of it to Queen Fire.

The queen messaged back on a job well done, and the only—and most important—step left was for Bella to sneak Queen Fire into the castle to get it.

Now goose bumps suddenly dotted Bella's arms, even in the warm air. Today was The Day. The day that Queen Fire was coming for the crystal. Bella had waited and waited for the right opportunity over the past couple of days, but there hadn't been a good time to sneak Queen Fire onto the castle grounds. It had been driving Bella crazy that she was *so* close to keeping Glimmer safe, but she had to keep waiting. But no more.

If I don't do it today, she thought, *I lose Glimmer. Forever.*

Bella sat up straight, squared her shoulders, and took a deep breath. *No one* was taking her unicorn. Not after everything she had done to try to keep Glimmer safe.

It's not like Queen Fire is a beginner at all of this spying and hiding stuff, Bella reminded herself. *She is an evil queen. She doesn't want to get caught.*

Bella looked at the drawbridge, which was guarded like usual with someone on each side. Not as though she had planned to meet Queen Fire and walk—

"Bella?"

The princess jumped at her mom's voice.

"Oh, honey! I'm sorry that I scared you," Queen Katherine said from Bella's doorway. She walked over and put her arms around her daughter. "Is everything all right? You've been jumpy lately."

Bella *hated* that she was about to lie to her mom.

"I'm fine, Mom!" Bella declared. "Promise! I think it's all of the clarity berries I've been having at breakfast. They give me so much energy that I'm all squirmy until bedtime."

The queen laughed.

Part of what Bella said *was* true. Clarity berries, named after how they looked, were clear square berries. The princess *had* been eating more of them than usual.

Queen Katherine squeezed Bella's hand. "Okay. Sweetie, I'm sorry that your dad and I have been so busy lately. This is the last weekend that we'll be in and out—I promise."

Bella squeezed her mom's hand back. It was the only time *ever* that she hadn't been sad that her parents were very busy.

"It's okay, Mom," Bella said. "I'm fine. Promise."

In a couple of hours, Bella hoped that what she had just told her mother would actually be true.

"C'mon, please, c'mon!" Bella murmured under her breath.

If someone had told Bella that she would soon be standing in her great room, wishing for Queen Fire to hurry up and appear beside her, Bella would have laughed hysterically. But that was exactly what she was doing.

Ivy and Clara had split up—Ivy trailing Queen Katherine and Clara keeping an eye on King Phillip. Their jobs were to come and give Bella a heads-up if either one of her parents were headed into the castle. Moments earlier, Ivy had messaged via Chat Crystal that Queen Katherine was busy gardening, and Clara had sent word that King Phillip was inspecting the royal stables.

If only Queen Fire would get here already, take

her crystal, and go! *What if her new spell isn't working?* Bella thought. She crossed her fingers that she was wrong.

Over the past few days, Queen Fire had been working out the best way to enter the castle's property. The queen had messaged Bella that she had also been working on her disappearing-into-smoke act, trying to keep the noise and smoke to a minimum.

"I like what my sister has done with this room."

Bella jumped, clapping her hands over her mouth as she almost screamed. She whirled around.

"You scared me!" Bella said to Queen Fire. "I was starting to worry that you couldn't find a way to access the castle."

"I had to finish my tea first, Bella."

Bella tilted her head, forcing back her annoyance. It didn't matter. Nothing else mattered but the crystal. "This way," she said.

Bella faced the bookcase that led to the small room. She still couldn't believe that the vault's hidden door was nothing more than a bookcase in the great room. All of the time that she and her friends had been searching, the vault had been hiding in plain sight after all.

Bella had to press on the spine of one "book" that looked no different from the rest. But it was quite different. She slid a finger along the spine and *bzzzz!* The book vibrated ever so slightly. The bookcase slid to the side, allowing a space just wide enough for a person to enter. Bella was grateful for the button. It allowed her, Ivy, and Clara easy vault access.

"Okay, we're in," Bella said in a whisper, turning to her aunt. "And I think . . ."

Bella let her sentence trail off. The queen wasn't behind her. Her aunt stood near the end of one of the cream-colored love seats near the fireplace. She had a large, silver-framed photo in one hand

and swiped at her cheek with the other. Her nails weren't painted bloodred.

I can't believe I missed that, Bella thought. She had been maybe a teensy bit preoccupied with, oh, making sure her parents were gone, worrying about the guards, hoping the dogs wouldn't pick up her aunt's scent. . . .

Bella left the hidden door and quietly walked up to her aunt.

"You were so tiny then," Queen Fire said. She ran her finger across the glass, stopping near a toothless, smiling baby Bella, who was in a bouncy chair in a pink ruffly outfit. "I bet you didn't know that pink is actually my favorite color."

Before Bella could respond, Queen Fire put back the photo, slid past her, and entered the vault. Bella quickly pressed the button to slide the bookcase back into place. Lights flickered as soon as they stepped inside.

"This is it," Bella said with a wave of her hand. The smallish room had shelves from wall to wall. Every possible inch of shelf space was filled with books—a lot of them, Mom and Dad had pointed out, were from their school days. The rest? She looked up at the white shelves that towered over her head. Bella just *knew* those books would be hers someday. Fun things like how to dress like a queen, the master interior design book of the castle, and a list of every royal unicorn that had been at Crystal Castle.

"So it was in a book right here," Bella said. She reached for the book, frowning. It was heavier than she remembered. She opened the book to find, well, a book. Pages. Lots and lots of pages.

"What's wrong?" Queen Fire asked.

Bella put the book on a table behind her. "Nothing. I'm sorry—I grabbed the wrong book. It's this one."

She grabbed another book off the shelf and

flipped it open. There was no cutout box. No sparkling crystal. Just words.

"All right, what's going on?" Queen Fire asked. "If this is some sort of trick to lure me to the castle . . ."

"It's not a trick!" Bella said, pleading with her aunt. "I promise, the book was right here! I opened it and saw the crystal. I'm not lying."

She yanked another book off the shelf. And another.

"I'm guessing that this is your first experience with a book shuffle spell," Queen Fire said.

"A what?" Bella asked.

Queen Fire sighed. "It's a kind of protection magic. You found the correct book, and to make it a little harder, the books reordered themselves when you left."

"Oh no," Bella said. "We have to start all over again."

Queen Fire moved toward a shelf and plucked

off a book. She opened it, then set it on the floor.

"One down," she said.

"We have to move faster than that," Bella said. "I mean, I don't think anyone is going to come in here, but I can't stay too long."

"Did it seem as though I wanted to spend the night?" Queen Fire asked, annoyed. She shook her head, her signature red earrings clinking back and forth. "I have a home to get to as well."

After what seemed like forever, they had made a dent in the amount of books on the shelves, but there were still hundreds of books left.

"I probably need to go see if my parents are home," Bella said. "I'll sneak back in. Do you want anything?"

"Water, please."

"Okay, be right back." Bella eased the bookcase to the side, opening it just enough for her to get through, then slid it back.

The great room was quiet and the kitchen still empty. Whew. Not having to sidestep Dad or—

"Mom, hi!" Bella said.

"Whoa, that was close," her mother said, smiling. "Careful, Bells. I'm old, and you can't plow into us old folk."

"Sorry!" The princess froze, unsure of what to do. *Act normal. Sit on the couch. Turn on the TV.* But what if Mom wanted to talk more? *Put on something that she hates. But—*

"What time is company coming?"

Bella tried not to react, but a streak of panic ran through her. Her ears started to feel warm, and she knew she was blushing—something she always did when she tried to lie.

"Bella, come on." Queen Katherine reached out and touched her elbow. "I was just teasing. Are you sure everything is okay?"

"Completely sure," Bella said. "I'm just really

thirsty." Bella dashed to the kitchen and got bottled waters from the fridge.

She twisted the cap off one of the bottles and started drinking the water quickly. She skirted around her mom and sat on the couch. She flicked on the TV.

"I'll be on the back patio if you need me," Queen Katherine said.

Bella smiled and nodded.

After the back door shut, she counted to twenty before she leaped off the couch and ran to the bookcase.

"I'm so sorry," Bella said. "Here's your—"

The vault was empty, and all of the books had been returned to the shelves. Queen Fire had clearly found the crystal and gone home. The princess's debt to Queen Fire was paid. But that didn't mean Bella wanted the queen or king to know that she'd been in the vault and start asking questions.

One book near the end was upside down. Bella pulled it out and flipped the book over. STABLES was scratched into the back.

"Ugh," Bella said. She stamped her foot, not caring that she wasn't five. "I just want this to be over." Bella groaned again and rolled her eyes as she put the book back right side up.

She turned and smacked directly into Queen Katherine, with Ivy trailing close behind. Ivy, looking pale, mouthed, "I'm sorry" to her best friend.

Bella felt her heart drop to her toes.

10

Reunited . . . but Are They United?

Queen Katherine took off for the stables, and Bella had to work to keep up with her mom.

"Mom, wait. Can we talk first?" Bella pleaded.

The queen ignored her and made a beeline down the stable aisle.

"Where are you going?" Bella asked.

"To the exact spot where my sister and I used to almost live when we were your age," the queen said.

She stopped in front of Glimmer's stall and slid the door open.

"Katherine," Queen Fire said, locking eyes with her sister.

In one of her hands was the crystal. Queen Fire halted, quietly closing the stall door.

"Were you going back on your word?" Bella asked. "You obviously found the crystal in the vault and then you came *here*. Why?"

"I did find the crystal. My locator spell worked perfectly." The queen eyed Bella, her gaze settling on the "stables" book. "So you figured out how to find me," Queen Fire said. "But I also found the book that you had seen, Bella, with this note. I knew it wasn't some childish act of vandalism. The word "stables" was the only clue that I needed. It led me here."

Bella's eyes wandered from her mom to Queen Fire. Six guards flanked Bella and her mom. They had been so silent that Bella hadn't even heard them approach. Bella looked over her shoulder, and three more guards stood silent and still behind Queen Fire. Bella locked eyes with Glimmer. As much as the unicorn disliked Queen Fire, she was standing still and on her best behavior.

"Tell me the truth, Fawn," Queen Katherine said. "Did you come here for the crystal or for something else?"

The guards tensed, ready to pounce if Queen Fire said the wrong thing. Whatever "wrong" was.

"The crystal," Queen Fire said. "I came for the photographs it holds, Katherine. Of us. Of our childhood."

Bella shook her head, sure she'd heard wrong. She hadn't allowed herself to think much about what the crystal did. That somehow made it easier to steal from the castle and give to Queen Fire.

"Guards, I have the situation under control. You're free to go." Queen Katherine leaned down to face Bella. "As for you, I can tell you that we are going to have a very, *very* long talk about all of this when your father gets home."

"I know." Bella cast her eyes down. "I'm sorry."

She was ready for Queen Katherine to tell her to go to her room and not expect to ride Glimmer for weeks. Months.

Queen Katherine let out a big breath. "I know you are," she said. "Why don't you take Glimmer out for a walk and let me talk to my . . . sister. We clearly have a lot to discuss." Bella looked from her mom to Queen Fire. The sisters exchanged small smiles.

"Come on, Glimmer," Bella said. Glimmer sidestepped Queen Fire and trotted after Bella as she left the stables. Bella felt lighter than she had in a week. She knew that she was still in big trouble for lying to her parents. As she looked back at her mom and aunt, she tried to imagine how close they used to be and hoped this might help them speak again. Maybe one day they would all end up at Queen Fire's castle, enjoying that Dark Forest cake as one big family.

But for now, the one thing Bella knew for sure? Glimmer was safe and all hers.

Acknowledgments

Many, many thanks to my team at Simon & Schuster who made *The Hidden Treasure*, well, magic! Hugs to Mara Anastas, Alyson Heller, Fiona Simpson, Jessica Handelman, and everyone from sales to design who had a hand in crafting this book.

Victoria Ying, your illustrations brought Bella, Glimmer, and their friends to life—thank you!

Endless appreciation to my friends, Cali Family, and the amaze Agent Jenn.

Thank-yous to the teachers, librarians, booksellers, and reviewers everywhere!

Finally, to my readers—you are the true princesses and princes!